Chapter One

Welcome to Terra

Abaddon stepped out of the portal and was met with a tumult of sounds and smells as he found himself standing amongst a massive crowd of people. It took several seconds for his ears to adjust to the barrage of noise and snatches of conversation, only some of it in languages he could understand. There were various clerks behind desks, and a recorded voice was telling everyone to get into orderly lines. Not quite sure where to go, Abaddon followed the movements of the crowd and was shuffled into a line behind what he could only assume was some kind of elf dressed in leaves. The person behind him moved unexpectedly and he was pushed forward, his horns jabbing into the elf's back.

"Hey, watch it bu-" the elf stopped mid-sentence as he turned to see Abaddon standing behind him.

"I'm really sorry, it's this line and I didn't mean to-"

"Don't-don't worry about it," the elf looked scared.

"I'm Abaddon," Abaddon held out a dark grey hand.

"Karl," the elf shook it, clearly uncomfortable.

"Look, I really didn't mean to-" Abaddon was cut off as the line moved forwards and the elf stepped up to the desk, eager to get away from him.

Well that could have gone better. Abaddon hoped his next interaction would be... well he didn't really know what he hoped it would be, but not that. He looked around at all the various people standing in their respective lines. The building they were in was massive, but he was still impressed it could hold them all. That one gentleman in the hat and coat appeared to be at least fifteen feet tall, and made of wood. He'd never actually seen someone like that before, even in his books. His musings were interrupted by a voice right in front of him calling out, "Next."

"Welcome to New Eden Extraplanar Immigration Offices," the man behind the desk said in a bored voice as Abaddon stepped forward. Apparently the sight of a demon was nothing out of the ordinary, because his tone didn't even change as he continued, "Name?"

"Abaddon."

"Which plane of existence are you coming from?"

"Hell."

"Did you bring any invasive or dangerous plants/animals from Hell with you?"

"No."

"Any scrolls, wands, staves, magical or cursed objects, or greater or lesser artifacts to declare?"

"Um, well I have an obsidian bracer and the mighty war hammer Spellbreaker, capable of-"

"Greater or lesser artifacts or magic objects?" the man behind the desk cut him off, his tone suggested he wanted to speed this along as quickly as possible.

"The war hammer is a greater artifact and the bracer is a lesser one."

"Hold on," the man sighed, reaching under his desk. A second later he came back up with a set of forms. "Please read through and sign these forms, acknowledging that you know the rules and procedures for the carrying and use of greater artifacts within city limits."

Abaddon started to scan the documents, then stopped halfway down the page. "Actually, on line four I don't really-"

"Just sign the forms. Other otherworldly beings are waiting to come through here."

"Uh, okay," Abaddon was taken aback, but put his signature on the documents.

"Reason for stay?" the man asked as he put the forms back underneath his desk.

"Work."

"Do you possess the required certification allowing a demon of the lower planes to be employed in New Eden?"

Abaddon fished around in the pocket of his leather jacket. It took him longer than he would have liked, and the man's staring didn't help matters at all. Eventually he pulled out a small scroll.

The man took the scroll from Abaddon's gray hand and unfurled it, revealing the dark twisted runes burned into the paper. He pulled out a glowing object, emblazoned with holy script. He ran the artifact over the scroll, and the golden letters turned green, accompanied by a snatch of choir music.

"That seems to be in order. Please enjoy your stay in New Eden," the man gestured to another portal that opened up directly to his left. Abaddon barely had time to step through it as the man called out, "Next."

As always, it took Abaddon's eyes several seconds to adjust after exiting the portal. He blinked blearily, registering a bright light coming in through his eyelids. When everything finally came into focus, Abaddon felt as though he'd pass out right there on the street. So much movement, everywhere he looked, so many sights, people running about, buildings stretching to the Heavens. Speaking of the Heavens, there was the blue sky he'd only ever read about before. It was so much more breathtaking than Gorath Soulflayer's Guide to Terra had made it seem in the illustrations. And the warmth of the sun, it was so different from the hellfire back home. He couldn't tell if he liked it more or not, but he didn't care. It was all just so incredible. So incredible in fact, that Abaddon almost didn't notice the thunder of hooves from the horse bearing down on him. At the last second he dived out of the way.

"Watch it, I'm charioteering here!" the driver shouted as he barreled past.

Abaddon made sure to find a safe spot, off of the road, before continuing to gawk at all the sights and sounds. After several more minutes of letting the splendor of it all wash over him, Abaddon reached into his pocket and pulled out another scroll. Unfurling this one, he read the address aloud, "Jacob's Ladder Apts. 15th and Adam, #415."

Abaddon looked around for signs of some sort. He knew that the primary means of transportation through New Eden was the Teleportation Nexus Network. So all he needed was to find a station. He chose a random direction to walk in. After several minutes of not finding anything he hailed a passerby.

"Excuse me, I need directions to the nearest nexus station."

The woman pointed, not even bothering to look up as she went by.

"Thanks," Abaddon called after her, then headed in the direction she had indicated.

When he finally arrived at the station, Abaddon was once again surprised at the size of the building. He was used to great obsidian castles looming over the cursed plains, but something about the buildings in New Eden was just so much more breathtaking. As he approached the entrance, a glowing portal appeared in the wall, letting him and a bunch of other travelers through. Abaddon was beginning to suspect he wouldn't be able to go anywhere in New Eden without being part of a large crowd or line. He was shepherded with the group into a big atrium of sorts where he was met with even more sights and sounds. Signs and flashing lights were everywhere, and various hallways were branching off in different directions.

He heard another recording, this one a soothing woman's voice, go out over the room. "Passengers please head to the appropriate gate for your next destination in a calm and orderly fashion. If you have a nexus pass, please show it to the conductor for your portal. All other passengers please be ready with the appropriate fare. We would like to remind you that we are no longer accepting first born children."

Abaddon spun slowly, looking in every direction. He had no clue where to go, but after several seconds he spied a small booth with a sign that said "HELP". Since that was what he sorely needed, he headed straight for it. Behind the desk was a friendly looking woman. She seemed in a much better mood than the man at the immigration office had been.

"How may I help you?"

"Hi, I need to get to this address," Abaddon held out the scroll. "Sorry, I just arrived here in the city and don't know my way around."

"That's perfectly alright," the woman smiled, taking the scroll. "I see, you'll want gate C, over that way, down the east hall. Once you exit the portal it should be just a few blocks south of the nexus station."

"Thank you very much."

"Happy to help. And welcome to New Eden."

Well, Abaddon's fourth interaction in New Eden had seemed to go pretty well. But it just showed that he still had so much to learn, and he'd have to learn what all the things he would need to learn were before he could start learning them. This would be very difficult, and take a lot of getting used to. But one thing was for sure: it would definitely be exciting.

Chapter Two

Trouble Day One

Abaddon felt the rush of air and light, accompanied by the strange sensation that his body was being stretched. He didn't think he'd ever get used to that. Even the portals were different in Terra. This street looked a little less busy than the others he had been on. Abaddon checked his wallet. Good; he still had a decent amount of money. It would have been nice to make a completely fresh start on his own, but having some emergency cash in case things didn't go well was necessary. With everything in order, Abaddon put his wallet back in his pocket and headed in the direction of his apartment.

He was now on Adams street, so the apartment should be very close by. He stopped in his tracks as he saw a blue shape out of the corner of his eye. Was it… yes, it was! a real live wyvern. To think he'd get to see an actual domesticated riding dragon on his first day. It was a bit smaller than he'd thought it would be, but he supposed that made sense for an urban area. He quickly crossed the street to take a closer look. The wyvern snorted as he approached.

"It's okay fella, I just want to say hi."

Abaddon slowly held out a hand. He waited patiently as the wyvern sniffed at it. After a moment, the wyvern decided that Abaddon was not dangerous, and noticeably relaxed.

"Wow," Abaddon started to pet the back of the wyvern's head, which it seemed to rather enjoy.

"Hey kid, is that your wyvern?"

Abaddon turned to see two figures striding toward him. Both wore identical golden suits of armor and had swords at their sides. Great, he got to deal with the local law enforcement on his first day.

"No, this isn't mine."

"What're you doing with someone else's wyvern?"

"I was just looking-"

"I think he might have been trying to steal it."

"No I wasn't-"

"Were you stealing this wyvern kid?"

"No, I was just looking at it," Abaddon was getting frustrated.

"Hey, Phil," the first templar turned to the other. "I think he just raised his voice at me."

"I believe he did Roy."

"Hey, I was just looking at this wyvern. I didn't do anything."

"Then why are you getting hostile?" Roy sneered, leaning in close in a clearly condescending gesture.

"I'm not getting hostile," Abaddon was starting to get angry now.

"Whoa, whoa," Roy held up his hands and backed off in an overdramatic fashion. "I just wanted to make sure you weren't wanting to add assaulting a templar to your list of crimes."

"List of crimes! I haven't even-" Abaddon had to forcibly calm himself. "Look, as I already explained, I was only looking at that wyvern. I'm new in town and have never seen one before."

"Not a lot of wyverns in Hell are there?" Phil chimed in.

"No, there are not. So I was just looking is all."

"You were grabbing it," Roy corrected. "Looked like you might make off with it."

"I was petting its- I was just petting the wyvern. It was very friendly and liked being petted."

"Oh, so first you were just looking, and now you're just petting? Are you sure you weren't just taking it?"

"I WASN'T TRYING TO STEAL THE SAVED WYVERN."

Both templars drew their swords. Runes of light flashed on the blades. Abaddon put his hands in the air, fighting down a roar that would have shaken the templars' very bones.

"Just don't move, and keep your hands up."

"Hey Roy," Phil gestured to Abaddon's back.

"Hey kid, you have a license for that war hammer?"

"It's bonded to my soul. Only I can wield it."

"I don't think he has a license."

"I don't think he does."

"Kid I'm going to have put a level five restraint on that war hammer until you can get the appropriate license to operate that thing."

"You can't do that."

"Telling an officer what to do now are we?" Roy moved up to Abaddon, holding out his empty hand, which was now glowing gold.

"No I mean you literally cant-"

Golden chains of glowing runes snaked their way up the handle of Spellbreaker, binding the weapon tightly in holy magic. The next instant the chains shattered with an audible crash and burst of light.

"ON THE GROUND NOW," Roy had both hands on his sword.

Abaddon dropped to his knees, hands still in the air. Anger swelled again, but Abaddon pushed it down as hard as he could. This was all just a misunderstanding, it was all just a misunderstanding, it was all just a misunderstanding….

"Looks like you're resisting arrest now, huh kid?" Roy growled. "Phil, call it in."

"I was not resisting arrest," Abaddon forced himself to be calm with all his might. "My war hammer shatters magic that it comes into contact with. It cannot be enchanted. I'll gladly come with you and fill out whatever forms I need to get a license or-"

"Filling out forms eh?" Roy turned to Phil with a sneer. Phil returned the look. "We're past filling out forms. So far I think you committed attempted theft, were hostile to two officers, and just resisted arrest. I suggest you come down to the station quietly so you don't make things worse for yourself."

"That won't be necessary officers," a grand voice interjected.

All three figures turned to see who the speaker was. They were met with a tall muscular man in a silver breastplate, with a large sword on his back. Abaddon couldn't be sure, but he thought the man's long blond hair was actually flowing majestically in the lack of wind.

"Hey, you're Adonis!" Roy took a step backwards.

"You mean the legendary hero Adonis?" Phil followed his partner's suit.

"That's the one. W-what are you doing here? There aren't any monsters around or anything... are there?"

"No need to worry officers," Adonis' chest seemed to puff out as he spoke, or maybe it was just the hands on his hips. "For now, New Eden is safe, and I can lay down my sword for a while. I simply noticed my friend here was in trouble and thought I should lend a hand."

"Friend? You know this demon?"

"Indeed. I was supposed to show him around the city. New arrival and all that."

"Well your friend just broke the law. And we were about to arrest him."

"I saw the whole thing officers. A hero's eyes are ever vigilant. That weapon of his repels magic. He was not trying to resist your binding spell."

"Yeah well, we still need to bring him in."

"He meant no harm officers. He is new to the ways of the city. I will take full responsibility for his actions today. For is it not our duty to guide those with less wisdom? You may be a noble templar, but that does not mean you cannot also be a true hero in your own right."

Roy stood for a moment, clearly annoyed, but weighing his options carefully. "Alright, since a great hero of your stature made the request, we will trust your judgement. But I don't wanna see any more trouble around here," he motioned to Phil and the two templars turned and left.

Abaddon's anger had been replaced by sheer astonishment. He hadn't even gotten up off the ground. His mouth moved wordlessly for almost a minute, until finally he sputtered, "Y-you're Adonis!"

Chapter Three

A True Hero

"I know who I am," Adonis' voice now sounded like a normal person's; the change was jarring enough to snap Abaddon out of his stupor. "Man that voice is hard to keep up for very long."

"So wait, you're Adonis? As in the most famous hero in New Eden Adonis?"

"Yeah, that's me."

"Slayer of the black hydra, vanquisher of the dark horde, smiter-"

"Of the infernal warrior Bagdath. Yes, I am familiar with my many heroic deeds."

"Sorry," Abaddon finally got up off of the ground. "It's just, to see you, I mean meet you in the flesh. And not to be rude, but what are you doing here?"

"Like I said, helping a friend," Adonis paused, then continued in his grandiose voice, "For are not all citizens in need, friends to a true hero?"

"But being here, helping me. I mean you're a legend."

"I was being serious," Adonis' voice was back to normal. "And I did see everything. A citizen was getting hassled by some templars, so I stepped in. A true hero does help people on the street as well as perform earth-shattering deeds."

"Well thank you so much. I mean, I didn't even know what was going on, those templars just came out of nowhere and-"

"Forget it. All part of the job. Not to mention common decency. But unfortunately some templars like those two think throwing their divine authority around to boost their fragile egos is all part of *THEIR* job. Plus it doesn't help being a demon and all."

"I'm starting to see that," Abaddon sighed.

"I mean, not that being a demon is a problem or anything. Hey, one of my best friends is a demon- wow that came out wrong."

Abaddon burst out laughing, "Sorry, sorry," he clutched his side, barely getting the words out. "This is just so absurd. Not only do I meet the most famous hero in New Eden, but now I have him flustered? I didn't even think you could get flustered."

"Hey, despite the painstaking amount of time I have spent getting people to think otherwise, I am still a person, just like anyone else," at that Abaddon gave him a look. "Okay, maybe not *JUST* like everyone else. But yeah, I love, I laugh, I learn, all that cliché stuff. Just because I can bench-press a great wurm doesn't mean I can't get embarrassed."

"Now you're just showing off," Abaddon chuckled, then realized he was having a casual conversation with Adonis, and almost went into a daze again. "But why do all this? I don't mean the saving me stuff. I mean, talking to me like this. You just said you've crafted this epic hero image for yourself, and it took a very long time. Aren't you just kind of blowing it all right now?"

"Eh, call it a whim if you want. Something about you just felt different to me. It would be really corny if I said I see great things in your future or something like that, and that's not really true anyway. But I get an interesting sense from you. I can't really think of a better way to phrase it. It just seemed like I should be 'myself' around you, so to speak."

"I still can't believe I get to speak with *THE* Adonis."

"Which reminds me, I never got your name."

"Abaddon," Abaddon held out a hand.

"Like the Demon Lord of Destruction?"

"Well, yeah, I mean I suppose," Abaddon rubbed the back of his head awkwardly. "I mean I'm not him, I mean I know you know I'm not, or at least you would have assumed I'm not, but like I said I'm not, I mean-"

"Herschel," Adonis shook Abaddon's hand.

"Wait, your name's Herschel?"

"Jewish," at that Abaddon gave Adonis a look, "on my mom's side. Scandinavian on my dad's." There was a moment's pause, then, "Wait, how did you know that Jews aren't usually tall and blond? Come to think of it, it's weird to see a demon with hair. Especially bright red hair. Though I suppose I'd have no idea what demon hair is supposed to look like, I mean given that I didn't even know they had hair."

"No, most don't," Abaddon was still feeling a bit awkward. "It's not super uncommon though…." there was an awkward pause. "I guess it's kind of silly to think that Adonis would be your real name huh?"

"Hey, it's just you and everyone else in New Eden. Adonis sounded much more heroic, so I made the change. Mom would be rolling over in her grave though."

"Because heritage is really important to Jews?"

"Something like that. Wow, you seem to know a lot about humans. Sorry, I just wouldn't have expected that."

"My dad really emphasized reading. My favorite subject was A.D. humanity."

Adonis whistled, "That's a pretty broad subject."

"Demons live a long time, so I was able to do a lot of reading."

"But a demon emphasizing reading. I mean, no offense, but your dad must have been rather odd."

"My dad is-" Abaddon paused, hoping his face wasn't showing how uncomfortable he suddenly felt. "My dad is…. special."

"That must be a greater artifact you've got there," Adonis abruptly changed the subject, Abaddon hoped coincidentally. "I mean, to be able to passively shrug off a level five restraint like that."

"Yeah, Spellbreaker's a greater artifact."

"I take it that bracer of yours is an artifact as well."

"Yeah, but only a lesser one."

Adonis gave him a look that perfectly mirrored the one he'd given early. "Only a lesser artifact? Even for a demon those look like some fancy toys."

"Well I am looking to be a hero. That's actually why I came to New Eden."

"No kidding. I'm assuming you wanna be a monster-slayer, right?"

"Yeah, that's the plan anyway."

"Well good luck with that."

"You have no idea how much that means to me."

"Hey, knock 'em dead. The monsters I mean," Adonis was interrupted by a beeping sound. He pulled out a watch from his pants pocket. "Oh shit, is it really 1:30 already? Damnit, my boyfriend's going to kill me," Adonis started to run off.

"Wait, boyfriend?!"

"Good day citizen," Adonis called back as he ran out of sight.

For several minutes, Abaddon just stood there, trying to absorb everything that had just happened to him, and failing miserably. Then he remembered what he had been doing before the templars arrived, and following Adonis' example, ran off.

Chapter Four

Hellaphone Call

Abaddon sat alone in his small apartment. A lot had happened to him on his first day in New Eden. He was tired, but he couldn't sleep yet. There was still one last thing he needed to do. He breathed out slowly than began to speak. His words hissed, bringing about a darkness with them. Had anyone else been present they would have noticed the corners of the room turn to shadows, and the whole space close in on itself, as a strange sense of claustrophobia encompassed the apartment. Flames licked at the edge of his speech. Abaddon finished his black spell, and as he did, the air in front of him began to rip at the seams. A portal showing darkness and flame appeared before him. The spiraling hellfire gave way to a new form. In a dark room was a great throne of bones. Sitting atop it was an imposing figure. Clad in armor of blackest obsidian, even sitting, he towered. Great gray wings unfurled at his back, and wicked horns like those of a bull curved forwards, causing shadows to move across his face. His eyes looked straight into the dark portal in front of him, their red flame piercing right into Abaddon's dark soul. The very air grew chill as Lucifer, king of the Ninth Circle, fixed his gaze upon Abaddon.

"Hi Dad."

"How's my prince of darkness doing? Did you make it to New Eden okay?"

"I'm fine. And I made it to my apartment fine too."

"This is your new domain?" Lucifer peered through the portal. "It's a bit small, isn't it?"

"It's fine Dad, and it's affordable."

"I still liked that place we looked at over on the East Side better."

"Beverley Hells? If I wanted to live in a blasted hellscape I would have moved to the Seventh Circle."

"Your Aunt Lilith lives in the Seventh Circle. Remember how much fun you had as a young spawn, visiting her at the summer Pandemonium?"

"Dad, you know I don't have a problem with blasted hellscapes, and of course I loved visiting Aunt Lilith. It's just that the whole reason I came to New Eden was to see Terra, and all of the wonderful new things it has to offer. There wouldn't be much point in that if I just ended up living in Hell on Terra."

"I know son. I just hope you're getting everything you need."

"I'll be fine Dad. How is Aunt Lilith anyway? Is she still seeing Belial?"

"Heh, it's been almost twenty years. She's probably had at least fifteen concubines since him."

"But I thought she liked Belial?"

"Well, you know how your aunt is. But yes, he was a fine concubine. One of the better one's she's had."

"And no one could barbecue imp like he did."

"I'd forgotten about that. It was the Festival of the Seven Deadly, wasn't it?"

"Yup, best I'd ever had."

"I know. I could have eaten it all night. Would have too, but it wouldn't have been fair to the other six sins."

"I assume nothing much has happened in the few hours I've been gone."

"You know, same old same old. Some fool challenged me for the dark throne, so I flayed his soul for his insolence. How was your first day? No problems or anything?"

"N-no. No, it all went smoothly."

"You hesitated there."

"It was nothing, really."

"Trying to lie to the great deceiver? Remember, I was the father of lies before I was your father."

"Look, it was just- it was just some templars giving me a hard time. No big d-"

"WHAT?!" Lucifer's roar shook the very walls of the apartment, and the floor was almost rent in twain.

"See Dad, this is why I didn't want to tell you. I knew you'd react like this."

"Did you strike down those arrogant fools of Heaven? Do their brood now weep at their torturous passing?"

"No Dad, you know I can't do that. They're the law around here."

"They are mere servants, lapdogs of Heaven, while you are Abaddon, son of Lucifer, prince of the sulfury void."

"Not while I'm in Terra. Here I'm just Abaddon: a demon trying to make a living like everyone else."

"I will not stand for such disrespect!"

"Yes you will Dad. Remember how I said I wanted to do things on my own? You never fought my battles before, so why should you start now that I'm living on my own?"

"Well that's because you always used to *FIGHT* your battles."

"I can't take on all the templars in New Eden."

"You think that holy scum would stand a chance against-"

"I didn't mean I wouldn't be strong enough. I meant, that's not how it works here. The rules say no. And I have to listen to the rules, just like everyone else."

"I know, I know," Lucifer had calmed down considerably. "It's just I can't stand those cocky divine warriors. Always acting so smug with their golden armor and holier than thou attitude."

Abaddon gave him a look. "They're templars Dad, it's their job to be holier than thou. And you're the demon king of the Ninth Circle, I think literally anyone else in existence is holier than thou."

"Yeah, but they don't have to be so in your face about it. And when the world gets reforged anew, of course they get to create the bastion of a new glorious age. Do you see any demons rebuilding the civilizations of man? Typical."

Abaddon sighed. "We were the ones who started the apocalypse, remember?"

"Remember? I was right by your grandfather's side as he slew the first angel. But that was over three centuries ago. We lost, we signed all the treaties, and even now, my own son gets attacked just because he's a demon."

"I wasn't *ATTACKED*. Those templars were just waving their authority around. All they were doing was boosting their pathetic egos," Abaddon was saying this as much to convince himself as his father. "Look, it all turned out fine, I made it to the apartment; no one was arrested, nothing bad happened. I'm going to have to deal with a lot of things like this from now on. And you unleashing the fury of blackest pits every time I hit a stumbling block won't help anyone."

"I know," Lucifer growled. "But thinking of a world where weak scum can boss around someone stronger like you…"

"Yes, we've been over this Dad, it's not Hell. And stuff like this doesn't even matter. I've already seen and experienced so much, and it's only been one day. The infernal tomes don't even come close to the real thing. I even got to meet Adonis! It was my first day!"

"You met the greatest champion of man on your first day?"

"Yes, and he practically spoke to me like an equal."

"Ha!" This time Lucifer's voice only shook the hanging light on the ceiling. "Now that's my spawn. Day one and you're already showing them what for."

"Well, I don't know if I would go that far, but it was really exciting. And I've got so much more to do and see."

"And you won't see any of it if your eyes are closed. Wait any longer to go to sleep and there'll be no rest for the wicked tonight."

"Yeah, you're right."

"Love you."

"Love you too Dad."

Chapter Five

The Interview

Abaddon was sitting in a nice little office. He was on a very comfortable couch, with a small glass table between him and Ms. Weathers. She was a smart looking woman in a gray business suit. She had straight brown hair and wore sensible shoes. All in all, not someone he had expected to be the representative of a heroes guild.

"So, Mr. Abaddon was it? It seems you wish to be a hero with the White Pegasus Guild."

"Yes ma'am."

"Well, let's look over your application, shall we?" Ms. Weathers made various 'hmmm' and 'tch' sounds as she read the document. "Impressive, it says here that you slew Nidhogg, the dragon of destruction. Please tell me about that."

"Oh well you know, classic monster slaying," Abaddon was rubbing the back of his head, trying not to look as embarrassed as he felt. "I took my mighty Spellbreaker and brought low the beast."

"But doesn't Nidhogg breathe the very fires of Hell? How were you able to best such a foe with a war hammer?"

"Well see, Spellbreaker is actually a greater artifact. It shatters all magic it strikes, so it was uh, able to deal with Nidhogg's fire breath quite easily."

Abaddon hoped he wasn't showing his nervousness as much as he was feeling it. Technically he *WAS* responsible for Nidhogg's death, but actually there had been no slaying involved. In truth, Nidhogg had been his Uncle's pet, and it died when it got into Abaddon's secret stash of holy water. Boy had his father been mad at him when he found out.

"I see," Ms. Weathers had a pensive expression. "And here, you checked the box for being multilingual, but in the space below, you did not write down a language. Care to elaborate as to what other language(s) you speak?"

"Uh, dark tongues that should not be spoken by mortal men."

"I see," Ms. Weathers said again, this time giving Abaddon a very sharp look. "I would assume mortal women should not speak these tongues either. For that matter, mortals of any kind, regardless of gender should not speak them yes?"

"Well yeah, but I mean it's just a way of phrasing-"

"I'm afraid it's more than that. I don't want to seem like I'm picking on small details here, but this sort of thing does matter. Image is important for a hero. How people perceive you is relevant, even if it may not seem like it. This is the third century, and we cannot have our heroes talking like they're from A.D."

"I'm sorry, I didn't mean to offend anyone."

"I'm sure you didn't. And like I said, I do not mean to nitpick or be overly touchy, but someone in your position cannot be too careful about this sort of thing."

"Someone in my position?"

"Yes, and on that subject," Ms. Weathers seemed to intentionally take that as a statement rather than a question, "we need to do something about your name."

"My name? What's wrong with it?"

"The White Pegasus Guild cannot represent a hero named Abaddon."

"Why not?"

"Do I need to spell it out for you? Abaddon is the Demon Lord of Destruction."

"Well yeah, but I don't see what that has to do with me. I mean, I'm not him."

"Obviously, but that's not the point. It's the association. I mean, it's the third century A.A. but you still don't see many Adolf's around, do you?"

"Abaddon may be the Demon Lord of Destruction, slayer of angels, and dark spawn of blackest pits, but don't you think comparing him to Hitler is a bit much?"

"Look, all I'm saying is that you're going to have a hard-enough time as it is trying to be a hero while being a demon. You don't need the extra baggage that comes with a name like that. Hmmm? I know, how about Abe."

"Abe?"

"Yes, it can be short for Abaddon, but it's also a neutral name. A lot of people will think it's short for Abraham. A holy angle, people will eat it up."

"But isn't Abraham famous for attempting to kill his own son, just because God told him to?"

"No one's going to care. Hell, most of these people you'll be saving won't have even read the Bible, or paid much attention at any rate. What's important is how they will view you. A name like that could really help offset your-" Ms. Weathers paused for a moment, "less advantageous qualities."

"I suppose so," Abaddon was really feeling uncomfortable with the way the interview was going, but he was much too nervous to say anything.

"Well we can come back to that later. Obviously image isn't as important as your abilities. I notice that where it asks you to check the box for warrior or magic hero, you didn't check either one."

"I didn't know which one I should check."

Ms. Weathers looked him up and down. "I would have thought it'd be obvious. You fight with an enchanted war hammer, and you have a history of slaying monsters."

"Well yes, but my demonic lineage has natural magic abilities. I was born with many dark powers such as curses, manipulating hellfire, and so on. I've spent as much time honing my magic as I have my martial skills."

"Well, there are certain cases where a hero has equal aptitude for magic and fighting. A special appeal would have to be filled out and sent to HR for review. In the meantime, I suggest we put you down as a warrior."

"Does that mean I can't use my magic on the job?"

"Oh no, you still can, though I don't know that I'd advise calling upon your demonic powers in public that much. This just means that for now you won't be listed as magical officially. This really only affects client call-ins, not your everyday acts of heroism."

"So basically, being cross-listed means there would be more jobs I'd be called out for."

"Yes. For instance, while you're listed as a warrior, someone looking to exterminate a vengeful spirit wouldn't ask for you. They would pick another hero, unless of course you have a magic weapon that can destroy them or some other item like that."

"Well, my Spellbreaker destroys magic, so it could banish spirits summoned with magic, but that's about it."

"Mhm. So until you get the cross-listing, you will only be called for things like giants or hydras, or dragons. Speaking of dragons: can you fly? It wasn't listed as one of your abilities on the application, but seeing as you're a demon, I figured I should ask."

"Not all demons are born with wings. It is actually a rare genetic anomaly. So even if a parent is a winged demon, there's a good chance the child will not be. So it's actually more normal for a demon to not have wings"

"I see," Abaddon was starting to think he should keep an 'I see' count going in his head. "Are there any other abilities not listed on the application I should be made aware of?"

"Well, as you can see, my horns are fairly small, and actually not good for fighting or anything. My physical abilities are a decent bit above the Human Standard Deviation, but not enough that I thought I should write it down. Oh, and I have excellent night vision, and overall hearing. And also a very high resistance to heat and flame, though I think I put that on the application."

"Yes, that appears to be here. Oh, and one more thing. Under the section that asks you to list your training, you put down Baal, who you said may also be referred to as Moloch. Am I to take it that this is the same warrior demon Baal who served under the demon king of the Ninth Circle during Armageddon?"

"Yup, that's him."

"I see, that's quite the reference. And may I contact him?"

"Oh right, I forgot to put a number down for him there, sorry. That's 666-524-9917"

"Well, your resume is definitely quite impressive. We will contact you shortly with a reply after looking over your application again, but it does look very good for you," Ms. Weathers stood up to shake Abaddon's hand.

"Thank you very much Ms. Weathers."

Everything seemed to be going really well. It was looking like Abaddon would get the job. But then why was he feeling so uneasy?

Chapter Six

Getting Started in New Eden

"I got the job!" It was several days later and Abaddon was talking to his father again.

"That's great news. Just the other day Baal came up to me and told me that someone from a White Pegasus Guild had called him up and asked about you. I figured that had to be a good sign."

"Now I'm a little worried about what Baal told them."

"Don't be, no one here is in doubt about your martial abilities. And the power of an elder demon doesn't hurt either."

"Well it won't hurt me anyway," both laughed at that. "But now I have to go into the guild later today for basic orientation and all that. I'm getting kind of nervous thinking about it."

"Why be nervous? You'll be the strongest one in the guild. You'll make a fine hero."

"I'm not doubting my combat abilities Dad. You and Baal and all the others gave me great training. It's just, there's more to being a hero than being good at fighting, even for a monster-slayer."

"What more is there? They point you to a monster, you slay it, they pay you."

"Well that's sort of what I thought it would be like at first too, but as it turns out, it's more complicated than that. Apparently how you look, and how you act are also important. Being a hero is also about how the public sees you."

"Let me guess, the people down at the guild were giving you talks about how a demon can't be a hero."

"Not exactly, in those words."

"Then in what words did they say it?"

"I mean, it wasn't that I can't be a hero, well, obviously, seeing as I got the job. It's just, at the interview, Ms. Weathers was coming up with all these strategies to help downplay the fact that I'm a demon."

"Are you becoming ashamed of your great lineage now?"

"Of course not Dad. But I'm starting to get the feeling that some of them think I should."

"Well to heaven with them!"

"I still have to work with these people."

"Then work. Work like you never have before. Become a hero whose deeds are even greater than those of Adonis. Show all those puny mortals what a true demon can do."

"That's... actually good advice."

"Ouch."

"I didn't mean it like that," Abaddon backpedaled so fast he almost fell over. "I was just expecting you to tell me to slay them and assert my dominance or something."

"And I would have, before our conversation the other day."

"I don't understand."

"It's all well and good to talk about slaying and destroying in Hell, but you're on Terra now. Like you said, the rules are different there. And when you talked about those saved templars, I could tell how much it bothered you."

"What do you mean? I wasn't bothered. It was just some stupid humans showing off."

Lucifer gave Abaddon a look. "My spawn, I can read you better than anyone else. I should be able to, I mean good Heavens I raised you. I know you wanted to slay those templars, but you knew you couldn't. It burned you up that you had to sit there and take it, and my telling you to rip them apart wasn't helping. Believe me, none of this makes me happy, but you're not in Hell anymore, and you can't keep doing things the same old way you have in the past."

"Then what do I do? What happens when I get into another situation like that?"

"You're the one who wanted all the new experiences; you figure it out."

"I'm seriously asking for help Dad!" Abaddon was close to crying out in frustration.

"And I'm being serious too. You need to figure this out. I know battle, and I know deception. We've already established that you won't be able to fight your way out of every situation, and I don't think the ol' Faustian bargain is looked upon favorably by the people of Terra. And even if it was, I don't think tricking and manipulating these people is what you want to do. As painful as it is to admit it, I can't help you when you need me most."

Abaddon just sat in silence for a minute. "You always help Dad. Even just by talking. And like you said, I just need to become the greatest hero I can. I'll just show everyone."

"That's the spirit. But you can't become the greatest hero if you're late to your own orientation. What time do you need to leave?"

"Yeah, probably in a few minutes."

"Well then, talk to you later. Love you."

"Love you too Dad."

Abaddon blinked in the bleary sunlight. He wondered if he would ever get out of a nexus portal without temporary blindness. He waited for his vision to return, then checked the street signs. The guild office was on the corner of Eve Avenue and 43rd Street. He was currently on Eve and 41st. A few minutes later he arrived. The building was unmistakable. It was larger by far than the two on either side, and there was a grand placard above the doors that showed a gleaming white Pegasus and a sword-wielding rider. Abaddon took a deep breath and went on in.

He found himself in a large lobby. He headed straight for the front desk. Behind it sat a skinny man with short hair and glasses.

"Name," the receptionist asked as Abaddon approached.

"Abaddon."

"Oh yes, the new hero," the receptionist's voice took on an excited tone. "Welcome to the team. From what I hear, you're quite the talented little monster-slayer. Good luck. I know things can be tricky at first around here, but I think you'll pick it up fast."

"Thanks. I was supposed to have an orientation meeting?"

"Right, you want the elevators on your left. Take one to the third floor. Then find room A. There should be several other new heroes there already."

"Thanks...again," Abaddon headed off to the elevators.

When he entered room A, Abaddon saw four other individuals already present. Three of them were sitting in chairs, and the fourth, a figure who looked like they were made of crystal, was leaning against a wall. Finding an empty chair, Abaddon sat down, consciously trying to avoid making eye contact with anyone. After a few minutes of awkward sitting, he heard the door open, and a new figure walked in. She was a woman with mid-length black hair, done up in a ponytail. She wore jeans and a red sports jacket. As soon as she came into the room, Abaddon noticed her glasses, and the crossbow and quiver of bolts on her back. The crossbow and quiver, as well as the glasses, were all clearly magical objects of some sort. He could feel a strange energy coming from them.

"Welcome, new heroes, to the White Pegasus Guild!" the woman's voice was jarringly upbeat. That coupled with her big smile made Abaddon half expect her to jump up and down and start clapping. "My name is Artemis, and I'll be leading you through our little orientation process. Now as you may have guessed, Artemis isn't my real name. But it is quite common for Heroes to give themselves new names that sound more heroic. As you are probably aware, I am named after the great hunter. But new names are not required. Now then, let's all get to know each other and the guild. And let's all have lots of fun!"

Chapter Seven

Orientation

"Now I know this might seem a bit middle school," Artemis still had a big smile on her face, "But I would like everyone to come up one at a time, and introduce themselves. Tell us your name, which hero specialization you picked, and the special skills or abilities that got you a job here at the White Pegasus Guild. Let's start with you Sir." Artemis pointed to an aged elf in blue robes.

The elf stood a bit unsteadily, holding on to a large wooden staff for support. He made his way to the front of the room slowly, then turned to address the others.

"My name is Valerius. I am a great wizard and sage. I have just been hired on at the White Pegasus Guild as a savior, and as a magical consultant. In my many years, I have studied a variety of arcane disciplines, and my specialty is magical theory relating to leylines."

"That is wonderful," Artemis chimed in, clapping for him, and not noticing or caring that no one else was. "Not many people realize, but a lot of saviors spend most of their time doing important research into magic and natural phenomena, so as to prevent potential Apocalypses before they even begin."

At the mention of the word Apocalypse, a blond teenage boy in a black trench coat who was sitting in front of Abaddon, turned in his chair and gave him a pointed look. He then got out of his chair, and moved up to the front of the room.

"I'll go next. My name's Brad van Helsing. That's right, a descendant of *THE* Abraham van Helsing. Going back for generations, my family is the greatest line of monster-slayers in the world. And I've been trained since birth to be the greatest of the greatest."

Brad sat back down in his chair without even waiting for Artemis to say anything. He turned to Abaddon and gave him another look, this one dripping with self-importance.

"Okay then," Artemis' smile faltered just a bit. "How about you there, the golem leaning up against the wall."

With each step the golem took, the floor shook ever so slightly. Abaddon had read about golems before, but he'd never actually seen one in person. This was so exciting. Abaddon suddenly realized he was grinning like an idiot and quickly turned his head under the pretext of coughing. He hoped no one had noticed.

"Hello there," the golem said in a voice that was much lighter than Abaddon would have expected. "My name is Mary. As Ms. Artemis said, and as I'm sure you already noticed, I am a golem. In case you weren't aware, that means I'm a being made of living rock. I don't really have any special skills or notable family members or anything. But golems are very resistant to magic, as well as physical injury. And our physical strength and endurance are at least three degrees above the Standard Human Deviation. I also happen to be a diamond golem. I uh, guess we are pretty rare, and our bodies are the toughest among golems. Starting today I am a defender of the people. I don't really believe that all heroes need to be of legendary quality. And I think that helping an underprivileged individual who's down on their luck can be just as important as saving the world or slaying a dangerous monster," At that Brad snorted audibly.

Artemis glared at Brad as Mary stomped her way back to the wall. She was replaced by a girl around Brad's age, who had olive skin and short black hair. She was wearing robes similar to the elf's, but hers were white instead of blue.

"Hello there, my name is Alethea. I come from a tradition of oracles and prophets going back to Greece, in earth B.C.E. I am a new savior here at the White Pegasus Guild. My specialty is predicting the future, obviously useful in preventing world shattering disasters. I also have other divinely granted abilities such as healing injuries, and curing disease. While I may not be able to fight monsters or anything like that, I hope my abilities to help and heal others will make me a great savior. Thank you," Alethea bowed and went to take her seat.

"Excellent," Artemis looked even happier than before, if that was possible. "It's good to remember that not all heroes are big strong warriors who are only good at killing. There are also great healers and protectors in our ranks as well. Okay, that just leaves you in the back."

If he were a more cynical demon, Abaddon would have thought Artemis had planned that. Either way, as far as setups go, he probably couldn't have asked for a much worse one. He was nervous enough already, and his nervousness only grew as he got to the front of the room.

"Hi there," Abaddon gave an awkward half wave. "My name is- well I uh, suppose you can call me Abe," he almost winced at the name, but continued. "I'm sure you noticed that I'm a demon. I'm actually originally from the Ninth Circle of Hell. Starting today I guess I'm going to be a monster-slayer, just like Brad over there, though uh, my family doesn't have a history of slaying monsters," no, they had a history of slaying angels and humans, but he wasn't going to say that. "But I have spent most of my life training in the arts of fighting and black magic. Aside from my demonic magic, I also have this war hammer named Spellbreaker. It's a greater artifact, and as the name suggests, it shatters any magic it comes into contact with. And I guess I have this obsidian bracer. It's a lesser artifact that can conjure obsidian armor forged in the blackest pits. But that's uh, that's standard issue for demon warriors. At least in the Ninth Circle anyway."

Abaddon stood awkwardly in front of the rest of the new heroes for several moments before seeming to notice, then quickly returned to his seat. Artemis clapped enthusiastically again as he sat down.

"Alright everyone, now wasn't that fun? Well, I'm sure you all have a lot of questions. Soon enough you will get to meet with other heroes of your given hero specialization, and they will be able to answer any specific questions you have pertaining to that. But in the meantime, I am happy to answer any general questions about being a hero or working at the White Pegasus Guild, or any questions relating to monster slaying, as that is my hero specialization. Alright, who's first?"

Brad raised a hand, "So do I get paid for each monster I eliminate, and do the bigger and badder monsters get me more money?"

"No, actually. Contrary to what many people think, heroes get paid a salary just like in most jobs, not a pay based on commission."

"But then what's the point of me actually slaying any monsters? I mean, if I get paid regardless."

"Well, aside from the desire to help others," at this, Artemis' smile tightened, "the more heroic deeds you perform, and the more impressive the deeds, the more likely you are to receive a promotion. You see, you all will start out as basic heroes. A hero can be promoted to a noble hero, a noble hero to a hero of great deeds, and a hero of great deeds is promoted to a hero of legend. A promotion of course means better pay and benefits, but also more dangerous call in jobs. Also, every hero must submit monthly reports, detailing their heroic deeds, or lack thereof, for that month. If a hero goes too many months in a row without performing any heroic deeds, barring special circumstances, they could be liable to lose their job. Though this only happens in very rare cases, and you have to miss at least four months in a row before you can even be considered for being let go. Also, I know the rules are different for saviors, given that worldwide catastrophes are much rarer than monster attacks or people in need of defending, but I don't know what those rules specifically are."

"But wouldn't it still make more sense to get paid based on commission?" Brad pressed on. "I mean, then you wouldn't get paid for not doing work."

"Oh heavens no. Pay based on commission would be a nightmare. Just think about it. If your livelihood revolved around the number of monsters you killed, then pretty soon people would be letting chimeras loose on the city just so they could slay them. And can you imagine how it would be for saviors? We'd have a new apocalypse on the horizon every other day. Now sure, this system may not be perfect, but it's a lot better than that. And besides, we aren't going to find a system that is. So all we can do is the best we can. Any other questions?"

Mary spoke up, "Beyond getting called in for specific jobs, how do acts of heroism work?"

"Could you clarify the question please?"

"I mean, how does doing our jobs work? Do we have specific hours? Do we sign in and out, or what?"

"Oh, I see. Yes, that's a very good question. Actually, you are assumed to always be on the clock as it were. If you see monster attacking, or something like that, it is up to you to decide whether or not to get involved, assuming you haven't been specifically called in for the job. But this doesn't mean you have to just wait for an opportunity to fall into your lap. If you know a basilisk is on the loose for example, you can totally make a point of hunting it down. Just make sure you detail your heroic deeds fully in your monthly report. If you spent a week hunting down and killing a basilisk, you want to make sure the management knows how much time and effort you put in, so you're more likely to get promoted."

Brad started to say something in reply, but Artemis cut him off. Abaddon wasn't sure if it was intentional or not. "Any more questions? If not, then I can take you all to your assigned lockers. These are where you can store your personal equipment, such as weapons and armor, trophies from your kills and the like, though you do not have to store things there if you do not want to. They are simply for your convenience. In some cases," Artemis looked at Valerius, "individuals might get their own offices, alchemical labs, and such. But that is less common, especially starting out. Now if you'll all follow me," Artemis bounced out of the room, humming a tune to herself as she went.

As Abaddon made his way out of the room, Brad pushed past him roughly. Given that he had been sitting behind Brad, Abaddon had to assume that he had intentionally hung back, just to bump into him.

"Watch it Hell boy," Brad snapped.

Abaddon sighed deeply. This time it was easier to stifle the urge to reach for Spellbreaker, but not by much. This job was going to be much more complicated than he had initially thought.

Chapter Eight

Altercation

"Alright, here are the lockers," Artemis waved a hand into a very large room. "As you can see, the lockers are divided into three sections, based on your hero specialization. The lockers are alphabetical, and will have your name on them, so they should be easy to locate. Now if we could all-" Artemis was interrupted by a beeping sound. "One second, I'm getting a sending spell," she turned to answer. "Yes, mhm, yes, yes, I see. Yeah, I'll be right over." Then turning back to the group. "I'm sorry, I just got a call in job. It's a request for me personally, so I can't turn it down. That will have to be it for orientation today. Everyone feel free make yourself at home, unpack in your locker, etc. You can also find other heroes around the guild if you have more questions. Again, I'm really sorry, but I have to go," Artemis turned and headed out the door.

"Well then," Velarius headed toward the door as well. "Seeing as things are finished here, I shall retire to my study. I have much important research waiting for me," and with that, he too was gone.

"Yeah, *SOME* of us have important hero work to do," Brad started to follow the other two. "Oh, and I'm keeping an eye on you, Hell boy. So just stay out of my way."

"What's your problem asshole?" now that Abaddon's embarrassment was gone, he was becoming pretty mad. And his pent-up anger from the templars probably wasn't helping matters either.

"My problem?" Brad stopped and turned back to Abaddon. "My problem is having to work with a damn demon."

"Hey, that's not very nice," Mary was looking really indignant, and had he not been so mad himself, Abaddon would have marveled at the amount of expression a face made of diamond was able to make.

"Not very nice is starting the god damn apocalypse and ending the world!"

"Don't blame me for that. That was over three centuries ago. I wasn't even born yet."

"Yeah? Well if you had been, I bet you'd have lead the charge against the gates of Heaven. And I'm supposed to buy that you wanna play hero? I may not have as long a life span as you demons do, but that doesn't mean I was born yesterday."

"Get off my freakin' back already. I doubt you even know the first thing about me."

"I know everything about you. I've spent my whole life training to *KILL* monsters like you."

"Oh please," Abaddon almost reached for Spellbreaker. "You haven't been trained to kill me."

"What, you think you're so tough?" Brad actually did reach for a weapon: a silver dagger. "I kill shit like you for a warmup."

"Just stop it Brad!" Mary stepped in between the two of them.

"Yeah, Brad. You wouldn't want to shame the *PROUD* van Helsing lineage-"

"That's it! DIE DEMON SCUM."

Brad dodged around Mary, lunging at Abaddon with incredible speed. His dagger flashed out, point aiming for Abaddon's heart. Holy runes of silver glowed on the blade as it aimed true. Abaddon pulled Spellbreaker from his back, and swung with the war hammer. The two magic weapons clashed, and the silver blade shattered into pieces, barely even halting Abaddon's swing. With his free hand, Abaddon grabbed Brad's stunned face. Then, in one quick burst of speed he moved to the side, slamming Brad's head into the wall.

"FOOLISH MORTAL," Abaddon roared, his voice echoing the dark flames of the pit. "YOUR SOUL SHALL NOT BE SPARED MY WRATH."

Brad could not respond, but only jibber incoherently. His eyes were alight with true terror, the emotion seared into them by Abaddon's fiery gaze. Through his haze of anger, Abaddon felt a sudden pressure. And then he was moving backwards, his hand pulling free from Brad's face.

"THAT'S ENOUGH. BOTH OF YOU," Mary had Abaddon in a bearhug, pinning his arms at his sides. Formidable though he was, he was no match for the golem's strength, and struggle as he might, he could not free himself. "Everyone just calm down," Mary stopped shouting, but did not loosen her grip. "Brad, you had no right provoking and attacking Abe like that. And *YOU,* you took things way too far. Self-defense is one thing, but you were going to kill Brad. Now chill the hell out or I'm going to have to keep squeezing until you do."

Abaddon blinked. Using all of his willpower, he forced his blood to cool. He pulled the rage from the corners of his eyes and took a deep breath. Or at least he tried to. It was proving difficult with Mary's arms around his stomach.

"I'm sorry," Abaddon deliberately spoke very slowly. "I got out of control, but I'm alright now. You can let me go, but I understand if you do not want to yet."

Mary's arms relaxed, and Abaddon dropped to his feet. It was only when he touched the floor, that he realized she had been holding him several inches off the ground. Brad was on his knees, still shaking. After a moment, he collected himself and quickly got to his feet.

"See?" Brad was pointing at Abaddon, his hand shaking. "He's just another monster. And they want him on the team? This is some kind of sick joke," he turned and ran out of the room.

"Thank you for stopping me Mary, I-" Abaddon stopped short, at the sound of suppressed sobs.

Both Abaddon and Mary turned to see Alethea pressed up against a set of lockers behind them. Her whole body was so stiff it almost made Abaddon sore to look at. The tears were unmoving on her face, which was a frozen visage of terror, exactly like Brad's had been.

"Alethea, I-" Abaddon stopped, not sure of what to say. He started to move towards her, but her eyes got wider, it seemed as though her head were shaking, if just barely, and it looked like she might pass out at any moment. "I didn't mean to-"

"Let's just go," Mary put a hand on Abaddon's shoulder.

"Well at least you aren't terrified of me," Abaddon and Mary were sitting in an empty hallway in a back corner of the guild office.

"Alethea isn't terrified of you either."

"Did you see the look on her face?"

"Yes, but it wasn't you she was afraid of."

"Oh, was it the guy whose face I indented into the wall?"

"No. Look," Mary put her hand on Abaddon's shoulder again, "Alethea may be a hero like us, but she's also just a girl. Sure she can predict the future and cure diseases and all that, but she comes from a tradition of oracles, not warriors. I doubt she's seen any fighting or violence before in her life. To have a fight like that break out right in front of her, well that would terrify anyone."

"It didn't terrify you, and you're not a warrior, are you?"

"I'm different. My body is made of diamond. I'm used to not getting hurt by anything. When I was five years old, I was playing with a ball and it got away from me. I chased it into the street, and got hit by an oncoming chariot going well past the speed limit. The horse pulling the chariot got killed, and the man driving it was concussed. I didn't have so much as a scratch. I may not be trained to fight, and I've never seen real violence up close, at least not until today, but I know there's almost nothing out there that can hurt me, not even you. I remember what you said during the introduction. That war hammer destroys any magic it comes into contact with. You shattered Brad's silver dagger because it was magical. But even with the strength of a demon behind it, that weapon probably wouldn't make a mark on my body, let alone hurt me."

"But that doesn't mean you shouldn't be scared of me. Brad's reaction was perfectly justified."

"Brad's a prick. He made that pretty clear during the introductions."

"So, you don't think what I did was wrong?"

"Oh no, you were way out of line, but that was only because Brad intentionally provoked you. Plus, he struck first. I don't think you would just attack anyone out of the blue or anything," Mary was cut off by a beeping from a sending spell. "Oh shit, sorry, I got to go," she got up and started to lumber off. "But we should definitely continue this conversation some time," she called back. "And maybe we can even talk about something other than your demonic rage."

"Y-yeah," Abaddon said to the now empty hallway, "sure."

Chapter Nine

A Rather Stern Talking To

"Let me get this straight," Ms. Weathers was pacing in her office, as Abaddon sat uncomfortably on the couch. "You barely even finished your orientation, and you almost killed another hero?!"

"Well he-"

"Don't give me that he started it crap. I am well aware that Brad started it, and he will get yelled at too. Do you have anything to say for yourself?"

"He attacked me, I defended myself, and I took things too far," Abaddon wasn't sure how apologetic to sound, and he wasn't even sure how apologetic he was.

"Took things too far? After defusing the situation, you slammed his head into a wall and threatened his very soul if the accounts are correct."

"In my defense, just stopping his initially attack and destroying his weapon was not enough to defuse the situation."

"I don't care! Maybe in Hell you can kill someone just for looking at you funny, and that's considered alright, but not here. Here we have rules."

"Hey, he pulled a holy silver blade on me. He was aiming for the heart."

"And I already told you that Brad will be getting his own talking to. But Brad isn't in as delicate a position as you are."

"What does 'delicate position' mean?"

"Look, you may not like it," Ms. Weathers stopped pacing and was now staring directly at Abaddon, "but your situation is very different from his. There was some definite controversy about hiring you; not everyone was on board with the idea. You ended up with the job because you quite frankly have incredible credentials. But you are still an unknown demon, fresh from the pits of Hell. Meanwhile Brad, whatever less than stellar personality quirks he may have, is also quite skilled, and just so happens to be the next heir to one of the most prestigious monster hunter families in the world."

"So what, the rules are different for him?"

"No, but people's reactions to when he breaks them are. Brad has centuries of good credibility already built up, meanwhile you have the exact opposite. All he has to do is point to his lineage, and most people will give him the benefit of the doubt. You on the other hand have to fight yours every step of the way."

"What does that mean? Am I going to get fired on my first day?"

"No you won't. However, someone like Brad gets a few free tries, a couple of do-overs, and that's just a luxury you don't have. Short of you *ACTUALLY* killing someone, there is very little that could legally allow us to fire you on the spot. Thank your dark lords and the Infernal Equality Act for that. But like I said, a lot of people here at White Pegasus weren't thrilled about you coming on in the first place, Brad wasn't the only one, and now you've just given them more ammunition to use against you. I wouldn't be surprised if they're writing up a petition to get you fired right now. And I have to say, anymore incidents like this one, and I might just be signing it myself."

"This won't happen again; you don't have to worry about that."

"And what guarantee do I have?" Ms Weathers looked understandably skeptical.

"I'm not an idiot. I mess up again like that, and I'm probably out of here. Aside from this being one of the best jobs I could possibly find, if I get kicked out of White Pegasus for playing rough, do you think another heroes guild would hire me? Just like you said, I can't afford to make mistakes."

"But demons are known for their tempers. Can you give me good reason to believe that your anger won't get the better of you again? Isn't that what happened with Brad: he made you mad and you snapped?"

"So demons are just mindless beasts who cannot control their rage?"

"No, but they come from a society where they don't have to."

"Now you're just being diplomatic," even as he was getting mad, Abaddon had to realize the irony of going into a rage at the prospect of being told he couldn't control his temper, so he forcibly calmed himself.

"Fine, that is part of it. My *JOB* is to be diplomatic. I help heroes to craft a good image, that's what I'm paid for. And no, even if I thought it were true, I wouldn't insult you to your face. But personally, I do not think demons are just mindless beasts who cannot control their rage; I think that's just a cheap cop out. If you want the truth, I think you are an intelligent person who can control your rage but chooses not to, and that just makes you weak and lazy."

That shut Abaddon up. He tried for several seconds to think of a response to that. At first he wanted to respond with angry, but that would only prove her point. Besides, she wasn't really who he was angry at. Then he thought to respond by being apologetic, but that was no good either. First, he would have to feel sorry about what he did, and honestly, he didn't. He felt bad about how he had made Alethea break down from fear. He felt bad about how Mary had seemed disappointed in him. And he felt bad about how he had let Ms. Weathers down after she'd hired him. But no, Abaddon just couldn't feel bad for Brad no matter how hard he tried. What Abaddon finally settled on, was not settling on an emotion.

"You're right," his voice was flat, giving away no feeling behind the words. "Regardless of what I think, you're right. So now what do I do? Is there a reprimand? Some anger management classes? What?"

"Now, you get to work."

That was not the answer Abaddon had been expecting, "Excuse me?"

"Well you are employed here to be a hero, aren't you?"

"Yes, but after what happened-"

"After what happened, believe it or not, the world kept spinning, and still needs saving. And people are still calling in with requests."

"So wait, I got a call-in job on my first day?"

"This normally never happens, but we got a request, and you just so happen to be our most qualified hero to tackle it. It only seemed appropriate to send you. Since you're still starting out here, you don't have an official guild agent yet to handle your call-ins and promotions and whatnot, so I made the decision to give this one to you. No one complained."

"Alright, so what's the request?"

"Well, it seems a cerberus is rampaging through Little Purgatory, causing all sorts of problems."

"A cerberus? Are you sure it isn't a normal hellhound?"

"Nope, three heads and everything. Apparently the damn thing's been starting fires, knocking down buildings, and you don't want to know what it's been doing in the public fountains. Needless to say, this must be dealt with immediately. I assume there won't be any problems?"

"I've dealt with a cerberus or two before; I can handle it."

"Good, then see that you do."

Chapter Ten

Dog Fighting

Ms. Weathers hadn't been kidding. When Abaddon arrived at the edge of Little Purgatory, he could see the signs of something having rampaged through the area. If nothing else, it made it easy to find what he was looking for. Once he got to the center of Little Purgatory, Abaddon could hear a growling roaring sound. Then he saw the jets of flame. And there it was, the first beast for him to slay. The cerberus stood at around fifteen feet tall, all dark fur and gnashing teeth. The three heads were yowling in different directions, the left-most head spewing flames.

Abaddon stuck his fingers in his mouth and whistled a sharp note. The cerberus turned all three of its heads to look in his direction. Abaddon drew Spellbreaker from his back and struck it on the ground several times, calling out to the beast. The cerberus charged, each bound of its paws shaking the ground. The middle head shot down, teeth aimed right at Abaddon. He swung in with the war hammer, and the beast caught it in its jaws. The two struggled for several seconds, locked in a grim contest for the weapon. Finally, Abaddon wrenched it free, causing the cerberus' middle head to swing to the side. It collided with the leftmost head. As it steadied itself, Abaddon took this opportunity and lunged forward. Bringing Spellbreaker to bear, Abaddon swung with his full might, striking the middle head right on the snout. The beast recoiled, flames billowing from its nose in agitation.

Abaddon spoke words of the cursed speech of hell. His tongue twisted as the world went dark. He leapt back, striking the ground with his hammer once more. The great beast's mouths opened, acid dripping to the ground with a hiss like a thousand serpents. Bearing its teeth, the cerberus lunged at Abaddon once more. This time when he spoke in the dark tongues of demons, Abaddon touched the ground with his hand, calling forth a great red circle to appear. Dark flames erupted from the earth, hurling chucks of rock into the air. Undaunted by the blast of fire, the cerberus kept coming, its mouths lashing out, biting the stones, and crushing them into dust.

Abaddon was moving to the left, trying to get around the beast. But the cerberus' tail, formed of a great black snake, swung wide, striking Abaddon, and sending him crashing into a wall. Abaddon slowly rose to his feet, picking up Spellbreaker as he stood. Readying himself, he swung with his mighty weapon, striking the rubble on the ground, sending more rocks hurtling at the beast from Hell. The cerberus leapt into the air, once more crushing the stones with its fearsome jaws. When it descended, the ground quaked.

Again, the black snake that was its tail whipped around, but this time Abaddon was ready. He rolled under it. When he stood, the middle head of the cerberus spouted flames. Abaddon raised his left hand, turning the flames aside as they sought to engulf him.

Again, Abaddon's words darkened the air, the blackest tongues that brought madness crawling to the corners of mortal minds. The cerberus moved low, and its tail swung forth a second time. Again Abaddon moved aside, avoiding the blow, continuing to utter the dark words of the damned. Now came forth a brutal command, spoken with such force and finality that even mortal ears, not versed in the tongues of demons would hear and obey. The cerberus heard and submitted its will, crashing to the ground, falling onto its back. Abaddon leapt onto the great beast's stomach. Standing atop it, he raised one hand high. With great swiftness he brought it crashing down and…. began to scratch the cerberus' stomach.

With sounds like roaring thunder, the cerberus' tail slapped against the ground, and one leg began to twitch. The long tongues of its three foul mouths whipped forth, acid dripping as the beast of darkness drooled happily.

"Awww, you were just playing, weren't you?" Abaddon continued scratching the cerberus' belly as it thrashed excitedly. "Who's all tired out? You are. Yes you are, yes you are. Ooh, yes you are."

Then Abaddon's voice changed, reverting to the dark tongue which damned the very souls of man and beast alike. He issued forth another cursed command. Flames erupted from the ground as chains of purest darkness shot from the earth, binding the cerberus in shadow. As the great chains constricted, so too was the cerberus' form constricted in turn. In moments the cursed spell was cast, and the great beast was now brought low, little more than a puppy of the damned.

"Who wants to come live in my apartment?" Abaddon grabbed the cerberus, scratching its three heads as it licked him with its wicked tongues. "Yes, *YOU'RE* going to come live in my apartment."

"What is that thing?"

Abaddon's landlady was a short and irritable looking goblin. As much as she smoked, Abaddon was quite frankly surprised she hadn't keeled over long ago. Then again, he knew very little about goblins. Maybe smoking wasn't bad for them like it was for other creatures.

"It's a cerberus," Abaddon scratched the back of his head awkwardly. "You know, a three-headed hound of Hell? They're quite rare actually."

"That little thing is a mythological cerberus?"

"Well, I used black magic to shrink it down so I could bring it with me."

"And why would you want to do that?"

"So it could be my pet?"

"Let me get this straight," the landlady gave him a look. "You want to keep a guardian of the gates of hell in my apartment complex as a pet?"

"Well, I don't think this little guy was a guardian of any gates to Hell, but yes."

"What does a hellhound even eat? Cuz if you're gonna be sacrificing the blood of the innocent all over my carpets-"

"That would be awful. The blood of the innocent is very hard to digest, and provides little nutrients. An energetic little cerberus needs a solid food diet. He'll eat meat, just like other dogs. You know, dragon, manticore, phoenix, anything really."

"And how are you planning on feeding this 'little cerberus' of yours anyway? The local supermarket doesn't sell phoenix."

"I'm a monster-slayer. I'm allowed to collect trophies, so I can feed him with that. And if I need to, I can always get him food at the pet store."

"You mean like dog food?" the landlady seemed very hesitant in asking the question.

"Well, not dog necessarily. Whatever pets they have in stock will do just fine."

"And why should I let a foul creature from the pits of Hell stay in my apartments?"

"Well, you're renting to me, aren't you?"

"*YOU* pay eight fifty a month."

"I'll bump it up to an even nine hundred."

The landlady paused for a moment, then sighed, "Obviously you need to do everything: feeding, walking, all that crap. And speaking of, I don't want 'surprises' waiting for me around here. That thing goes outside just like any other dog, three heads or no."

"Oh, thank you, thank you, thank you," Abaddon grasped both her hands and shook them so vigorously that she was almost lifted off the ground.

"Just get the damned thing inside before I decide an extra fifty bucks a month ain't worth it."

"Welcome to your new home," Abaddon smiled as his new pet raced around the small room. "We're going to have lots of adventures in New Eden together. Yes we are, yes we are."

Well, Abaddon's first day as a hero had definitely been exciting. He hadn't been too hopeful when it started with him almost killing one of his new teammates, but it had ended with him getting a new friend. So, all in all, he considered it a good day. He gave the little guy a big smile.

"From now on, I shall call you Sir Boris."

Chapter Eleven

Even More Friends

Abaddon was sitting in a chair at a table outside a small coffee shop called Sacred Grounds. Abaddon half thought Mary chose this place to meet up at just to be ironic. He sipped his coffee, not sure exactly how to start.

"So's how's your first week at White Pegasus been? I hear you got a call-in job on your first day."

"Yeah," Abaddon took another sip. "A cerberus was tearing up Little Purgatory, and I was sent to deal with it."

"Heard all about that. So how's it feel to be a big bad monster-slayer?"

"Well, to be honest, I haven't actually slain any monsters yet."

"But the cerberus-"

"Is my pet now. He's living with me in my apartment."

"But aren't hellhounds supposed to be huge? How would one even fit inside your door?"

"Oh, I shrunk him with a black magic curse. He's about the size of a puppy now, and just as playful."

"Wow," Mary laughed, an altogether odd, but not unpleasant sound.

"What?"

"Oh nothing, it's just, that's really adorable. You never really think about demons having pets. And you especially don't think about them playing with puppies."

"Well we do, some of us anyway. How's your first week on the job been?"

"I've actually been helping to rebuild Little Purgatory, after you and the hellhound trashed it."

"Hey, Boris did most of the trashing. And besides, he was only playing."

"You named your hellhound Boris?"

"Well, his full name is Sir Boris, but yeah, that's what I call him."

"Wow," Mary laughed again. "That's even more adorable."

If Abaddon could have, he probably would have blushed, "So anyway, when you say helping to rebuild Little Purgatory-"

"I mean it literally. I've mostly been moving debris and construction materials, you know, heaving lifting jobs."

"Odd, I wouldn't have thought a hero would do that sort of thing."

"And why not? It's like I said in my introduction: being a hero is more than just slaying monsters and saving the world. And being a defender of the people means defending them from all manner of things, not just some thug with a sword and something to prove."

"Oh well, I didn't actually know that. I just sort of assumed defender of the people meant vigilante style crime fighting."

"Oh no, there's a whole social justice angle to it as well. Though some people do focus primarily on beating bad guys up. But I think they miss the point of being a defender of the people."

"Wow," Abaddon took another sip of his drink. "When you say it like that, being a monster-slayer seems rather small-minded. I didn't even think about how those people would rebuild after I defeated Boris."

"Hey, not everyone can be looking out for the little guy. If it weren't for you, there would have been nothing left to rebuild. You definitely cut down on the number of buildings that I have to fix."

"Thanks... or.... You're welcome.... I'm not really sure."

"Both are fine," Mary smiled. "You almost seem as nervous as you were during the introductions."

"I was just wondering why you were doing this?"

"What? Being a hero?"

"No, I mean, asking me to meet you here."

"Hey, I may not eat or drink, but I figured you'd appreciate it."

"No, not this place specifically. I mean, why did you want to talk to me again? When you left after my 'fight' with Brad you said we should definitely continue our conversation. I just don't know why you wanted to."

"I find you interesting. There's a lot more to you than just some battle-hardened monster. I wanted to get to know that you."

"Oh, well, uh, sure I mean-"

"You seem totally caught off guard. Are you that unaccustomed to making friends?"

"Um…. yes?"

"Okay then," Mary was now the one who seemed totally caught off guard. "I wasn't actually expecting that to be the case. I would have assumed even demons have friends."

"Oh we do, after a fashion. It's just that I never really…. well…."

"What the hell happened? Wow, didn't realize that until I said it. Anyway, what happened. *I* had friends growing up, and I'm an eight-foot-tall diamond?"

"Wait, did you actually like *GROW* up, grow up, or…."

"Okay, no, I have always been an eight-foot-tall diamond. But, golems still mature and age, same as everyone else, well, we age much slower than everyone else but-"

"I'm two hundred and fifty," Abaddon took another sip of his coffee.

"Wait, what? I'm only forty seven, and I thought I was the oldest hero at White Pegasus, other than Valerius of course."

"Yeah, demons live for thousands of years. Well, in theory anyway."

"In theory?"

"Yeah, most of us get killed way before then. A demon who makes it to their first millennia is considered incredibly powerful, or perhaps insanely lucky. But no one remembers those guys. Insanely lucky means they probably avoided ever getting into any fights or danger, so you know, not really worth-" Abaddon stopped. "Now that I think about it, I don't really know how to finish that sentence in a way that doesn't sound terrible."

"Yeah really. I can't think of one either. But don't feel too bad. Hell is a different place than Terra. I imagine strength and power and all that are what's valued most."

"Yup, might makes right is pretty much how things work in Hell. For example, in theory anyone can be a ruler of one of the circles of Hell, they just have to kill the current ruler."

"So you could sneak up on them, or kill them in their sleep, and suddenly you rule Hell?"

"Well, that circle anyway. But the thing is, if you weren't strong enough to best the current ruler in a head-on fight, no way you're gonna be ruler for more than a few days. Someone else is going to come along and kill you real quick."

"Hell doesn't sound like a very pleasant place."

"Well not to visit, no. But if you grow up there, well, you learn to fight, and how to be strong. It's not that bad really."

"I see," Mary looked him over for a minute, then. "You still haven't answered my question. You know, about why you never had friends."

"Well that's," Abaddon struggled for a few moments. "You see the thing is I- well- I…. should probably get back to the apartment. Boris will need a walk or he might start trying to tear up the place," Abaddon very quickly stood up. "Thanks for talking," he turned and left.

"Yeah, okay then…. good talking to you too…. I guess…."

Chapter Twelve

Going for a Walk

"Well I could have handled that better, huh Boris?" Abaddon addressed the three-headed pup as they walked down the street.

Abaddon was mad at himself when he thought back to how he had left things with Mary. He didn't want anyone to know about Dad, but that had definitely been the wrong way to go about it. He just hadn't been expecting to have to address that issue so soon. But what was he supposed to say? "Well, when you're the son of Lucifer, it's a bit hard to make friends." That would have just complicated things. Wouldn't it? No, no, he didn't want anyone in New Eden to know he was the son of Lucifer, and that was the right decision. But regardless, freaking out like that and just up and leaving had been really dumb. Mary was looking like the one coworker he hadn't managed to distance himself from on the first day, and now he might have just blown that too.

"Ah well, at least we're good friends," Abaddon kneeled down and scratched the cheeks on the left and right heads. "Yes, we are, very good friends."

Abaddon kept on walking, but his internal musings on his lack of social skills were quickly interrupted by a voice calling out from the other side of the street, "Help us, oh dark brother."

Abaddon turned to see a pair of young guys, one a human, and the other an elf, both dressed in unnecessary amounts of black leather and spikes. A golden-armored templar was standing in front of them. Abaddon thought they were looking in his direction, and was very confused.

"Excuse me," Abaddon crossed the street, "do I know you?"

"We too are servants of the great lord Lucifer," the human declared.

"Yeah!" the elf made the rock symbol with his right hand and stuck out his tongue. "Strike down this unbeliever who mocks our dark lord."

"What in Heaven's name is going on here?"

"These two were spray-painting their praises to Satan all over the walls of these buildings," the templar held up a can of red paint. "They claim to have association with you. Where you an accomplice to their actions?"

"Good heavens no; I've never seen these two in my life."

"But we also serve your dark master. Help us oh great warrior of the infernal pits."

"Yeah, kill this non-believer. He cannot silence the voice of the dark one."

"What is this?" Abaddon had no idea what was going on. "Officer, these two are clearly delirious or something. I don't know what they think they're talking about, but no humans or elves serve in the dark armies of Hell."

"What are you? Some kind of demonic soldier?" the templar eyed Spellbreaker.

"No," Abaddon pulled out his ID glyph. "I'm a hero employed with the White Pegasus heroes guild."

The templar snatched the glyph, "Let me see that. Huh? It seems the White Pegasus will hire anyone these days," he handed the glyph back

"What's that supposed to mean?"

"Yeah, slay him for his insult against you, oh dark-"

"Shut up," Abaddon turned to the two teens and gave them a look that instantly rendered them silent.

"Whoa, whoa," the templar held up his hands. "I'm just surprised that they hired a demon as a hero is all."

"And why should that be a surprise?!"

"Geez buddy, do I need to spell it out for you?"

"Whatever," Abaddon turned to leave. "And you two idiots don't know shit about Lucifer, or demons, or Hell in general. C'mon Boris."

Well great, now Abaddon was in an even worse mood. Even now that he was a hero, the templars still gave him crap. And he still couldn't do anything about it. He really just wanted to smash them in the face, but obviously that wouldn't solve any of his problems. It probably wouldn't even make him feel better. And what was with those punks? They sought to serve his father? They were a couple of idiots graffitiing walls, and they dared invoke Lucifer's name? And for what, so Abaddon could slay a templar for them? They were mere pathetic mortals, claiming to command him?! The worst part of all of this was that the more he thought about it, the more Abaddon wanted to slay them for their insolence. Had he been in Hell, he would have ripped them apart and hung their eviscerated corpses on the walls of Pandemonium. Definitely not something a hero would do. Good heavens, the saved templars had a point!

"Raaah!" Abaddon smashed his fist into a lamppost, causing an indentation.

Several people on the street stopped to look at him. A few hastily went around him, clearly wary of getting too close. Now all of Boris' heads were barking excitedly. Abaddon took a deep breath, and he forced his face to assume a less terrifying visage. He knelt down again, this time scratching Boris under his chins.

"Calm down, Boris, it's okay. I just got a little angry. Nothing to worry about."

Abaddon sat down on a bench at the edge of a small park. With a quick word in the damned tongues, he bound the infernal chains around Boris' necks to the leg of the bench and stretched his arms above his head. Well, it was a nice day if nothing else. And it had started out good. The optimistic part of him thought that he probably hadn't blown things with Mary. After all, if she had still wanted to talk to him after he nearly killed a fellow hero, something like running away unexpectedly was probably not going to be a deal breaker. But then the more pessimistic side of him piped up, pointing out that if he acted that way the first time, he was liable to make more mistakes the next time.

"Well I gotta learn how to interact with mortals at some point," Abaddon sighed. "I suppose the best way is firsthand experience."

After all, hadn't that been the whole reason he had come to New Eden in the first place? Reading books had been great and all, but they couldn't compare to the real thing. And sure, he'd known there would be a lot of tough times, and a lot of adjustments. This was just another thing he would have to power through. Good heavens, he couldn't be expected to get it right on the first try, could he? Mr. Pessimism piped up for a second time, pointing out that him being two hundred and fifty, and this being his first try making friends, was quite sad. But hey, was it really his fault that he'd never really had friends before? Sure, demon friendship worked differently than mortal friendship, but even then, the fact that he was the son of Lucifer had to have been a big problem. He was a prime target for challenge. He had to spend most of his time training to fight. And it wasn't just him, it was the honor of the line of Lucifer at stake. He couldn't be the first of that line to lose the throne. But he hadn't been training 24/7. Surely if he'd wanted to he could have- No, who would have wanted to be his friend? Everyone feared him. There were few demons in the Ninth Circle who could match him. He was better than all of them.

"Is that the best you can come up with?" Mr. Pessimism sneered. "You're better than they are, so you don't need them?"

"It's not my fault those other demons were so weak."

"Oh, I didn't want to be in their stupid club anyway, nyaah."

"Shut up. The son of Lucifer does not have time for such pathetic creatures."

"But the giant rock might not want to be my friend now, waaah."

Abaddon shook his head. This was getting ridiculous. Trying to psychoanalyze his childhood was one of the most idiotic things he'd ever done. Things were different in Hell. He would learn to adapt to life in New Eden and everything would work itself- Abaddon's assurances were cut off by shouting coming from an alley on the other side of the street.

"You bastard, I'm going to kill you!"

Abaddon turned to Sir Boris, "Stay," then proceeded to run off towards the alley.

Chapter Thirteen

A Man with Some Sticks

When Abaddon arrived on the scene, he saw four figures in the alley. On the left side, stood a big female with dark green skin that Abaddon assumed must be an ogre or troll of some kind. She was carrying a mean looking knife. At her side was a smaller figure of similar complexion. He was carrying a club. On Abaddon's right, there was a man in a dirty apron cowering up against the wall, and between him and the assailants was another man. He was muscular, though around average height. He wore jeans and a white t-shirt stretched across his broad chest. A white cloth headband adorned his brow, and he held a pair of thick wooden rods, one and a half to two feet in length. If Abaddon was correct, the man was of Asian descent, he thought Chinese, but wasn't sure.

The female moved in, shouting. Apparently, she had been the one who'd issued the death threat. Abaddon reach for Spellbreaker. A good fight, and some heroic deeds was just what he needed to brighten his day. But before his hand had even grasped Spellbreaker's handle, the man in white closed the distance. Abaddon was so surprised by the human's speed that he stopped in his tracks. The sticks were a blur. In the first instant, her knife was smashed from her hand. In the next, Abaddon counted six, no wait, eight, hits to her chest, four on each side. He wasn't sure, but he thought he heard a few ribs crack. And whether she was an ogre *OR* a troll, that would be quite a feat. By the end of about the fourth second, the female was kneeling on the ground, clutching her chest, letting out shallow, pained breaths. It took about one more second for the other aggressor to realize what happened. When he did, he shrieked, dropped his club, and ran down the alley as fast as he could.

"Th-thank you," the man in the apron said after a few moments of shocked blinking. "How can I repay you?"

"By finding the nearest templar as quickly as you can. This one will need to be put in custody, but I have to stay here and watch over her, make sure she doesn't get away."

"Of course," the man stood awkwardly for a moment, then bowed. "Thank you again," he ran off down the street.

Abaddon didn't quite know what to say or do, so he just stood there and waited. A few minutes later, the man returned with a templar in tow.

"The shop-owner filled me in," she said. "Thank you for capturing this dangerous individual."

"Happy to help. I assume you have everything under control here?"

"Yes, I'll be taking her in now. But he said she had an accomplice, a shorter male with a club?"

"He got away."

"Alright, we'll be on the lookout. You two stay safe," the Templar led the female away.

"Thank you," the shop-owner said again, before leaving as well.

"I guess you got quite the show," the warrior turned to Abaddon, putting the sticks into sheaths on his back.

"You beat me to the punch. I was all ready to help out, but you certainly didn't need it."

"Well thanks anyway, it's good to know that people will still come running when they hear something like that. Most people will just ignore that sort of thing."

"Well it is my job to help out in these sorts of situations," Abaddon scratched the back of his head and looked away.

"I see, so you're a hero then?"

"As of about a week ago, yes," a pause, then, "Wait, you're not?"

"No, just an unlicensed vigilante I suppose."

"Well you should become one. With skills like that it would be easy for you."

"It probably would be. But honestly, I have very little interest in that."

"Really? That seems strange."

"How do you figure?" the man leaned up against the wall behind him.

"Well, I mean if you're gonna be doing this anyway, and you're so good at it, why not get paid for it?"

"I make enough money to live on as it is. I don't really feel the need for a higher-paying job. Besides, I wouldn't make a very good hero."

"Are you kidding? I've only ever seen a few people kick that much ass, and I'm from Hell."

"Being a hero is about more than just kicking ass, as I'm sure you're aware. There is a whole persona that goes with it. I'm no good at crafting a grand image for myself or anything like that."

"I'm not good at that either. I'm a demon. That's about as far from a grand image as you can get."

"But I take it you still have that desire?"

"Excuse me?"

"You still want to be a hero, don't you? I don't mean just get paid to fight. I mean, a hero. You want to be liked and admired, looked up to as an example to live by."

"Well I don't know if I'd go that far," Abaddon paused for a moment. "I suppose I never really thought about that."

"Then why become a hero? In my mind, the two are inexorably linked."

"Well…. I guess it's like I said: I'm a good fighter, so why not get paid for the skill set I have. I suppose doing good in the process doesn't hurt."

"Well I couldn't bring myself to do it."

"Well shit, I probably look like a big fraud now or something huh?"

"Oh not at all. I could never be a hero, because I cannot divorce the job from the concept of a hero. I won't hold anyone else at fault if they don't share my views."

"Well that seems to be a rare opinion around here," Abaddon gave a dark laugh.

"I imagine you get a lot of grief for being a demon."

"Good heavens yes. And it doesn't make trying to be a hero any easier."

"I would think not." The warrior's laughter was lighter. "That's quite the path you've set out for yourself there."

"Yeah, well hopefully it's the right one."

"I wouldn't worry about that. Choosing the right path, I mean. In fact, I think the whole idea of a right path is somewhat absurd."

"What do you mean?"

"The way I figure it, everyone has many different paths they could take that would all be equally good. No one has just one skillset or talent. And even if you think you've found the perfect opportunity, there might be another even better one you haven't found yet."

"But what if you make the wrong choice?"

"Another absurd concept. It is very difficult to make the wrong choice. Especially when it comes to something like your life path."

"I find that screwing up is easy," Abaddon's thoughts went back to the coffee shop.

"Maybe so, but it's rarely as a result of making the wrong choice." At that, Abaddon looked confused, so the man continued. "A choice can really only be the wrong choice if you had a strong reason to believe it was wrong, but chose it anyway. Let's say I flip a coin, and I ask you to choose heads or tails. You have no good way of knowing which side the coin will land on, so either choice is just as good as the other. The odds are equal for both, so neither choice is wrong, because you have no reason to choose one over the other. It is the same with life paths. Usually we do not have the clarity to see if a path is good or bad until we have walked a good ways down it. So while the end result might be bad, the choice itself cannot be rightfully said to be so."

"Wow," Abaddon just stood there for a moment, not sure what to say, then. "Oh, right, I'm Abaddon by the way," he held out a hand.

"Angga Bayu," the man shook his outstretched hand.

"I know that name.... wait a minute! You're-"

"Just a man with some sticks," Angga smiled. "I'm no one special."

Chapter Fourteen

Checking in Again

Abaddon was sitting in the middle of his apartment with Boris. He had just finished chanting in the dark tongues and the portal was once again rent in space.

"So how's my big fancy hero settling in? It's been a week since you've been gone hasn't it?"

"I'm doing… alright."

"Oh? What happened?"

"Well, it's been mostly good. I mean, I did get into a fight with the van Helsing's brat."

"Van Helsing?! Those two-bit demon hunters? Just hearing the name makes my blood burn. Do you know that the van Helsings tried to kill me on five separate occasions? The last one walked right up to the gates of Pandemonium. She tried to put a true silver crossbow bolt right through my heart in the middle of breakfast. That crazy mortal threw off my entire day's schedule."

"Wow, I didn't know our families had such a history."

"I swear, it's like they never even bothered to go after any of the other demon kings. I mean, Surt never had mortals bust down her door and interrupt her morning meal. Anyway, what happened with you and their latest spawn?"

"You're not going to believe this, but we're actually both monster-slayers working for White Pegasus."

"Ha! If there was a one true god I'd think this was one of their divine jokes. To think you have to work with that weak scum."

"Oh, it gets better. When we first met, he got incredibly mad, what with me being a demon and all. We traded some insults, and when I called him weak, he pulled a true silver dagger on me. He attacked me right in front of all the other new heroes."

"Did you crush that weak mortal in front of all the other new blood?"

"I almost did. If it wasn't for Mary stepping in, I probably would have."

"I wish you had. Saved van Helsings deserve a good crushing."

"You know I can't go around killing mortals Dad. Especially my coworkers."

"Yeah, yeah, I know. But come on, the latest heir to a family of demon hunters tries to kill my spawn. How do you expect me to react?"

"I'm perfectly fine Dad. You know a van Helsing wouldn't stand a chance against me."

"Well obviously. It's the principle of the thing! You keep getting attacked by these weak mortals, and you can't even fight back. It almost makes me want to start another apocalypse just to teach them a lesson."

"Oh, come on Dad."

"I'm not actually going to invade Terra or anything. Don't worry. I'm just mad. I'll get over it, but it might take a while."

"Yeah, you and everyone else at White Pegasus. A lot of them weren't too thrilled about a demon being hired as a hero in the first place, and now that I almost killed one of my coworkers…."

"But he started it!"

"Dad, how many centuries old are you?"

"Hey, just because little spawn use that line doesn't mean it has no merit. You gave the brat no reason to attack you, but he goes at you with a true silver dagger? And somehow it's your fault that he gets what's coming to him as a result?"

"Not entirely my fault. He got yelled at also. Believe me, he's in hot water too, it's just that, well…."

"They're more forgiving when a human does it than when a demon does?"

"Yes actually. It's not like they don't have good reason to think that way."

"I suppose," Lucifer folded his arms in begrudging acceptance. "We never had a good rapport with the mortals. And your grandfather didn't do anything to help matters what with the whole Armageddon thing. But you think after over three centuries, people would start to get over it. I mean, aren't they the ones always talking about how you should be more accepting of everyone else?"

"Yeah, I know. Believe me, I'm not happy about any of this either. But it's the way things are around here, and if I'm gonna live in New Eden, I just have to get used to it."

"Well, if things don't work out, you know you can always go to Hell. We'd be happy to have you back."

"I know Dad."

"He won't admit it, but your Uncle Abaddon really misses you."

"I miss him too."

"He'd probably try to destroy me for saying this, but he actually still has your baby armor."

"Aw, that's sweet."

"So you'll always have a home in the deepest pits of the abyss."

"Thanks dad. But I need to tough it out. A fight with a van Helsing is no reason for me to give up."

"That's my spawn. Though I must say, that was one impressive brat. I mean, taking on the son of Lucifer single-handedly. As much as I hate those saved demon hunters, they're nothing if not ludicrously brave."

"Well that's the thing Dad," Abaddon tried to make his voice not betray just how awkward he felt. "You see…. no one in New Eden knows that I'm your son. I haven't actually told anyone that yet."

"What? Are you embarrassed of your old sire?"

"Oh no, no. I mean, it's not that I'm *EMBARRASSED*….."

"Ha!" Lucifer let out his telltale lamp-shaking laugh. "It's a law of the universe that parents embarrass their spawn. It's one of the few things that binds all creatures, mortal and demon alike."

"I'm *NOT* embarrassed Dad. I'm just worried. I mean, I have a hard-enough time being a demon. If people knew I was the spawn of Lucifer.... well....."

"I suppose that wouldn't do you any favors in the friends department."

"I'm sorry Dad...."

"Sorry? After all these centuries, I *STILL* make the mortals quake in their boots. I take it as an honor."

"But it's not just that. I want whatever I do here in New Eden to be *MY* accomplishments. I don't want anyone thinking of me as just the spawn of Lucifer."

"Don't want to be overshadowed by your father? Believe me, I know that feeling. I was quite the rebel back in the day. Don't worry, there're no hard feelings. You want to be your own demon. You're moving out and doing things by yourself. Any father would be proud of that."

"Thanks a lot, Dad."

"Well this is just getting dark and depressing. And this is coming from a ruler of Hell. I assume you have some good news too?"

"Oh right, I have a new friend," Abaddon picked up Boris and held him in front of the Hell portal.

"And who's this cute little guy?"

"His name is Sir Boris. I was actually supposed to slay him, but I made him my pet instead.

"Ha! Remember when you were just a little spawn? You always wanted a cerberus. And I told you you'd have to walk it, and play with it, and slay the lesser demons to feed it."

"And you said if it ever did its business inside Pandemonium you'd rend its cursed flesh yourself."

"I don't remember that part, but that's definitely something I'd say. Well that's great. And keep it up. I know you'll make one *HELL* of a hero."

"That means a lot, Dad."

"Oh shit, sorry. It looks like some templars are seeking to redeem themselves by besieging my dark gates. I'm going to have to hang up now. Talk to you later."

"Bye Dad. Cleave their souls once for me."

"Will do. Love you."

"Love you too Dad."

Chapter Fifteen

A Half-Assed Attempt at Making Things Right

"I don't know what I'm doing here," Brad crossed his arms and stared out the window obstinately.

"I have to admit I'm a bit confused myself," Abaddon was looking at Artemis, who was standing where they had all introduced themselves on the first day.

"Well, since I am the senior monster-slayer at White Pegasus, not to mention your orientation leader, I was asked to help you two deal with your little 'disagreement' from the other day," she was still smiling as always, but this was her weakest one yet.

"I don't think disagreement covers trying to stab me in the heart with a true silver dagger."

"And I'd do it again. You're just a monster. Come on Artemis, you know it's our job to kill those things."

"He's not a monster, he's a hero, and a monster-slayer just like us."

"Oh really? He didn't even slay that cerberus in Little Purgatory. I heard he has it as a pet now."

"And so what if I do?"

"It's a cerberus! You're supposed to kill them, not take them on walks in the park. I mean seriously, you can't be okay with him having a monster like that as a pet can you?"

"He's just my pet."

"Until you set him loose on everyone in the guild."

"Set him loose-You paranoid wretched spawn of-"

"That's enough, both of you!" Artemis' change of tone was so surprising that both Abaddon and Brad shut up and sat in their seats, looking directly at her as if they were disobedient school children. "Look, you both have already gotten yelled at. And I have no intention of being your babysitter. I was excited to have some talented new monster-slayers in the guild, but if you guys are going to behave like children then I suggest you leave now. Kids have no place fighting monsters."

"How am I being childish?" Abaddon was legitimately confused. "I mean, sure I went too far, but he's the one who attacked me and tried to kill me."

"Yes, Brad's an immature prick."

"Hey!"

"But you keep rising to his taunts and insults. Just because someone calls you a monster doesn't mean you have to go and try to prove them right. Fighting between heroes is not allowed. You *BOTH* need to get that through your heads."

"*YOU'RE* the ones who need to get something through your heads," Brad stood up angrily. "I can't be the only one who has a problem with this. No fighting between heroes? Who in their right mind would ever consider a demon to be a hero?"

Artemis held up a hand to stop Abaddon before he even started, "Tell me exactly what reason you have to think a demon can't be a hero?"

"Hello. Does the word Armageddon mean anything to you?"

"Does the word slavery mean anything to you?"

"What's that got to do with anything?"

"In A.D. earth, white men enslaved black men. Does that make you a monster?"

"That's completely different. Humans don't come from the infernal pits of Hell!"

"That's-"

"Don't," now Abaddon was standing too. "I'm not going to pretend I'm not a demon. I'm not going to pretend I'm not from Hell. And I certainly am not going to pretend that I don't want to kill this pathetic bastard."

"SEE?!" Brad was waving his arm at Abaddon.

"But I have no intention of killing him. In Hell, fighting and killing is normal. It is a violent and brutal place. Terra is different. I have every intention of playing by the rules. And I legitimately want to do things the mortal way. Good heavens, I would have probably wanted to be your friend if you weren't such a saved asshole!"

"This is getting even more ridiculous by the second. If I were friends with a demon I'd have to kill myself. Even that might not wash away the shame it would bring."

"For the divine entities sake," Artemis was sounding really annoyed now. "This is three fifty-seven A.A. but you're still acting like it's frickin' nineteen fifty A.D. I had hoped humanity had moved past this stupid intolerant bullshit. Abe chose to come live in New Eden. He *WANTS* to be a hero. Clearly he's one of the good demons."

"How can you say that with a straight face? Who ever heard of a good demon?"

"Uggggh!" now the smile was actually gone. "It's like you're specifically trying to not hear a word I'm saying. Do you think I want to be here moderating you two? I have a life. Hell, I'm missing lunch with my girlfriend right now to try and help you two with your shit. So I'd really appreciate it if you tried to at least meet me half-way here."

"I can't stand by while a demon walks around the guild."

"And I just can't stand to be in the same room as this prick."

"And I don't care! You two are contractually obligated to get along. While you are both heroes at White Pegasus, you are required to at least be civil towards each other. "

"So what," Brad snapped, "They'll fire me for exorcising this demon?"

"YES. Because this demon just so happens to be your coworker. And whether you like it or not, he's a legally registered citizen of New Eden and, hero or not, you aren't allowed to just go around killing whoever you want. That's it, no more arguing. We have to find a way to stop you two from fighting like spoiled brats. Otherwise you're both fired, and I will have used up my whole Saturday afternoon for nothing."

"I don't have any problems not fighting with Brad, I just expect him to pull a knife on me at any moment. And I'll be saved if I don't fight back when some demon hunter tries to kill me."

"Fine, whatever," Brad turned his back on the both of them. "I'm still not letting this go. But I'm not about to risk my job just to fight some lowly demon. You're not worth it. But count yourself lucky. Last time was a fluke. You caught me off guard. If I tried, I'd kill you in a second."

Abaddon had to use all of his willpower to not reach for Spellbreaker. He managed it, but barely. He started to say something, but forced himself not to.

"Finally. But at the risk of dragging this on longer, that's not gonna do it. I don't care if you two have to avoid each other or get restraining orders or what, but just agreeing not to fight isn't enough. You guys will need to get along. What I mean is, no fighting, literally or otherwise, no antagonizing each other, and no going out of your way to cause problems for each other. The bare minimum is that you two are neutral towards each other."

"Fine," Brad still had his back turned.

"Fine."

"Thank my namesake we have an agreement. Now we can actually get back to work around here," she started to leave. "And don't forget you have to fill out your reports before the end of the month. Pro tip, actually fighting something other than each other might help with that."

Chapter Sixteen

A Heroic Deed

Abaddon was still angry. He could only hope that he never actually had to do any work with Brad. The thing that made him angriest was the fact that Brad made him mad in the first place. Such an insignificant little ant shouldn't have been able to get to him like that. Then again, that was the problem. In Hell that would have been the case. He could have slaughtered Brad and no one would have looked twice. Things were different here though, and that's exactly what he had wanted: different. And not only that, but he wanted to fit in. He didn't want to be angry. The plane of Terra had so much to offer, and he wouldn't get to experience it all if he was just going to keep acting like a demon straight out of Hell. He *WAS* a demon straight out of Hell, but that was beside the point.

Abaddon had hoped going for a walk to the supermarket would have helped him get out of his foul mood, but the weather was not cooperating. Sunlight seemed nice enough, he had decided, but rain was a different matter. He didn't know how people could stand it. After what seemed like half an eternity at least, he made it to the supermarket. He had never been so happy to enter a building. Seriously, the water just sank into the body and made everything uncomfortable. And he knew that if he summoned the flames of Hell in order to dry off, *SOMEONE* would raise a big fuss, and there would be a mass panic, and people saying he was going to devour their souls. Though he supposed the flames of Hell wouldn't be the best for drying off. Better than nothing, but mortal flames seemed much more suited to the task. But given that he couldn't use the former and was fresh out of the latter, he settled for unzipping his jacket in the hopes that it would dry out a bit before he had to return to the dreaded outside.

Too late, Abaddon realized he had meant to bring a bag, but had forgotten. Then he remembered that actually he had meant to *BUY* a bag, but had forgotten. He supposed grabbing a shopping basket would do for now, but he really didn't like using the plastic bags they had. They just seemed so flimsy; he was worried they'd break at any moment. Oh well, it was either that, or make an extra trip in the rain, and he definitely knew which one he would prefer.

On the upside, now he got to pick out new foods to try. He had never imagined so many choices. In his first couple of days he had been blown away by all of the options. He had been so eager to try all of the things that he ended up with five bags filled with snacks and treats. After that, though, he had decided to stick primarily with the humanoid food sections. That igneous sampler packet had really done a number on his stomach. Though the Chlorophyll Zero had been quite tasty. On the other hand, good heavens it had not been fun trying to get that stuff out of his system later.

Abaddon started with two bushels of bananas; those had proven to be his favorite food so far. Roast 'em with a bit of hellfire. Delicious. It was weird how often he saw the peels in trash cans; that was the best part. He passed right by the frozen vegetables. Those things were nasty: all cold and wet; it was like eating solid rain. No thanks. That pasta stuff seemed to be quite popular, but he didn't much care for it: far too hard and tasteless. He grabbed a few loaves of bread. He was always fascinated by how the minor variations made the various breads taste so different. This time he decided to try one of the ones with whatever pumpernickel was. It looked exciting. The supermarket didn't have any good demon options, but he hadn't really expected any. And besides, he'd rather try new stuff. Over in one of the refrigerators he grabbed several bottles of milk. He really liked that. And he'd been eager to try it ever since he'd read about cows in *Beasts of Terra: A Demon's Guide to What to Slay and What Not to Slay*. He had been surprised when the clerk had told him that that brown liquid was also milk. He'd decided against buying any. *Beasts of Terra* hadn't said anything about brown cows, and he was wary of the stuff. Finally, he grabbed various cheeses. He hadn't tried them yet. *Beasts of Terra* identified cheese as a form of solidified milk. It seemed rather strange to him, but apparently it was a common food stuff amongst the humanoid races, and he figured he'd finally get up the courage to try it.

As Abaddon was standing in line for the checkout, his eyes wandered to the candy bar selection. He was having a hard time deciding which one he wanted to get for a snack on the way home. He finally settled on the Mars bar. It was a candy endorsed by a divine aspect of war, but he figured it was worth a shot. Who was to say that Heaven couldn't have good food. Besides, that Mr. Good Bar had been surprisingly tasty. And he'd already tried most of the other ones.

Abaddon paid for his assorted foodstuffs and was heading out the door. As the doors slid open he steeled himself to venture back into the dreaded rain. His foot stopped on the threshold as he heard a scream from behind him.

"Give me everything in the register, now!"

Abaddon turned to see a haggard-looking man in dirty clothes carrying an obviously magical longsword, which he was brandishing at the clerk. Abaddon barely stopped to wonder how this bum had gotten his hands on an enchanted weapon, before springing into action. His hand reached up behind his back to grab Spellbreaker. When he grasped empty air, he remembered that he had left it at the apartment. For short trips like these he usually didn't bother to bring it with him; it tended to make people uncomfortable, and he was tired of always having to show them his hero ID glyph. Well, this was going to be a bit more complicated then.

"Stop," Abaddon called to the man, slowly walking towards him.

"Stay back!" the man turned, brandishing the sword wildly in front of him.

"I don't want to have to hurt you sir."

"I-I mean it! This sword is cursed: it consumes mortal flesh. Stay back or I'll stab you, I swear."

"FOOLISH INSECT," Abaddon roared. "I AM A GREAT DEMON FROM THE PITS OF HELL. DO YOU THINK THE WEAPONS OF MAN CAN HARM ME?"

"This-this is a cursed weapon. It can kill demons too!" the man had backed up slightly, still brandishing the longsword.

"REALLY?" Abaddon stepped in, reached out with his left hand and grabbed the blade. With a swift motion, he wrenched it from the man's grip and hurled it to the ground.

The man started to shake even more violently than had before. He tried to speak, but no words came. He then slumped to the ground. Abaddon turned to the clerk who was still cowering behind the counter.

"CALL THE- I mean, call the templars. This man will need to be arrested." The clerk nodded, still clearly afraid. "Everyone be careful. That sword is dangerous. No one touch it; it's cursed."

"I guess it's a good thing a hero showed up here," the head templar spoke with Abaddon as the other officers were taking in the man and sealing the weapon in a protective barrier. "Th- uh…. thank you for all your help."

"Well, it is my job after all. Though I am worried as to how this man got a cursed sword. Clearly anyone robbing supermarkets couldn't afford one."

"Yeah, we'll need to interrogate him once we get back to the station. But I wouldn't be too worried about it. It is possible that there is some supplier who is selling cursed weapons for cheap, but I doubt it. Usually culprits this desperate steal them from someone else. And in some rare cases they can be possessed by a dark spirit which causes the weapon to become cursed. Whatever the case, we'll get to the bottom of it, and if there are other cursed weapons around, we'll find 'em and purify 'em."

"Good to hear."

"Yeah, so uh, thanks again for the help here," the templar glanced around awkwardly, "But I think you've done your job, so you can probably leave now. That is, I mean, leave the rest to us."

Abaddon looked around as well. The few people who were still in the store gave him uncomfortable glances. Abaddon sighed. He supposed his display had scared them just as much as the robber. No reason to stick around any longer. The fact that he stopped the criminal probably meant he wouldn't be banned from the supermarket, so that was something at least. As he headed for the door, Abaddon winced. Looking down, he noticed the palm of his right hand was ripped open. Apparently the sword had hurt him after all. He guessed grabbing it by the blade like that had been a bit much, but it had definitely helped with the whole intimidation thing. Well that was something to look forward too for the next few days. Abaddon sighed again. Then those thoughts were pushed aside as he felt a tugging on his jacket. He looked down to see a little girl pulling on the zipper.

"That man was really scary," the little girl looked up into Abaddon's face. "Thank you for saving me Mister." she then ran off to her mother who gave Abaddon a weak nod before moving on into a different isle.

Abaddon stepped out into the rain. He felt the wet soak into his bones. He looked down at his shredded palm that was still stinging (the rain didn't do it any favors). Then he thought about the little girl as he began the walk back to his apartment and smiled. Today had been a good day after all.

Chapter Seventeen

Round Two at the Coffee Shop

"Thanks for coming back here," Abaddon awkwardly sipped his coffee.

"I must admit I was a bit confused by how you 'left things' so abruptly last time," Mary's voice implied the air quotes her hands didn't make.

"Yeah, sorry about that. I'm uh, I'm not that great at this sort of thing, and you kinda caught me off guard there so… yeah…."

"My bad, I shouldn't have pried like that."

"No, no, I was the one who messed up. Anyway, how've things been going with you? Still working on rebuilding Little Purgatory?"

"Yeah, progress is slow. Little Purgatory is one of the poorer districts in the area, so not a lot of help from outside. We'll get it done soon though. I mean, you did prevent a lot of potential damage, so it isn't too bad."

"Cool. That's good, I suppose."

"Hey, what happened to your hand?" Mary noticed the bandage Abaddon was wearing.

"Oh this? Some weird guy came into my local supermarket and tried to rob the place with a cursed sword."

"No kidding. I guess that was your second heroic deed in New Eden huh?"

"I almost had another one but someone else beat me to it. So I guess that does make this act number two."

"Not as exciting as fighting a cerberus I suppose."

"Yeah," Abaddon gave a little nervous laugh.

"I'm surprised the robber even managed to cut you. I mean, with your skills-"

"I uh, actually kinda grabbed the sword with my bare hand in order to disarm him. You know, sort of an intimidation thing."

"By the blade? You may be a demon, but remember, I'm the indestructible one. Why didn't you use your war hammer to shatter it like you did with Brad's holy dagger?"

"I didn't actually have Spellbreaker on me; I don't usually carry it when I'm doing simple errands. People usually give me weird looks. And then I have to explain that no, I'm actually a hero, and I show them my I.D. glyph, and I'm kind of getting tired of having to do that all the time."

"I could see that. Still though, as heroes, we're on the job all the time. You never know when you're going to run into a situation like that, so being fully equipped and ready to go at all times is not a bad idea."

"I suppose."

"It also helps to cut down on things like that," Mary gestured to Abaddon's hand.

"Yeah, yeah, I get your point. You don't have to worry about things like that, though; must be nice."

"Actually I wish I could."

"What in Heaven's name-" Abaddon paused for a moment. "Sorry, I was just surprised. I mean, why would you want to feel pain?"

"Did you just say, 'what in Heaven's name'?" Mary laughed.

"Yeah... are you laughing?"

"I just expected demons to be more cavalier about swearing."

"I was swearing though."

"So wait, you consider 'what in Heaven's name' to be swearing?" Mary tried to hold back her snickering, without much success.

"Sure. What were you expecting? I mean, why would demons care about phrases like hell or damn."

"Okay fair point. It's just odd-sounding."

"I mean, I don't have a problem with it or anything. I still say swear words like crap, or shit, or f-"

"Okay, I think I get the idea."

"Right…. Anyway, you said you wish you could feel pain? Seriously, what's that about?"

"I never have before. It's something that all biological creatures experience. It's just another way I'm reminded that I'm different from them."

"Wow…. I'm sorry, I didn't mean-"

"It's okay. It makes sense that it would sound crazy. And I know pain is an unpleasant experience. It just, well it feels lonely at times."

"I never realized how hard being a golem is. Wait! I didn't mean hard as in- I mean- not-"

"Don't worry," Mary laughed again. "You don't have to tiptoe around me or anything. It's not like I'm made of glass."

"Well of course you're not made glass. I mean- oh shit, I didn't mean-"

"Okay, sorry," Mary managed in between laughs, "I guess that one was just setting you up there. Look, just don't worry. You don't have to try so hard. I'm not going to hold it against you if you come off as less than sensitive. Besides, there's plenty of stuff I wouldn't even think of when it comes to being a demon. So no worries."

"Like what kind of stuff?" Abaddon was legitimately curious.

"How would I be able to think of the things I wouldn't think of?" Mary gave him a look.

"Okay, that would be kind of difficult."

"But here's something. What kind of a name is Abe? I wouldn't have thought a demon would have a name like that. Isn't it short for Abraham?"

"No, actually, Abaddon."

"You mean like the Demon Lord of Destruction?"

"Yeah, he's my- he's who I'm named after."

"But you go by Abe?"

"Ms. Weathers said I should change it if I wanted to be a hero."

"Oh, I suppose people would be a bit weary of getting saved by someone named Abaddon."

"Yeah, can't say I blame them, I suppose."

"But I like the name Abaddon, on you, that is. It suits you. Far better than Abe anyways."

Abaddon just sat in his chair with a big grin on his face for several seconds. Then realizing how stupid he must look, he quickly turned away, replacing the smile with an equally dumb embarrassed expression.

"What was that?" Mary snickered again.

"What?"

"Sorry, I just don't normally think of a demon as smiling that much, is all."

"Hey, we get happy, just like other people," now Abaddon was mildly offended.

"See, and there's one of those things I wouldn't even think about. Now we're even."

"Ha; I guess so," Abaddon was laughing too.

For a minute the two just chuckled. They continued talking for a while about various things. Abaddon was only half paying attention. He was too focused on the fact that he was having a conversation with Mary, and it seemed so natural. So this was what having a friend was like.

Chapter Eighteen

A True Battle

Abaddon slammed into a wall. That one really hurt. He wasn't seriously injured, at least as far as he could tell, but he was definitely going to be sore in the morning. He was very thankful for his obsidian armor, or that would have gone a lot worse. He got to his feet, brushed some rubble off his armor, and picked up Spellbreaker. He readied himself as the great twisting heads of the hydra lashed out towards him. He dodged right, narrowly avoiding the middle head. As he moved, he struck upwards with Spellbreaker, knocking the rightmost head aside. When he got to his feet, he was met with a massive claw that threw him aside.

"You're doing great," Artemis called from a nearby rooftop. "Just keep that thing distracted a little while longer. And whatever you do, do not cut off any of its heads."

"I've got a war hammer," Abaddon replied, dodging a vicious bite from the left-most head. "How would I even do that?"

The hydra attacked with another deadly claw. This time Abaddon swung Spellbreaker with full force, meeting the claw head on. He was able to repel the beast, but his efforts only seemed to make it mad. He had to quickly dive for cover as all three heads tried to chomp down on him at once.

"Alright, get back!" Artemis shouted.

Abaddon took her advice and started to run in the opposite direction of the hydra. The great beast shrieked in frustration and started off after him. Abaddon didn't look behind him; he just kept running. A second later he heard a different shriek, this one of pain. Now he turned. The hydra was still coming toward him, however now it had a crossbow bolt in its chest.

"Didn't work," Abaddon called up to Artemis as the hydra continued its advance.

"Give it a minute."

Abaddon readied himself, taking a defensive stance. The hydra's heads were only a few feet away, but then the beast suddenly stopped. Abaddon could see blue lines spidering outward from the bolt in its chest. It took a moment for Abaddon to realize that those were the hydra's veins being made extra prominent. The hydra tried to move, then it just keeled over. Abaddon just stood there for a moment, looking at the heads lying about a foot away from him.

"What in heaven's name did you do to it?" Abaddon asked as Artemis clambered down from the rooftop.

"That was an ice bolt I shot it with. It literally froze the blood in its veins. Works really well on reptiles."

"Wow, and people are scared of me."

"Hey, being able to go toe to toe with a hydra like that is no small feat. Thanks a lot for the assist. I would have had a really hard time killing that thing on my own."

"I'm just glad I was in the area when that thing attacked. Where did it come from anyway? Did it escape from the zoo or something?"

"No idea. When I got the call, they said it just sort of showed up. Well whatever the case, it picked a great time to do so. I hadn't actually performed any heroic deeds this month."

"What about when you got called out during orientation? You said that was urgent, right?"

"That? Some wealthy elf on the Upper East Side called that one in. His pet werewolf had escaped and he wanted me to hunt it down. Never did catch the damn thing."

Abaddon was about to reply, when he heard a strange noise. Turning, he saw a figure in a black cloak and hood, appearing atop the hydra in a strange dark cloud.

"Oh you poor creature," the figured crooned. "What did they do to you?"

"Who are you?" Artemis leveled her crossbow at the newcomer. "And what do you want with that hydra?"

"You will now learn the error of your ways," the figure pulled an eerie crystal charm from inside their cloak, and began to chant.

Artemis fired her crossbow, lodging a bolt squarely in the figure's shoulder. The figure didn't even seem to notice and continued chanting, a black circle, edged in purple, appearing underneath the hydra as they spoke. This time, Artemis aimed the crossbow at the figure's head. Before she could get a shot off, the ground exploded. As the dust cleared, Abaddon saw shapes moving. The hydra was once again on its feet, its three heads writhing. The great serpent lashed out. Abaddon dodged left, Artemis went right. Abaddon rolled free, but while Artemis avoided the middle head, the right-most one caught her with its jaws and flung her aside. She tumbled to the ground and fell limp.

The hydra turned its full attention on Abaddon. He activated his obsidian gauntlet, and the black armor appeared on him once more. The hydra's heads lashed out at Abaddon, and he swung with Spellbreaker. His war hammer hit the middle head squarely on the chin. There was a great flash as energy burst out from the serpent. However, at that exact same moment, the other two heads crashed into Abaddon, and he was sent to the ground once more. The creature fell shortly after he did. Abaddon got to his feet, his whole body aching even more now.

"You managed to destroy my reanimation spell with your hammer," Abaddon turned to see the cloaked figure behind him.

The figure's right arm shot out. Abaddon had a brief moment to register the black, rock-like exterior, and red glowing sigils, before it slammed into his still-armored chest. He was hurled backwards with surprising force. Abaddon crashed to the ground, his whole body momentarily stunned.

"I know what you are," the figure advanced on Abaddon, raising the strange right hand, "who you are. You do not belong here, spawn of Lucifer!" He punctuated those words with red lightning that shot from his hand, engulfing Abaddon.

Abaddon screamed. A thousand knives made their home in all of his nerve clusters simultaneously. He writhed on the ground as agony arced up every inch of his body, straight to his brain, only so it could register exactly how much pain he was in. His vision blurred into a red haze. He couldn't think. He couldn't even tell if he was still screaming. Suddenly, everything ceased. Abaddon called upon all of his remaining willpower to not pass out. Blearily, through eyes drowning in half formed tears, Abaddon saw the cloaked figure whirling around. A second bolt was stuck in them, this one in their back, and flames were eating away at the cloak. His whole body protested, but Abaddon ignored the cries and turned his head slightly to the left. He saw Artemis standing hunched over, her left arm hanging limply at her side, her right extended, pointing the recently fired crossbow at the now burning figure. Abaddon's willpower chose that moment to give up the fight, and he let the darkness take over his vision.

Abaddon bolted up in bed. Whose bed, he didn't know, but he was out of it quickly. He picked up Spellbreaker, which was resting against a nightstand. He started to head for the door directly across from him when a figure in a white coat entered the room.

"What are you doing out of bed?" the man asked. "You were just brought in here a few hours ago, unconscious I might add."

"And here is…?"

"White Pegasus. Artemis brought you into the infirmary."

"We have an infirmary?"

"Of course. Your job description is killing monsters that are too dangerous for other people to handle; why wouldn't we have one? But that's beside the point. You need to get back into bed."

"No, I'm fine, just a little sore."

"*NO,* you're not."

"Yes he is," Artemis came into the room. "Good work Phil. I'll take responsibility for him from here. You can let him out."

"Alright," Phil raised his hands. "But don't come crying to me when he gets seriously injured. Hard enough trying to figure out how to use healing magic on a demon. But I did it. And does anyone listen to me?"

"Come on," Artemis grabbed Abaddon by the arm. "You've got some explaining to do."

Chapter Nineteen

Who's Your Daddy

Artemis sat Abaddon down at a table in an empty room nearby the infirmary, "Alright, what was up with that cloaked guy?"

"What? Why in Heaven's name would you expect me to know?"

"He was specifically targeting you."

"I have no clue what that was about."

"Come on. He said 'you don't belong here, spawn of Lucifer' and then attacked you. You've got to know something about that."

"Hey, just because Lucifer is my dad, does not mean-" Abaddon stopped mid-sentence. Artemis was staring at him, mouth hanging open. "Oh... hehe, yeah.... I guess I never told anyone about that."

"Your dad is Lucifer?" Artemis was saying the words slowly, the stunned expression still on her face.

"Um.... yes?"

"*THE* Lucifer?"

"Yes."

"The prince of darkness? Father of lies? *THAT* Lucifer?!"

"Well actually I'm the prince of darkness. He's the king of darkness so-"

"LUCIFER?"

"Would you please stop saying that," Abaddon was looking nervously around the room.

"But your dad is-"

"Yes, we've established that my dad is Lucifer, but I specifically didn't bring it up because I don't want anyone to know; so could you please stop freaking out?"

"I-I don't- how did this even happen?"

"Well... uh, several centuries ago Lucifer met this really nice she-demon and-"

"No, I mean- you- and he- and you. I just slayed a hydra with you five hours ago."

"Well yes, we're coworkers. We're bound to work together sometimes."

"But you're the son of Lucifer!"

"What did I just say?"

Artemis took a deep breath, "Sorry. I just can't believe this. I mean, you're important, like, *SUPER* important. I'm not sure important even begins to cover it. Your father is the ruler of the Ninth Circle of Hell."

"Yes, yes he is."

"Your father started Armageddon!"

"He did not," Abaddon stood in his chair. "My grandfather started Armageddon. My father was actually one of the demons who supported the ceasefire between Heaven and Hell."

"But I thought Lucifer-"

"Lucifer is a title. My family has sat on the dark throne of the Ninth Circle for millennia upon millennia. Each time the next demon ascends to the throne they gain the title of Lucifer."

"Still, this is ridiculous. I mean, what are you doing here?"

"You brought me here to ask questions."

"I meant in New Eden."

"I know what you meant, but why does me being the spawn of Lucifer make any difference? You were fine slaying that hydra with me before you found out about it."

"Hey, if you didn't think it made any difference, then why did you hide it from everyone?"

"I didn't hide it. I just.... didn't tell anyone."

"You *JUST* said you didn't want anyone to find out."

"Well that's only because I knew people would react like this."

"See, so it does matter."

"Well it shouldn't. I'm just a demon trying to make a living in New Eden."

"No way are you 'just a demon' or anything even close. No wonder you were able to defeat Brad so easily."

"Most demons probably could have. I've had several more centuries to train than he has. I mean, what is he, twenty? Even being a van Helsing doesn't make up for that gap in experience."

"But you were able to shatter his true silver dagger like it was nothing. That's what I heard. And I saw you destroy the reanimated hydra with one strike. I was surprised during orientation when you mentioned your war hammer, but now it all makes sense."

"Well technically I didn't destroy the hydra, I just destroyed the magic reanimating it. But yeah, Spellbreaker was my coming of age gift from my dad."

"Divine entities, you probably could have handled that hydra on your own. Oh shit, I was using the son of Lucifer as bait," Artemis suddenly looked terrified.

"Woah, woah, it's okay; that was a sound battle strategy. Of course the ranged fighter goes in the back while the melee fighter takes the front. No one's going to come after you or anything for that. See, these are exactly the kinds of things that made me not want to tell anyone about Dad. People had enough of a problem with me already, and I didn't want to be treated like some scary monster all the time. I get enough of that shit at home."

"Oh, I didn't realize…." Artemis' expression changed to one of mild embarrassment.

Abaddon realized what he had just said, "No, I didn't mean to- I mean- sorry about that."

"What are you apologizing for?"

"Look, I didn't mean to say that. And I definitely do *NOT* want anyone to feel sorry for me or anything; I just want to experience what having a normal life in Terra is like."

"And so you came to New Eden and became a monster-slayer?"

"Well.... it's the only job I'm qualified for. I mean, I have to make a living somehow."

"When your father is the ruler of the Ninth Circle of Hell?"

"I said I wanted to have a normal life in Terra. I don't want my dad paying for everything. I want to do this on my own, be my own person."

"Oh, believe me, I get that," Artemis leaned back in her chair.

"What are you supposed to be, some kind of rebel or something?" Abaddon couldn't picture the smiling happy Artemis as being very rebellious. He tried to imagine her in black leather and piercings but it just didn't work.

"Are you kidding? My family can trace its lineage back to Merlin. My dad threatened to lock me in the family tower when I said I was going to become a monster-slayer. My mom still won't speak to me."

"Wow, that's gotta suck."

"It's not fun, but I get by. I was never interested in learning magic. It always felt like I was just the next descendant of Merlin, and didn't have an identity of my own. But that's nothing. I can't imagine being the child of Lucifer. No wonder you wanted to get out."

"Hey, I love my dad."

"Oh no, I didn't mean-" Artemis held up her hands. "It's just, the feeling of being overshadowed must be much greater for you than it ever was for me. Look, I'm sorry I freaked out."

"No, it's okay. I understand why you would have that reaction. But please, I still don't want anyone to know so..."

"Don't worry, I won't tell anyone. But you've gotta tell me what it was like growing up as the son of Lucifer some time."

Abaddon was inwardly smiling, and trying very hard not to let it spill over into a stupid grin on the outside. He couldn't be sure, but it looked like he might just have a second friend.

Chapter Twenty

Another Talk with Ms. Weathers

"So, am I in trouble again or something?"

"Really," Ms. Weathers gave Abaddon an almost tired look. "It's not like I'm not your mother or your principal. You don't only get sent to my office so I can yell at you. I already got Artemis' report about your recent joint heroic deed. I wanted to follow up with you about it."

"Oh, alright then," Abaddon was a little concerned about what Artemis had said, but then he reminded himself that she had said she wouldn't tell anyone about his dad. He needed to trust his fellow heroes. Well, okay, not Brad, but everyone else.

"First off, I would like to congratulate you. Even with the help of a veteran hero like Artemis, taking on a hydra is no small feat. Good job."

"Thanks, but I really just acted as a diversion."

"I read the report. Being able to go toe to toe with a hydra is quite impressive. Then again, I never doubted your martial skills. But anyway, on to the more pressing matters. Artemis' report said that after you two slew the hydra, a man in a black cloak appeared. This man reanimated the hydra and proceeded to attack you. Is that correct?"

"Yes."

"You are positive he reanimated the hydra?"

"Yes, I took it down myself. And Artemis had literally frozen the blood in its veins, so I'm pretty sure it was dead before the cloaked man cast his spell on it."

"Wait, you took down the hydra by yourself? That is impressive even for someone with your credentials."

"Sort of. I didn't really do much of anything actual. My war hammer Spellbreaker is a greater artifact that destroys any magic it strikes. One hit was all it took to undo the reanimation spell. I would have had a really tough time defeating it if it had still been alive."

"Good to see you have such an objective view of your own capabilities. One of the worst things for a hero is overconfidence. I have personally represented five different heroes who all got killed by it. Be that as it may, not just anyone can get their hands on a greater artifact. In fact, almost no one can. So that's something in-unto-itself. Just keep in mind that under-confidence can be just as bad as overconfidence. But back to the mysterious assailant. If he really was engaging in necromancy, then this poses a big problem."

"Really? What's so bad about that?"

"You're kidding," Ms. Weathers gave Abaddon an astonished look. He responded with a blank stare. "Wow, apparently you're not kidding. Necromancy is literally top on the list of forbidden magic. Necromancy is considered a worse crime than murder. How could you not know this?"

"What? I don't know all the rules in New Eden."

"So you're telling me that necromancy is perfectly acceptable in Hell?"

"It's a non-issue in Hell. It's seen as a useless form of magic. Well, I suppose in some parts it might be used, but very rarely if at all."

"Why was I surprised? Whatever. In any case, here it is quite the issue. Necromancy goes against the natural order and can cause serious problems with the cycle of life. I don't know the specifics, but I do know that it is very dangerous. We've already alerted the templars that a suspected necromancer is on the loose in New Eden, so for now, it's out of our hands. But that doesn't mean it isn't our problem. From what Artemis' report indicated, the cloaked man seemed to be targeting you specifically. And he apparently used some strange form of magic she had never seen before to attack you."

"Oh that. He used the sigils of agony, forged in the Seventh Circle of Hell. Their magic triggers all of the enemy's nerves at once to register the signals for excruciating pain,"

Ms. Weathers just stood there, her face not quite sure what expression to make. It seemed to be caught between dumbfounded and horrified.

"Oh don't worry, they're not dangerous at all.... unless they kill you."

"My sanity begs me not to ask, but I have to know."

"The sigils of agony don't do any lasting harm. Well, I suppose if you get some form of PTSD or something from extended torture, that would count as lasting harm. Point is, the body isn't actually hurt. You just experience pain directly without any injury."

"But it can still kill you?"

"The signals are sent to your brain from all the nerves in your body at once. If this goes on for too long, the brain will get overloaded and shut down. Think of it like running too much magic energy through a mana battery, or too much electricity through a regular one. Wait, does Terra still use regular batteries? Or electricity for that matter? Come to think of it, I never checked if the light in my apartment worked off of magic or electricity. Huh."

"Well that's fascinating, and the previous part's horrifying. At least it's good to know you weren't seriously hurt. But that raises more questions. The cloaked figure was a demon and not a man? Artemis' report said that he was human, though it also said she shot him in the shoulder with her crossbow and it didn't seem to hurt him."

"He was definitely human. Well, now that I think about it, I couldn't rule out some kind of elf, but he wasn't a demon, I'm sure of that."

"But he used demonic magic? I didn't think that was the type of magic that humans could learn."

"They can't, at least not that I'm aware of. His right arm was…. well I guess the best term would be a demonic prosthetic. It was made out of obsidian, and the sigils were carved into the arm itself."

"Hmmm, and Artemis' report said that he had a strange talisman he used in the reanimation of the hydra. It's possible that this man doesn't actually possess magic of his own, but is just using magic items."

"I honestly have no idea."

"You recognized his right arm, but do you have any idea who the man himself is?"

"No clue. And no, I have no idea why he would be targeting me. No idea as to why he would be targeting me specifically anyway; he could just have wanted to kill me because I'm a demon."

"Unlikely. If he hated demons so much, why have a right arm forged by them?"

"Good point, but that's the only reason coming to mind for why he might want me dead." Well, that wasn't strictly true. But any other suspicions he had would involve his dad, and he didn't want to bring that up.

"Great, so we have a necromancer literally armed with a demonic weapon trying to kill you, and we don't have the faintest idea why. Oh well," Ms. Weathers sighed. "I don't know what we can do about it now. I guess we just have to let the templars track him down."

"Are you sure they'll be able to handle someone like him?"

"They *ARE* the divinely appointed protectors of New Eden. You may be a big-shot hero now, but they are pretty strong as well. Plus they have divine protection that shields them from magic of a cursed/demonic nature. And if they do face this necromancer, there will be more than two of them."

"Fair enough, I suppose. Is there anything else we need to talk about? I still need to get around to filing my monthly report."

"No, that should be all," at that Abaddon got up to leave. "Oh, but before you go."

"Yes?"

"Well.... just try to be careful. He could still come after you."

Chapter Twenty-One

The Next Fight

Abaddon was getting bored. He couldn't really believe those words, even as he thought them, but it was true. He had been in New Eden for over a month now, and in the past few days, he had had nothing to do. When he first arrived in New Eden, everything about it had been exciting and interesting, but now…. It wasn't that he had now seen everything there was to see in New Eden; far from it. In fact, most of the city was still unexplored territory. When he actually stopped to think about it, the parts he had seen directly made up an incredibly tiny portion of the city. Then again, he hadn't needed to roam very far. Just going to the grocery store was an adventure. But if that was the case, then why was he actually starting to feel bored? How could this be? He was still doing the same stuff he had been before.

Abaddon had been sitting in his apartment for at least half an hour, trying to figure out what could be the reason for his sudden feeling of lethargy. The consensus he came to was that if half an hour in his apartment didn't help, then he might as well go outside and see if a change of scenery would do the trick. Since he was going outside anyway, he decided to slay two cursed fell-ravens with one fatal blow, and take Boris out for a walk. He may have been at a low level of energy the past few days, but the same could not be said of his three-headed best friend. And sure enough, he had barely conjured the infernal chains of dark binding around Boris' necks before the cerberus was scrabbling at the door and barking excitedly. The barks were even harmonizing quite nicely.

Well, if nothing else, the weather was back to being relatively nice. That put him in a bit of a better mood. It wasn't overly warm, but it was at least dry. Abaddon thought back to his torturous trip in the rain to the grocery store, and he smiled. That was odd. He had expected to have a negative reaction to that memory. He thought more about that synaptic bait-and-switch as he walked down the street. It didn't take him long to realize that it wasn't that memory specifically he had been smiling about. In fact, that memory *WAS* a very unpleasant one. He could still feel the saved damp seeping down into his core. But that little girl thanking him for saving her was a very good memory indeed. That whole day was just associated with that one good memory now.

"Maybe that's it," Abaddon laughed to Boris. "I should find a crazy man robbing a convenience store. That will get me out of my funk."

It was a few minutes later when Abaddon stopped. Boris made it quite clear that they needed to. Abaddon sighed. He knelt down next to the cerberus and began to softly speak in the damned tongues. A small amount of hellfire appeared in his palm. A few passersby gave him odd looks. Yes, Abaddon supposed kneeling down next to your dog as they relieved themselves was a bit out of the ordinary, but he was just being extra careful. Last time a Templar had yelled at him when the poisonous plants grew and he didn't clean them up. That was one thing he hadn't considered when having a cerberus for a pet. After Boris was done, Abaddon burned any unwanted remains and got back up to resume the walk. It was only then that he noticed exactly where they were. Not five feet away was the bench across from the alley where he had met Angga Bayu.

Abaddon hadn't thought about Angga much since they had talked. He hadn't really known what to think to be honest. At one point, Angga had been a literal legend, almost as famous as Adonis. Abaddon had just assumed that him mysteriously vanishing meant he had died. But apparently, he had just dropped off the radar to go pick street fights in alleys. To be fair, that was sort of what he had always done, but still. Angga had been the most legendary mortal warrior. If the stories Abaddon had read were true, then no one could best him without the use of magic or other supernatural powers. According to *"Famous Humans and How to Kill Them,"* he had once defeated an entire gang and driven them out of the lower west side single-handedly. But apparently he was now "nobody special". At the time, Abaddon had been so surprised by that remark that he had just walked away without saying anything. He actually facepalmed when he thought back on that. Well, he may not have had any monsters to fight, but the battle with his social skills was still going on.

Abaddon sat back on the bench. It was only as he started to think back to his conversation with Angga Bayu, that he realized he had been purposefully avoiding doing so up until then. For some reason, Abaddon was really bothered by it all. Abaddon just got frustrated thinking about that encounter. He couldn't figure out why, but he knew it wasn't because of his apparent habit of walking out on people unexpectedly. Well, it wasn't *JUST* because of his apparent habit of walking out on people unexpectedly. The more Abaddon tried to figure it out, the more it got to him, and the more he wished for something to take his mind off it: preferably something he could take a few swings at with Spellbreaker.

It is a rare moment when a demon's prayers are answered. Even rarer than an off-white unicorn or a sincere politician. Red energy flew straight at Abaddon. He leapt aside, drawing Spellbreaker in the same motion. Boris was now yapping very excitedly. Abaddon absentmindedly said a word in the dark speech of demons, and Boris' chains tied themselves to the bench. Of all the people Abaddon might have expected, the cloaked necromancer wasn't one of them.

"Back already? I thought you would have gone into hiding now that the templars are looking for you."

"You do not belong here."

"That's what you said last time!" Abaddon punctuated his remark with a full-powered swing from Spellbreaker.

The necromancer raised his artificial right arm to block Abaddon's strike. As the weapon and arm clashed, a massive burst of golden light radiated from the point of contact. Abaddon was sent flying, crashing into the ground with incredible force.

"That weapon of yours won't work on me," the necromancer advanced.

"Impossible," Abaddon slowly got to his feet, picking up Spellbreaker. "Your right arm is magic. I should have destroyed it."

"Like I said, your weapon doesn't work on me. Well, at least not now that I have taken precautions against it."

Abaddon raised Spellbreaker and took a defensive stance. As the necromancer moved forward, he raised his left arm from under his cloak. This one was definitely flesh and bone, but it was covered in strange white markings. The man began to intone a deep chant. As he spoke in words Abaddon could barely conceive, let alone understand, the markings started to glow gold. It hadn't worked out well for Abaddon last time, but he'd be saved if he'd let this man finish casting his spell. Abaddon charged in, this time aiming Spellbreaker at his opponent's left arm. His attack didn't even reach the limb. A golden force blocked Abaddon's strike. The backlash from *THIS* blow was several times stronger. As he hit the ground a second time, Abaddon felt Spellbreaker go flying from his hand. He must have taken on more damage than he thought. He was having trouble getting to his feet.

"My left arm wards me from all forms of cursed power," the necromancer advanced again, "even a greater artifact such as your Spellbreaker." He continued to slowly approach, a smile on his face. Abaddon was barely paying attention, mumbling the black words of Hell under his breath. "Didn't you hear what I just said? My left arm protects me from all of your black magic."

"Oh, that wasn't for you," Abaddon smiled from on the ground.

For a moment, the necromancer stopped. Then he noticed the massive shadow he was standing in. If Abaddon could have seen his face, it probably would have borne an expression of fear, as realization hit him, about two seconds before the massive three-headed hellhound. Abaddon started to get to his feet as Boris ripped and toe at the necromancer. So maybe it wasn't his preferred method of dealing with an enemy, but whatever got the necromancer killed.

Abaddon was just about to turn around to go pick up Spellbreaker, when an all too familiar sound stopped him in his tracks. Rather than the screaming he had expected to hear from necromancer, his ears caught the dread-infused tones of the hellish tongues. Moreover, it was a curse of binding, very similar to the one Abaddon had used to first shrink Boris. A second later, Boris crawled off the necromancer, and knelt down in front of him, whining in the subservient manner of a bad dog who had just been scolded.

The necromancer got to his feet, blood visible beneath his now tattered cloak. "That will be enough of such tricks."

"What in Heaven's name are you?" was Abaddon actually feeling fear?

"In the name of Heaven, I am forsaken, in the name of Hell, I am damned, and in the name of Terra, I shall wipe you from it."

Chapter Twenty-Two

The True Face of a Demon

"Why do you want to kill me? What have I done to you?" Abaddon readied Spellbreaker.

"What have you done?" The necromancer advanced on Abaddon again, though this time slower, clearly pained by his injuries. "You are a demon, spawn of Lucifer. You are a blight upon creation."

"You want to kill me because Lucifer is my dad?"

"You shall not bow down to them or serve them, for I the Lord your God am a jealous God, visiting the iniquity of the fathers on the children to the third and the fourth generation of those who hate me."

"You think you're God? You know about the divine beings, right? About the lack of God?"

"Of course, there is no one God. No, I am *YOUR* god. Here to pass judgment on you for your father's sins, just as I sought to pass judgment on him for the sins of *HIS* father."

"What are you talking about?" Abaddon was stepping back, making sure to keep the distance between them. The necromancer seemed in no mood to close and attack, or maybe it was his injuries that prevented him. "Wait, are you telling me that you are after me because of my grandfather?"

"You have no idea who I am or what brings me to eradicate you. And I see no reason to tell you. Simply know that you are my enemy, and you shall be destroyed in the name of Heaven for your crimes, and the crimes of your family."

"If you really know who I am, then don't you think trying to take me on is a bit foolish?" Abaddon had regained his composure. The necromancer had caught him off guard, but that was all.

"You've seen what I can do. Your cursed weapon can't hurt me, your demonic powers can't hurt me. But I can hurt you."

"Spellbreaker may not be able to hurt you, but you know nothing of my demonic powers. Come at me again, and I will destroy you."

The necromancer moved forward now, showing great speed despite his injuries. Abaddon spoke the words of the pit and dark flames rose in his hands. He hurled the hellfire at his attacker, but the necromancer brushed it aside with his left arm. Abaddon started to recite another black spell, but the necromancer's right fist caught him in the chest and sent him crashing to the ground.

"You have proven weak," the necromancer stood over Abaddon as he struggled to move. "You are far too weak to face me. Now suffer and die!"

The necromancer held out his right arm, and the sigils of pain glowed bright red. As the crimson lightning shot towards Abaddon, he responded with a single sharp command in the demonic tongues. Right as the lightning struck, it seemed to vanish, almost as though absorbed into Abaddon's body. This time there were no screams. Abaddon didn't writhe in pain. Marks appeared on his body, dark symbols made of shadow. These symbols burst out from him, as though he was being released from ebony chains. A black miasma rose up from his body, coalescing into an aura of night, bringing with it the cold of the deepest pits. Abaddon's breath became frost, and the piercing cold filled the air.

"This is my power," Abaddon's voice darkened and chilled. "This is the power of my father, of the line of Lucifer. You thought you could kill me? Try and kill me now. You meet only your own death."

The necromancer tried the sigils of pain once more, but again they were just absorbed. He raised his left arm, and the holy symbols began to glow. Abaddon raised his right hand, and the symbols dimmed, as though a candle extinguished by a great darkness. It was Abaddon's turn to advance, the necromancer's turn to feel fear. He could barely even move as Abaddon's hand reached out and grasped his throat.

"Drown in the darkness of the abyss."

The necromancer could only sputter incoherently as shadows crawled forth from Abaddon's body. The shreds of darkness crept like insects from Abaddon's flesh to the necromancer's, slowly engulfing him, piece by piece. Abaddon could see skin beneath the hood begin to turn lifeless, as all heat left the body. Suddenly, a blinding, brilliant light, descend from the

Heavens, enveloping both of them. Abaddon was momentarily stunned. When he regained his senses, he saw the necromancer pulling a dark stone from his cloak. Gasping, he crushed it in his hand. In an instant, he vanished into black smoke

"NO!" Abaddon leapt forward.

"STOP, NOW," a booming voice commanded.

Abaddon looked up to see a figure descending in the now fading pillar of light. As the brightness dimmed, he made out the shining form of a woman in pure white armor, six luminescent wings of white and silver arose from her back and shoulders, and long silvery hair cascaded around her wild face and searing visage.

"IN THE NAME OF HEAVEN, AND BY THE ARMAGEDDON ACCORDS, YOU ARE ORDERED TO CEASE AND DESIST YOUR DEMONIC MAGIC IMMEDIATELY," the figure boomed.

"No," Abaddon was half furious and half desperate. "You let him get away!"

"YOU ARE USING CLASS SEVEN RESTRICTED MAGIC. CEASE IMMEDIATELY, OR I WILL BE FORCED TO APPREHEND YOU."

"I have to finish him," Abaddon started to move.

The seraph held out her arm and spoke a divine word. A blast of concentrated light flew from her outstretched hand, smashing into Abaddon and hurling him back with force. It was being absorbed into his body, just as the lightning had been, but this divine light was coming too fast for his dark powers to keep up. Abaddon was forced to the ground. As the light continued to pour into him, the seraph held out her other hand and again intoned string of divine words. Now golden chains wrapped around him. This was very similar to the binding the templars had tried to place on Spellbreaker, only this was many times stronger. Abaddon felt the dark powers being pushed back deep inside of his body. The seal he had broken moments before was being forcibly remade. As the binding stuck to his very being, Abaddon could feel the clash of heavenly light and demonic darkness shake through his whole body, ripping all strength and sanity from him.

Abaddon tried to think as he collapsed to the ground, tried to bring his mind back under control. He was having a very difficult time achieving anything other than scattered thoughts. Even at the best of times, breaking the seal left him both physically and emotionally drained. Then there was the deep cold it left in him, worse than a hundred heavy rains. Add to that the holy magic searing into his flesh, and well…. Abaddon tried to remember a time he had felt worse. Getting hit full on with the sigils of pain wasn't even a contender.

The last thing Abaddon was aware of before he lost consciousness, was the sound of many footsteps. A group of templars arrived on the scene, swords drawn.

"Alright, everyone on the ground-" the lead templar stopped as she saw the seraph, still hovering in the air.

All the templars immediately kneeled, sheathing their swords as they did so. The seraph descended slowly, alighting on the ground without any noise, despite her full suit of armor.

"This demon used class seven restricted magic," the seraph's voice was no longer booming like thunder, but instead strict business. "I have apprehended him and am bringing him into custody."

"You were sent by the divine council?" the head templar did not look up as she spoke.

"Yes. The violation of the Armageddon Accords was deemed severe enough that I was given level one divine punishment magic to apprehend him. This matter will be taken to court immediately. I will be acting as the divine representative for the proceedings. Please direct me to the nearest courtroom so we may begin as soon as possible."

"Yes ma'am."

Abaddon woke slowly. He was having a hard time remembering where he was, or what had happened to him recently. As he tried to get up, he felt a sharp jolt as his movement was stopped dead in its tracks. His vision returned, and he looked around. He was in a cell, golden chains tied him to the wall, and holy wards were everywhere, inside and out. Then his memory began to return. He was still aching all over, but what was coming was going to be much worse.

Chapter Twenty-Three

One Sending

"Hey Dad," Abaddon was very aware of how hesitant he sounded.

"It's been a while. How are you doing?"

"Well…. about that….."

Lucifer looked quizzically through the portal, "This isn't your apartment, is it? Where are you sending from?"

"Prison…." Abaddon winced as he said it.

"WHAT?" Abaddon's cell shook. The templar outside who was regulating the wards on his cell lost his balance and fell over, whether from sheer surprise or the actual vibrations, Abaddon couldn't tell. "Who dares lock my spawn in chains?"

"A seraph from the divine-"

"A SERAPH?"

"Please stop shouting Dad; you'll destroy the whole building.

"How can I be calm when the forces of Heaven attack my own spawn? You've committed no crime and yet still they see fit to put you in chains? I shall rise up and-"

"No Dad, it's not that simple."

"What could be more simple than this rank injustice?"

"You don't understand, Dad."

"I understand more than enough to bring my force to bear upon these-"

"I had to break my seal Dad," Abaddon's voice was all frustration and desperation. Lucifer instantly became silent. "The divine courts had good reason to send a seraph to arrest me."

"You know the Armageddon Accords. What made you break the seal?"

"It was an enemy. A man. He-"

"A mere human forced you to break your seal?" Abaddon couldn't tell if Lucifer was shocked or outraged.

"No, he was different. I don't even know where to start. Look, I don't have time to explain this to you now, but I promise I will tell you everything once this is all over. But for right now, just know that I had a good reason for breaking the seal."

"Well it's not me you have to convince, but the divine courts. You realize how bad this could be if you lose this trial, don't you?"

"You made me memorize the Armageddon Accords by the time I was one hundred. I know exactly how much trouble I'm in. The other reason I used my one sending to send you, is because I want to contact…. Mephistopheles."

"Are you sure about this? You know the risks of dealing with their kind."

"I don't really have a choice. Can you summon him for me?"

Before Lucifer could respond, there was a large puff of black smoke accompanied by a shrouded form appearing right outside Abaddon's cell. The poor Templar fell over for a second time. As the smoke cleared, a demon in a black suit and red pinstripes stepped into view. His crimson tail swished silently on the ground as he walked forward. He bowed his small horns in Abaddon's direction.

"My lord Lucifer tells me his spawn is in need of a lawyer?"

Abaddon looked through the portal at Lucifer, who shrugged, and then back at Mephistopheles, "Yes I am."

"You-you can't be in here," the templar stuttered after getting up off the floor for a second time.

"I am this young demon's legal representative. He *IS* entitled to representation the same as anyone else."

"N-no, I mean you literally can't be here. The station has divine wards on it that make teleportation in or out impossible."

Mephistopheles gave the man a look, "Clearly," and then turned back to Abaddon. "So do you wish me to represent you?"

"Yes, you are the best option I have. What is the price for your services?"

"A favor, to be determined, by me, at a later date. But for the spawn of Lucifer, I have a special offer. The favor I ask cannot have a reasonable chance of harming you. And you may make one stipulation, a restriction on the favor. And if both parties agree, we will have a deal."

"How generous of you. Very well then, here's my stipulation: I am currently working as a hero in New Eden. Whatever favor you ask of me cannot jeopardize my standing as a citizen and hero of New Eden. I don't want you to make me a pariah or anything."

"Of course, of course, you have an image to protect. Believe me, I understand how hard it can be trying to win the approval of mortals. Ever since I agreed to let Christopher Marlowe use my likeness in that play of his I've had a really difficult time making deals with any of them. Now people say the term 'Faustian bargain' like it's a bad thing."

"So, we have a deal then?"

"Excellent, let's shake on it," with a second puff of smoke Mephistopheles was standing next to Abaddon, his hand outstretched.

"But that's-" the templar was stuttering again. "The wards on the cell are even stronger than-"

"Yes, yes, impossible, I know," Mephistopheles shook Abaddon's hand and turned to the still open Hell portal. "Don't worry my lord, your spawn is in excellent hands."

"A-alright, you've made your one sending. Now I'm going to have to ask the demon to lea-" In a third puff of smoke, Mephistopheles was gone. The templar just stood blinking for a minute. Then, "Screw this, I'm going to get some coffee."

"Well this is quite the mess you've gotten yourself into here."

"Believe me, I know Dad. But if anyone can help me, Mephistopheles can."

"Well, hopefully this will all work out. And remember, you promised to tell me everything that happened after all this is over. And I do mean *EVERYTHING*."

"I will dad. You know I wouldn't have undone the seal if it wasn't completely necessary."

"I know. Just make sure that saved seraph doesn't lock you away, or so help me-"

"Dad, the last thing we need is for you to start another Armageddon."

"I wouldn't go *THAT* far. Besides, you know that sort of thing is more your uncle's style. I really don't go in for the direct approach."

"Yeah, yeah, father of lies, I know. But either way, don't worry Dad. I'll be fine."

"I know you will."

"Love you Dad."

"Love you too."

Chapter Twenty-Four

Standing Trial

Abaddon was still bound by holy seals. He could feel them burning his skin, but now it was only a mild irritation. He barely even noticed it over his anxiety. He knew of Mephistopheles' reputation, though he hadn't worked with the demon personally before. He just hoped he would be able to help.

Abaddon was led out into a large courtroom. He was brought to a stand, inside of a cage covered in holy seals and wards. As soon as the door of the cage was closed, the bindings on his hands disappeared. He didn't like the feeling of the holy magic all around him, but was it better than being in direct contact with it. Looking around, he saw a wizened female elf in white robes covered in golden holy symbols, sitting at a large elevated podium. To the left of his cage, the seraph stood. Her wings were folded behind her, but she was still wearing her white armor.

"I see the accused has been brought to his stand," the elf turned to Abaddon. "Where is your legal representative?"

There was a puff of black smoke, and Mephistopheles was standing to Abaddon's right, "Here, madam justiciar," Mephistopheles bowed deeply.

"Yes," the elf gave him a look that showed obvious displeasure with his entrance. "Now that we are all present we can begin-"

"Excuse me," Mephistopheles interrupted. "If I may, before we begin."

"What is it?"

"I would ask if it is strictly necessary to keep my client in a cage. He has not, as of yet, been found guilty of any crime, and this makes it seem as though all concerned already view him as such."

"I assure you Mr. Mephistopheles, was it?" the justiciar looked at some papers in front of her, "that the cage is merely a precaution, as your client is accused of posing a significant danger to Terra. For now, no guilt or innocence has been proclaimed or assumed. That is for me to determine at this trial. However, while Mr. Abaddon poses a potential threat, he will be contained."

"But what danger could he be?" Mephistopheles gave a smile in the direction of the seraph. "Is that not why she is clad in her holy armor? Unless I am much mistaken, she took Abaddon into custody once already. Surely she could do so again, if the need arises."

"The cage stays," the justiciar gave him another look.

"Well, I tried," Mephistopheles addressed Abaddon, his tone apologetic.

"It's alright. If it makes them more comfortable, I'm fine in the cage."

"How very diplomatic of you; your father would be proud."

Abaddon lingered on Mephistopheles' words. He thought back to his father's rage in the cell, and wondered if they were talking about the same person. His father had always been quick to anger, and while definitely smart, fairly direct. Abaddon knew that many demons, Lucifer included, referred to him as the father of lies, but he had never seen any evidence of that.

"Alright then," the justiciar continued. "Assuming there are no further complaints to be raised, we shall begin. At this time, I would like to remind all present that this trial will be monitored with powerful magic. Everything that is said and done in this courtroom will be recorded. Magic is also in place to protect this courtroom from any outside intrusion or sabotage of this trial. And finally I will need each of you to agree to a geas, binding you to tell only the truth for the duration of this trial. Ms. Cassandra," the justiciar turned to the seraph, "do you hereby swear to tell only the truth while in this courtroom, by order of this geas?"

"I do," A glow of golden light appeared over her head, and then vanished.

"And do you, Mr. Abaddon, hereby swear to tell only the truth while in this courtroom, by order of this geas?"

"I do," the same light appeared over Abaddon's head, then vanished.

The justiciar turned to Mephistopheles, a very calculated look appearing on her face, "And do you, Mr. Mephistopheles, hereby swear to tell only the truth while in this courtroom, by order of this geas?"

"I do," no gold light appeared over Mephistopheles' head. The look on the justiciar's face turned to momentary shock, and the seraph began to move forward. Mephistopheles held up a hand. "Sorry, sorry. I always make sure

I have certain protection of my own against holy magic. I forgot to dispel it," he snapped his fingers, and there was a crackle of black energy above his head. "Please, madam justiciar, ask me again."

"Very well. Mr. Mephistopheles, do you, hereby swear to tell only the truth while in this courtroom, by order of this geas?"

"I do," and this time, the gold light did appear over his head, and then vanish.

"Then this trial will now begin. I would like Ms. Cassandra, as the divine representative who was tasked with bringing in Mr. Abaddon by the divine council, to state the charge she has brought against him."

"Madam Justiciar, I caught this demon using class seven restricted magic in an urban area. Upon my command to cease his magic, he proceeded to ignore me, and then attack me. I was forced to use level one divine punishment magic to restrain him."

"Well, Mr. Abaddon, do you deny this charge?"

"I do not deny that I used class seven restricted magic in an urban area, however I do deny attacking Ms. Cassandra."

"Well then, the record shows you freely admitting to the use of prohibited magic. This means you shall punished to the full extent of-"

"If I may, madam justiciar," Mephistopheles stepped forward. "My client has a right to defend himself, as it is my right to help defend him on his behalf. You cannot simply move to a sentencing without a due process."

"Defend himself from what?" Cassandra stepped forward in turn. "He admitted to using class seven restricted magic. The Armageddon Accords are very clear about that."

"Ah, but the Armageddon Accords are also very clear about the situations in which such magic is allowed."

"Such magic is allowed within the lower planes," the justiciar interjected, "i.e. Hell. However, such magic is expressly forbidden in Terra, or the upper planes, i.e. Heaven. "

"Yes, but there is another exception wherein restricted magic can be used in Terra or the upper planes, which you have neglected to mention."

"Are you referring to a situation in which there is magic present of an equal or greater restriction level?"

"I am indeed Madam Justiciar."

"Ms. Cassandra, was there any other class seven or higher restricted magic at the scene when you apprehended Mr. Abaddon?"

"No madam justiciar. His was the only restricted magic present."

"But my client was battling with a known necromancer when Ms. Cassandra showed up. And in her attempts to apprehend my client, she let said necromancer escape."

"There was another figure present, who did indeed escape when I showed up, I never saw this figure use any necromancy. There was no threat present of any restricted magic."

"If you think that, then you are more foolish than I would have thought an agent of the divine courts was allowed to be."

"How dare you!" Cassandra made an aggressive move.

"Both of you calm down," the justiciar's voice stopped Cassandra in her tracks. "Explain yourself Mr. Mephistopheles."

"It's quite simple. Just because one is not currently using necromancy, does not mean one is not *CAPABLE* of using it. The mere fact that Ms. Cassandra did not witness any necromancy means nothing."

"I was not relying on mere sight. If he had been in possession of any restricted magic I would have sensed it."

"But you were not aware of my client's restricted magic until he used it. Such magic can be concealed."

"He is under a powerful demonic seal. This necromancer would need to possess magic equaling that of an elder demon bloodline, one of the demon rulers of Hell, to achieve that."

"And this necromancer does."

Chapter Twenty-Five

It's a Family Thing

"Are you telling us," the justiciar's tone showed her skepticism, "that this necromancer was an elder demon?"

"No, this necromancer was human."

"Then there was no way they could have hidden such magic from me!"

"Yes Mr. Abaddon, I also find this claim hard to believe. You are saying that a human possesses demonic magic equivalent to that of an elder demon. How is this even possible?"

"I believe my client is best suited to answer that," Mephistopheles gestured to Abaddon.

"Very well, Mr. Abaddon, can you explain to us how a human has demonic magic from an elder demon bloodline."

"This necromancer had a demonic prosthetic of sorts. His right arm was made from obsidian of the pits, and the sigils of pain were carved into it."

"I am not familiar with this specific form of magic; would you please state for this court what the sigils of pain are?"

"They are a powerful form of magic from the line of Lilith, ruler of the Seventh Circle of Hell. The sigils of pain trigger all of the subject's nerves simultaneously, sending maximized pain signals to the brain. If one is exposed to this for too long, their brain will overload and shut down, killing them."

"Ms. Cassandra, are you familiar with this type of magic?"

"No madam justiciar, I have never heard of such a thing. As a holy agent of the divine courts, I have fought my fair share of demons, but have no knowledge of this magic."

"My- I mean, Lilith guards this secret closely. The secret of this magic is known only to her and her kin."

"Tell me Mr. Abaddon, from what circle of Hell do you come from?"

"From the Ninth Circle, Madam Justiciar."

"Then how is it, that you know so much about a secret magic, supposedly known only to the ruler of the Seventh Circle of Hell? One so secret even a specially trained angelic warrior does not know of it?"

"Well... you see... the thing is..."

"We don't have all day Mr. Abaddon. Please explain yourself."

"Lilith... is my aunt. I have visited her in the Seventh Circle on multiple occasions, and she has used the sigils of pain on me personally on at least three of those."

"You are spawn related to the queen of dominion?!" golden light glowed in Cassandra's hand. "Such a creature of darkness walks among us on Terra?"

"Hey, I have every right to live here!" Abaddon struck his cage with a fist and quickly regretted it as the holy magic seared his flesh.

"CEASE," the justiciar's voice held a surprising degree of command. Both stopped speaking, but glared at each other. "Demons have every right to live in Terra, assuming they follow the proper procedures required of all immigrants."

"But this fiend is of one of the cursed bloodlines! He hid his true nature so that he could walk undetected in New Eden. He clearly poses a significant danger to-"

"ENOUGH, Ms. Cassandra. There is no rule that states that a demon must reveal their heritage. The same is true for any other creature who immigrates to Terra. As for his level of threat, we are still discussing that in this trial. Now Mr. Abaddon, you say your aunt is Lilith, demon queen of the Seventh Circle of Hell. And you further claim, that as a result of this, you were informed of this special magic known as the sigils of pain, correct?"

"Yes."

"And you further say that this necromancer you fought possessed a demonic right arm with these very same sigils, thus showing evidence that he does indeed possess demonic power equivalent to that of an elder demon, also correct?"

"Well, in that particular instance. I would not say he possesses anywhere near the power of a true elder demon. That would be a grave insult to-"

"The *POINT,* Mr. Abaddon, is that you are claiming this demonic right arm of his, is proof of his potential ability to seal his forbidden magic in the same way yours is sealed, correct?"

"Yes."

"Excuse me," Cassandra interjected, "but we have no evidence that any of this is true. Are we to just take his word on this?"

"My client," Mephistopheles stepped forward, "is under the same geas of truth that you and I are Ms. Cassandra. He is incapable of lying."

"But at the beginning of this trial, you yourself showed an ability to counter or fool the geas. How do we know that you are not doing that now, with your client?"

"My dear Ms. Cassandra, I find the very accusation insulting. I would never do such an unseemly thing in a hallowed court of law," Mephistopheles smiled.

"Unfortunately for you, I must agree with Ms. Cassandra. You have shown evidence of a weakness in my geas spell. It is possible that you or your client are avoiding its effects. I am afraid I have to ask you for some sort of proof of your client's claims."

"Certainly," Mephistopheles held up a hand as Abaddon started to object. "I would be more than happy to provide the required evidence." He then turned to Abaddon. "Now Mr. Abaddon, would please describe for us exactly what the sigils of pain, and their magical effects look like."

"The sigils themselves are markings carved into the flesh, or an inanimate object. In this case, an obsidian arm. When activated they glow bright red. Then magic that looks like red lightning shoots from the sigils, hitting the target of the magic. And as I said they cause immense pain by targeting the subject's nerves."

"Thank you Mr. Abaddon. Now if you please, tell the court what current employment you possess in the city of New Eden."

"I am a hero."

"And which guild do you belong to?"

"The White Pegasus Guild."

"And do you know a person by the name of Artemis?"

"Yes, she is a fellow monster-slayer at White Pegasus."

"And on the day of July 7th, did you, or did you not, help her in defeating a hydra that was attacking New Eden?"

"I did."

"And did this same necromancer we have previously discussed appear there and attack?"

"Yes."

"And did he use the sigils of pain upon you at that time?"

"Yes."

"So, would Ms. Artemis be able to identify said sigils, and give a description of them and their effects that is similar to your own?"

"Yes."

"Then Madam Justiciar, I call Ms. Artemis of the White Pegasus Guild as a witness."

Mephistopheles snapped his fingers, and a large pillar of smoke appeared. This was accompanied by screaming, and a vicious snarling nose. Artemis fell backwards out of the smoke, her crossbow in hand. A second later came a storm of sharp teeth and wicked claws, as a massive wolf leapt out of the smoke, an avatar of murderous rage.

Chapter Twenty-Six

End Game

Artemis seemed completely stunned as she materialized in the courtroom. The werewolf was almost upon her, when Cassandra called out a holy word and hurled a bolt of radiant light at the beast. It struck the werewolf square in the chest, sending it across the room with a burning hole in its center. Then wasting no time, Cassandra flared her wings and shot across the room, grabbing Mephistopheles by the throat and slamming him into Abaddon's cage. He hissed as the holy magic burned his body.

"YOU FOUL DEVIL. YOU WERE PLOTTING AN ATTACH AGAINST THE JUSTICIAR AND ME."

"Please," Mephistopheles grunted, "I meant no harm. I had no idea she was battling a werewolf at the-"

"QUIET DECIEVER, I HAVE HAD ENOUGH OF YOUR LIES AND TRICKS."

"What the hell is going on?" Artemis had gotten to her feet, and was looking around.

Suddenly a golden chain shot out from the justiciar's hand. It wrapped around Cassandra's midriff and forcible pulled her back, wrenching Mephistopheles from her grasp.

"Please control yourself!" the justiciar snapped at Cassandra. "This was no assassination plot or anything of the kind. I will *NOT* have you attacking the other legal representative, do I make myself clear?"

"Thank you very much madam justiciar, but I bear her no ill-"

"And you," the justiciar pointed threateningly at Mephistopheles. "First you teleport into my courtroom without authorization, and then you bring an armed hero and a werewolf into it. Mistake or not, you pull anything like this again and I will personally exile you from this courtroom myself, and make damn sure that you can never get back in, teleportation or not. And you will be responsible for getting that burning wolf carcass out of my courtroom."

"My apologies Madam Justiciar, it will not happen again."

"What is this?" Artemis, had just noticed Abaddon in his cage.

"A legal trial, my dear Artemis," Mephistopheles stepped forward. "I am Mephistopheles, Abaddon's legal advisor for the proceedings," Mephistopheles gave a deep bow. "My client is being held here under suspicion of violating the Armageddon Accords by using class seven restricted magic. I have 'asked you here' to testify on his behalf."

"But how did I get here? The courthouse should be warded against all forms of magical intrusion."

"I've gotten that a lot lately. Right now though, Abaddon needs your help to clear his, ahem, neutral name. Can I assume you will be willing to testify and answer any questions, I or the lovely Ms. Cassandra might have?" At this he gestured to Cassandra, who stared flaming daggers back at him.

"Um yes…. I mean, yes, I will answer any questions."

"Very well," the justiciar turned to Artemis. "Now that this circus has gotten under control, I shall administer the geas. Ms. Artemis, do you hereby swear to tell only the truth while in this courtroom, by order of this geas?"

"I do," the golden light appeared over her head, then vanished.

"Very well, Mr. Mephistopheles, you may ask your questions."

"Thank you madam justiciar," He turned to Artemis. "On July 7th, did you team up with my client, Mr. Abaddon, to slay a hydra?"

"I don't remember the exact date, but yes, Abaddon did help me slay a hydra."

"Would you please state for this court, the events that directly followed the slaying of the hydra, in as much detail as you can."

"I had just killed the hydra by shooting it in the heart, and was talking with Abaddon. Then a strange cloaked figure appeared on top of the hydra. He pulled out an odd charm and began to chant a spell of some kind. Oh wait, first I asked him to identify himself, but he did not, and *THEN* he pulled out the charm and started to chant. After he began his spell, I shot him in the arm. He didn't seem to notice, but kept chanting. His spell reanimated the hydra. Its first attack knocked me to the ground. Abaddon then broke the reanimation spell on the hydra with his war hammer Spellbreaker. Then the cloaked figure attacked Abaddon. He knocked him to the ground."

"How did he accomplish this?"

"He struck Abaddon from behind, with his right hand. It was weird. The arm was black, artificial. There were glowing red marks on it. Once he had Abaddon on the ground, he shouted a threat at him, and then attacked him."

"What did he do?"

"He used some sort of magic. Red lightning shot from the marks on his arm. It seemed to cause Abe- I mean Abaddon, a great deal of pain. He was writhing on the ground and screaming. When I finally regained enough of my strength, I shot the cloaked figure in the back with a flaming arrow, and he vanished. After that I took Abaddon back to the guild so he could get medical treatment."

"Thank you, Ms. Artemis," Mephistopheles turned back to the justiciar. "As you can see. Ms. Artemis' description of the sigils of pain matched the one that my client gave. An artificial arm with red sigils that shot red lightning. Oh, and one more question Ms. Artemis: did my client seem overly injured after he was struck by this red lightning?"

"No, actually. He suffered enough pain to pass out, but strangely there was no sign of injury on his body after the attack."

"I see," Mephistopheles turned back. "Almost as though my clients' nerves were attacked directly. Well in my humble opinion, this second testimony should show without a doubt that the necromancer possesses the sigils of pain, a magic of Lilith herself. Which in turn gives precedence for the necromancer being able to hide his necromantic abilities."

"Without a doubt?" Cassandra scoffed. "This proves nothing. This woman could be in league with you two. If you did indeed fool the geas, who's to say she isn't in on it. For all we know, this could all be an elaborate set-up."

"You are indeed correct," Mephistopheles put his hands behind his back. "For all you know this could be a scheme concocted by me and mine to get

Abaddon free. But you have given no proof that our story is incorrect, only your word that you would have noticed if the necromancer possessed forbidden magic. Whereas we have given ample evidence for our case. Your word is nothing to go on I am afraid."

"You would dare question a representative of the divine council?!"

"Indeed I would. Just because you are an angel does not mean you do not have to provide evidence, just like the rest of us. But I would go even further. The fact that you question the strength of the geas spell is rather suspect as well. The second time I was subjected to it, I received the same glowing light that you all did, a telltale sign that the spell worked."

"But you could have faked that light easily to trick us!"

"The first time no light appeared above my head, but it did without any trouble above Abaddon's. No before you go too much farther into your declarations of my elaborate and vile scheme, I would like to point out that simply stating that I might have foiled the geas is no proof that I did. And if I might be so bold, I would venture to guess that you would not have brought up this point if it weren't for me and my client's demonic origin."

"I freely admit to not trusting the spawn of Hell."

"And there you go Madam Justiciar. Ms. Cassandra's assertions of my evil trickery are completely baseless."

"You make a valid point Mr. Mephistopheles. And you have given good evidence to suggest your claims. Not only that, but both Mr. Abaddon, and Ms. Artemis attest to this man using necromancy. Which would mean that Abaddon acted within the bounds of the Armageddon accords when he used class seven restricted magic."

"You can't be seriously dropping the charges against him?" Cassandra was fuming. "He used forbidden magic, and resisted arrest-"

"Which is why he will be put under probation, and you Ms. Cassandra, will be watching over him."

Chapter Twenty-Seven

Free at Last…. Sort Of

"Well, I'm back," Abaddon was once more in his apartment, communing with Lucifer.

"I can see that. So, Mephistopheles came through for you then?"

"Yes, although you were right to be wary of him. He knew a lot more about my 'case' than I had told him. And he seems to be able to casually avoid high-level divine magic. Do you know if he is from one of the elder bloodlines?"

"I don't think so. As long as I have been ruler, he has been a resident of the Ninth Circle."

"That means he's been around for a while. He doesn't seem like the warrior type though. Frankly I'm surprised he lasted that long."

"Well, for what it's worth, the Ninth Circle is one of the more ordered ones. And from the few times I've had dealings with him, I've gotten the sense that he's the type who can talk his way out of most situations."

"I'd believe that. He teleported into the courtroom without authorization, deflected a holy geas, and summoned a werewolf in the middle of the trial, and he still managed get me free…. well, mostly anyway."

"What do you mean, mostly?"

Abaddon raised his right arm, which had a golden ring of holy symbols locked around his obsidian bracer, "I have to wear this. This seal prevents me from using my demonic magic. And, should I remove it or the bracer, the seraph that brought me in will be notified immediately, and have full recourse to arrest me again. And trust me, she would like nothing more than to do just that. Well, on second thought, maybe she would rather just kill me herself, but you get the idea."

"*THAT* is what passes for free in New Eden? The court put you on an angel's leash. This is an outrage!"

"Well thank you for not shaking the whole building with your voice of the damned."

"I'm getting better about that," Lucifer sounded a tad offended.

"Besides, it's not permanent. I'm on temporary probation until I am deemed not a threat."

"You never were one. Leave it to the divine council to pull something like this."

"Dad, I already told you that I broke the seal. You know how serious this is."

"I do. But I also know how serious the situation must have been for you to do that. Look, I may be mad that a seraph arrested you and chained you up like this, but I understand why they did it. It is standard procedure when restricted magic is used. But the fact that you did that means the enemy you were facing was much, much worse, and yet you were the one imprisoned. You said this person you fought was human, right? Well, I'd bet my throne that's the reason you're bound by holy magic, and they aren't."

"No, that's not the reason. Okay, it might have a little something to do with it, but that's not the reason. The necromancer wasn't using any restricted magic during that-"

"Necromancer? You fought a human necromancer who was powerful enough to force you to break your seal? You will explain everything to me, *NOW.*"

Abaddon hadn't heard that tone of voice since Lucifer had found out about Nidhogg and his holy water. "Well, when I got captured, it was actually the second time I had faced this necromancer. I had just helped a fellow hero defeat a hydra. That's when the necromancer showed up. He pulled out some strange charm from his cloak and used it to revive the hydra. Spellbreaker was easily able to stop the reanimated hydra, but the necromancer got me as soon as I did it."

"What do you mean, got you?"

"His right arm is demonic. It's made of obsidian, and it bears the sigils of pain."

"You mean Lilith's-"

"Yes. The other hero, Artemis, saved me. The necromancer caught me off guard and would have killed me with the sigils of pain, but she got a good shot in and he retreated."

"How could this have happened? How could a human have an obsidian arm? How could a mere mortal have gained power like the sigils of pain?"

"You're asking me, Dad? I have no idea how he did it. But I know that's what it was. Aunt Lilith used those on me that time when I was one hundred and sixty, and I broke her favorite concubine. I definitely know what that feels like, and he *DEFINITELY* had the sigils of pain."

"But even so, that shouldn't have been enough to force you to break your seal. There has to be more to this necromancer."

"There is. When I fought him the next time, his left arm was covered in holy script. He was able to fend off all my demon magic. He could even repel Spellbreaker. I'd never seen magic so strong. I had Boris attack him, but the necromancer sealed Boris."

"Sealed a cerberus? His magic was really that strong?"

"No Dad, he commanded Boris. He can speak the demonic tongues."

"So, you're telling me, that a human possesses necromancy, a holy left arm strong enough to stop Spellbreaker, and a demonic right arm with the sigils of pain, *AND* he can speak in the cursed tongues of the pit?"

"Yes. I don't even know how this could be possible, but that's the situation. And to top it off, he seems to be hunting me specifically. The first time he appeared, he referred to me as the spawn of Lucifer, and said he would kill me. The second time, he came after me in order to finish the job. Breaking the seal was the only way I could kill him."

"If he actually had that kind of power…. well yes, I suppose you didn't have any other choice. But this, none of this should be possible. Someone like him should not exist. I can't image how powerful that holy magic must have been to be able to repel Spellbreaker, and there should be no way a human could get a demonic arm, or learn necromancy."

"Necromancy may be top on the list of magic that is forbidden in Terra, but that doesn't mean someone couldn't still learn it. It would undoubtedly be difficult, but not impossible."

"No, only one person in the entirety of creation should know the secret of necromancy."

"Just one? Are you saying it's banned everywhere? What's going on here?"

"One of the deals I had with Heaven when the Armageddon Accords were made, was that I would seal the secret of necromancy away and never let anyone else know about it."

"You? You're a necromancer?"

"No, but the secret of necromancy traces its origin back through our line, the line of Lucifer. I inherited the power from my father, he got it from his, and so on."

"I'm going to get it?"

"You're going to inherit the protection of it. Like I said, I promised Heaven that I would safeguard it, never let it be used or discovered."

"Do you know why it is forbidden? Why does Heaven hate it so much?"

"They think it perverts the natural cycle of life and death. Personally, I think they are scared of it, because it could weaken their power. I don't know, and do not care to find out. The deal is I keep it sealed away, so I will. But apparently someone stole that secret."

"Wait, you don't think the forces of Heaven will come after you for this? For going against the Armageddon Accords?"

"They very well may want to chat with me, but I wouldn't be worried about much more than that. They aren't any more eager to stir up trouble between Heaven and Hell than I am. Besides, you've got your own mess to deal with, what with being chained to a saved angel. But now that I know what is going on, this has become my problem. I will figure out what is happening, who this necromancer is. You just be careful. With that seal on, you won't be a match for him."

"I think the upside of an angel showing up is that he won't try anything for a while. But yes, while this seal is in place, I will try to do my best to avoid another fight with him."

"Good. While you do that, I will get started on figuring out who in Heaven's name this necromancer is."

"Alright, bye Dad. Love you."

"Love you too."

Chapter Twenty-Eight

Back to Work

Abaddon walked into the White Pegasus building. He still was impressed by the large ground floor every time he came inside. Which, admittedly had not been many times. He made his way to the front desk.

"Hey, Frank."

"Hey Abaddon, or is it Abe now? I hear you had a little run-in with the law. What happened?"

Abaddon raised his right arm, showing the holy seal, "This. I'm on probation."

"Oh my, someone must have been really bad to get one of those."

"It's complicated: one of those necessary evil type things."

"I see. Well you'd better hope so. I can only imagine that's what Ms. Weathers wants to talk to you about."

"Can't wait. I think I've spent more time in her office than the rest of the guild combined."

"Well don't break your streak on my account. She's waiting for you."

"So, a report came in that you were arrested," Ms. Weathers was pacing.

"I was."

"And?"

Abaddon held up his arm, "I'm now on probation."

"That's just great. You know I heard that an angel was spotted over by the park. People saw a golden pillar of light, and they saw her battling a demon. I can only assume-"

"That the demon was me, yes."

"And after all I said about you needing to be extra careful with how you present yourself; first Brad, and now this. What were you thinking?"

"About my own safety."

"You were acting in self-defense?" Ms. Weathers' tone was full of skepticism. "Angels don't get called down from Heaven to arrest someone acting in self-defense."

"They do if I defend myself with class seven restricted magic."

"Class seven- Are you out of your mind?!"

"It was that or get killed by the necromancer."

"He came back?"

"To finish the job, yes. It wasn't just demonic powers this time. His left arm was covered in holy symbols. He was strong enough to repel everything I had. The restricted magic was my only option."

"Do you know what you could have done if the angel hadn't shown up?"

"Create a rip in reality that would be connected directly to the darkest coldest pits of Hell. I know how my own powers work. It was a risk I had to take. It was in order to save my life and stop a necromancer."

"And how did that part work out for you?"

"Hey, it's not my fault the angel let him get away. She was so busy arresting me that he escaped before I could finish him."

"Oh gee, I wonder why that was."

"Look, I understand why you're mad, but-"

"No you don't," Ms. Weathers stopped pacing to gesticulate at him forcefully. "I am not mad because you used class seven restricted magic."

"You're not?"

"No. It may have been foolish. It may have been reckless. But that was your call. Heroes make tough choices in the field, and I don't have the right to tell them what they did was right or wrong, I wasn't there, so I couldn't know. No, the angel and the justiciar who prosecuted you were the ones mad about that."

"Then what *ARE* you mad about?"

"The fact that you didn't tell a potential employer that you possessed class seven restricted magic!"

"Well, I keep it sealed. And I thought you probably wouldn't hire me if you knew."

"You're damn right we wouldn't have. Do you think White Pegasus would have wanted that sort of liability?"

"Liability? Sure, I was in custody for a few days, and I can't use magic for a while due to the seal, but that's hardly-"

"Wow, you really don't get it, do you? What this is really about?"

"Clearly not."

"*OTHER PEOPLE*, seeing as I seem to need to spell it out for you. We are a highly-respected heroes guild within the city. We are one of the *MOST* highly respected. Do you know what could happen to us, to our reputation, if this gets out? If our heroes are going around committing crimes, it could ruin us."

"I did it to stop a necromancer."

"And who the hell knows that huh? Me, you, the justiciar who tried you, and the angel who is now your probation officer? How many times will I have to say it before you get it through your head: the truth is not always as important as what people think is true. If people see you as a criminal, then you're a criminal. And if they see us as associating with you then-"

"Associating?!" Abaddon got to his feet. "You're making it sound like I'm some terrible bad guy that White Pegasus is harboring."

"It wouldn't surprise me if that is what a lot of people will think if this gets out."

"It's not like my use of restricted magic is going to be made public knowledge."

"No, but all it takes is for one person to I.D. you as the demon that was fighting an angel in the park and it's just as bad. You lied to us in order to get this job, and now we might just be in deep shit because of that."

"Hey, I didn't lie."

"I don't care; a lie by omission is basically the same thing. You said yourself that you didn't put that on your resume or tell me because you thought it would cost you the job. You knew that this was bad, and intentionally withheld it. I don't think this will get out. Fortunately for us, you're still a relatively new hero; no one knows who you are yet. But that might also mean you'll have the shortest career of any hero I've ever seen."

"So I'm getting fired now?"

"Maybe. I told you when you almost killed Brad that a lot of higher-ups in the guild didn't want you to come on in the first place. Forget givong them more ammunition, you just gave them a damn siege engine! I'm not sure if I can convince them this time, and I'm not even sure that I want to."

"Look, you don't have to worry about this happening again. I'm not a little kid; I know how serious this is."

"Is that necromancer still out there? Does he still want to kill you? Yes? Well, then I *DO* have to worry about it happening again."

"Not as long as I have this holy binding on me."

"Great. If he shows up again he'll just kill you instead. Having a dead hero on our payroll is almost as bad as having a criminal on it."

"Well what do you want me to do?"

"Nothing. While we figure out what will happen to you as far as your employment with us is concerned, I want you to do nothing. No acts of heroism. In fact, I have already temporarily suspended your hero I.D. glyph. Until such a time as you are returned to full employment, *IF* you are returned to full employment, the magic on it will start working again, but until then, it won't be valid identification of you being a hero."

"Fantastic. No, magic, and I'm not even a hero. Got anything else you want to yell at me about?"

"No, feel free to leave my office at any time."

Chapter Twenty-Nine

Abaddon Does Some Explaining

"We need to talk," Artemis ambushed Abaddon as he left Ms. Weathers' office.

"Now is not a good time."

"I don't care. One minute I was fighting a werewolf, the next I'm in a courtroom, an angel kills my prey, you're in a holy cage, and I'm asked by a creepy demon in a suit to testify on your behalf. So even if Ms. Weathers just yelled at you, I deserve some answers."

"So, what happened?" Artemis and Abaddon were back in room A.

"I got arrested."

"I figured that part out. Why? It seemed to have something to do with the necromancer."

"Yeah, he showed up again and tried to kill me while I was walking Boris."

"Boris?"

"My pet cerberus."

"You kept that thing as a- never mind. Why would that get you arrested? And by an angel no less."

"Because I couldn't beat him, so I had to use class seven restricted magic."

"I assume that's really bad, right?"

"For a descendant of Merlin you'd think you'd know about this kind of thing."

"Hey, my family practices earth/Terran magic, I don't know about whatever it is you demons do. Sorry, you know what I mean."

"Using class seven restricted magic outside of Hell is a breach of the Armageddon Accords."

"Oh, that's *REALLY* bad. And you just got a slap on the wrist?"

"No, I got a holy binding on the wrist," Abaddon raised his right arm. "Not complaining though. I Could have been locked away. I'm just lucky that necromancy is even worse than what I did. I was able to convince the justiciar overseeing my case that what I did was the only thing I could do to stop a necromancer trying to kill me, which was completely accurate."

"And what *DID* you do?"

"You don't want to know."

"If I'm going to be working with someone who has magic banned by the Armageddon Accords, then I think I do."

"Well you probably won't be."

"What, did you get fired?"

"No, but Ms. Weathers is super pissed that I have restricted magic and didn't tell her during the interview. And it's not looking too good with the other higher-ups either. For now though, I'm just suspended."

"That really sucks, I mean it, but I can understand why they would feel that way."

"Yeah, they don't like the idea of working with a dangerous monster," Abaddon's tone got darker.

"That's not what I- well okay, that is what I meant. Not the monster part though."

"I get it, you're scared of me too, it makes sense."

"Yes, it does. You did something to get Heaven to send down an angel to arrest you; who wouldn't be scared of that?"

"I should just go," Abaddon turned to leave.

"No, you shouldn't," Artemis put a hand on his shoulder. "Well, I suppose it's more accurate to say that I don't want you to. Remember, I know you're the son of Lucifer. That was even scarier. To be perfectly honest, the fact that you have magic banned by the Armageddon Accords sounds par for the course for your family. But I also know you helped me kill a hydra, twice. Once? Let's call it one and a half times."

"So what, you think you owe me a favor now?"

"No jackass, I think there's more to you than your demon magic. I may be wrong, but you inherited these powers from Lucifer, right?"

"Yeah."

"So the fact that you have them is not your fault."

"The fact that I lied about having them is."

"Yes, as is the fact that you could cause some serious harm to this city if you wanted to, *IF YOU WANTED TO*. You lying about this just shows that you really wanted to be a hero. You shouldn't have done it, that's definitely true, but you did it for… mostly good reasons, as far as I can tell."

"So…. you're not scared of me?"

"Have you been listening to a word I've said? Yes, I'm scared of you, but I think it's worth moving past the fear. If nothing else, it would be a shame to lose a hero like you. I mean, I've never seen anyone as powerful as you. You were able to hold your own against an adult hydra, without any magic. And it may not seem like it, but the way you were able to defeat Brad so easily was quite impressive."

"Brad's just a pathetic weakling."

"Compared to you maybe, but that's my point. He's still a van Helsing. I have several years of hero experience on him, but he's definitely a better monster-slayer than I am. Did you know that he singlehandedly took down a dragon? I could maybe do that, but that was in his first month as a hero."

"He's still a dick."

"Okay, granted, but dicks can be strong too."

"I didn't know you had personal experience in that area," Abaddon smiled.

"Oh shut up Mr. Convicted Criminal, you know what I meant."

"Wow, kick a guy while he's down."

"I honestly never thought I'd get guilt tripped by a demon."

"Hey, guilt isn't just a holy thing."

"You learn something new every day, as the saying goes."

"Believe me, I know that feeling."

"I bet you would. You've probably learned enough new things for a lifetime."

"A human one anyway."

"Oh right, I keep forgetting how old you must be. Demons live a long time, right?"

"At least a few centuries, assuming another demon doesn't kill us before then. But it really depends."

"I can't imagine living in a place where you could die at any moment."

Abaddon gave her a look, "You're a professional monster-slayer."

"But that's a job. And besides, monster attacks aren't super common. It's not like getting into a life or death fight at any moment is perfectly normal around here."

"It's not usually the case in Hell either, at least not to that extreme. Demons would not have survived as a species if that were true. But it is still a really harsh and violent place, for the most part."

"Sounds like you had a rough childhood, whatever childhood is for a demon"

"Eh, it was fine. I'm one of the stronger demons around, and not many sought to challenge me or my father."

"That sounds about right. Listen, I should probably get going, but I would definitely like to talk to you some more. I wouldn't have thought learning about Hell could be interesting."

"Really? I mean, sure, if you want to be seen with a disgraced ex hero."

"Oh, come on," Artemis laughed. "Now you're just going for pity. Some proud son of Lucifer you are."

Abaddon laughed along with Artemis. It felt nice. It was definitely something he had not been expecting to do that day.

Chapter Thirty

Once More into the Coffee Shop

"So, we haven't talked to each other in a while," Mary sounded apprehensive.

"I've been a bit busy. Glad you still wanted to do this sort of thing though."

"Yeah, of course. So…. I heard you uh…. got arrested…."

"Yeah, that happened."

"What did you do?" Mary sounded almost awed.

"I….. did something that was potentially illegal," Abaddon was starting to feel really awkward, and wasn't quite sure why.

"Well obviously. But it's gotta be more than that. I heard some people talking about an angel showing up in the park and fighting a demon. And Ms. Weathers seemed really pissed."

"That's an understatement."

"So whatever you did was-"

"None of your saved business!" Abaddon was on his feet.

"Alright, alright. Geez, I didn't mean to pry."

"Aw shit, sorry," Abaddon sat back down. "I should *NOT* have yelled at you."

"I guess it's a sensitive topic."

"No, it's just…. I might be fired."

"What?!"

"I've been suspended temporarily, but we'll see if I get my job back."

"What happened? I mean, okay, you just made it clear you don't want to tell me about it, but this is crazy. An angel arrests you, and you almost get fired?"

"And put on probation," for the billionth time, Abaddon showed his glowing holy restraints.

"Really?"

"Yeah, the angel who arrested me can track my location, will know when I take this or the gauntlet it's attached to off, and I can't use any of my magic as long as it is on."

"That's gotta be rough."

"It's fine. It's just until I am deemed not a threat," Abaddon wasn't convincing himself either.

"I just- well I don't know what to say. Whatever happened had to have been serious if an angel got involved, and this," she gestured at his arm.

"Can we just drop it, okay?" why was he getting so defensive?

"Sorry, it's just hard. I mean, I called you out here because I wanted to make sure you were okay."

"I'm fi- I'm…. dealing with it."

"Well, do you need help dealing with it?"

"Not from you."

"Oh…. okay."

"Shit," Abaddon held up his hands. "That's not what I meant."

"Sounded like it."

"No, it's just- I don't know what I meant. I don't understand this, it wasn't nearly that hard talking to Artemis about this."

"Artemis was involved?"

"Well, she ended up at my trial. Look, I don't know if you heard about the two of us getting attacked by a necromancer a little while ago."

"I did hear about that. What's that got to do with it?"

"He came back to attack me again. I got arrested while fighting him."

"What? Why would you get arrested for that?"

"Well, in order to beat him, I had to use some…. illegal magic."

"Oh."

"Hence the released on probation. You know, it was allowable because self-defense, and all that."

"So what, do you think I won't want to talk to you anymore if I know what you're really capable of?"

"No, I know that- it's not important."

"It seems to be. You really feel uncomfortable talking to me about this, and I just want to understand a bit better. I'm not trying to get you to talk about something you're not comfortable with; I just don't like the idea of you getting arrested and me not even knowing enough to help."

"Why do you care so much anyway?"

"Um, us being friends comes to mind."

Abaddon started to speak, then stopped. He started again, but couldn't get words out, "Friends?" he finally managed.

"Yes, did you not think we were?"

"I- well- no- I- I mean- I thought- but I didn't know what you- that is- I didn't want to assume anything."

"So you *REALLY* never had friend before coming to Terra? I still find that hard to believe."

"Not everyone can make friends okay!"

"Most people can. Look, I'm not trying to judge you or anything. I just feel bad for you."

"Oh? Pitying the social outcast 'cus he can't make friends?"

"Whoa, that's not what I meant at all."

"Sure. Even the eight-foot-tall rock can make friends; I must be a real loser."

"Hey, I'm genuinely concerned, and you're just being an ass."

"Well when you're the son of- Maybe I don't care about being an ass?"

"If that were actually true, I wouldn't be here right now. Seriously, what the hell is going on with you?"

"Hell is exactly what's going on with me."

"What does that even mean?"

"I'm just a big nasty demon," Abaddon got to his feet.

"What are you talking about?"

"I'm an evil, vile monster," Abaddon turned to leave. "Why would you ever want to be friends with me?"

Chapter Thirty-One

A Low Point

Abaddon was trying to remember a time when he'd felt worse. Well, he supposed that depended on what he meant by worse. He'd suffered through pains mere mortals could only have nightmares of on at least seven different occasions, but pain was pain. Right now, he was very frustrated, very angry, and wasn't entirely sure why, or at whom. The fact that he had taken it out on Mary was just the icing on Terra's shittiest cake.

Abaddon's mood wasn't improved by the fact that every time he moved his right arm he could see the glowing holy symbols. Honestly, his dad had taken that part better than he had initially thought he would. He was half expecting a horde of demons to storm Terra. Then again, he hadn't told his dad the worst of it. That was what infuriated him the most. Potentially losing his job was one thing, as was getting put on probation. But now....
On some level he knew the justiciar was only thinking of his safety. But that level was deep, deep down. And frankly, he didn't care. Even though a crazy necromancer was after him, the fact that the justiciar had ordered the seraph to not only watch him, but *PROTECT* him? He hadn't told anyone, and was not planning to ever tell anyone. But, in addition to sealing away his magic, the binding on his arm would instantly alert the seraph if his life were in danger. If he didn't know any better, he'd had thought the justiciar was being incredibly ironic. He didn't know a single demon who wouldn't chose death over getting rescued by an angel.

"Yeah, all angels are the enemy. I'm a big dumb rage-filled demon like my grandfather," Mr. Pessimism was back.

"Shut up. Grandpa wasn't a big dumb rage-filled demon"

"Oh no, he only started the apocalypse."

"Okay, big and rage-filled, but not dumb. And I'm not like him anyway."

"Oh waah, waah, waah; the angels are always mistreating us poor demons; we're the victims in all this."

"I thought I told you to shut up."

"Ha! A demon fighting his inner demons? That's screwed up, even for me."

"SHIT," Abaddon slammed his fist into the wall of his apartment.

Well, punching a hole into his wall wasn't going to fix anything. Actually, Abaddon was pretty sure that was literally the opposite of fixing things. Boris came over to Abaddon and tilted his heads, the motion accompanied by a said whine.

"Sorry about that," Abaddon knelt down and began petting the heads. "I didn't mean to upset you, but Daddy's really pissed right now, and would very much like to blow off some steam."

Unfortunately, that was one of the few things he *COULDN'T* do right now. Going around and picking fights would be a very stupid idea. And even if it was technically allowed, he wouldn't be surprised if he got in trouble for beating up some thugs, now that his hero I.D. glyph was inactive. If nothing else the templars would probably enjoy another reason to hassle him.

Now Abaddon was thinking back to Adonis. Day One and he had practically gotten the whole hero mentor speech. Not only that, but Adonis had treated him like an equal, more or less. Now Abaddon was a criminal. He'd done a real good job of being a hero. Adonis would be so proud.

"Waah, waah; I'm a failure."

"Good heavens leave me alone!" Abaddon actually swatted the air this time.

"Wow, trying to attack the voices in my head."

"Shut up."

"Got a problem, so the only answer is to hit it. No, I'm not a big dumb demon, not at all."

"I said SHUT UP," a second hole in the wall.

Abaddon needed to get out and do something. If nothing else he'd be replacing a wall soon if he stayed cooped up any longer. He tried to think of what to do. For several minutes he came up empty. Then, all of a sudden, it hit him. Maybe that was the true irony: the voices in his head were actually good for something.

Abaddon stepped out of the portal in front of the West Point Library, "Would a big dumb demon do this?"

"May I help you?" the librarian at the reference desk was a young enthusiastic woman, who, to her credit, only briefly glanced at the holy binding on Abaddon's right arm.

"Yes, I was looking for books having to do with demonic, and holy magic."

"Alright then," the librarian gave him another quick glance. "Our magic section is one floor down and directly to your left; try checking there."

"Thank you very much."

Just because his magic was bound, and his hero I.D. glyph disabled, didn't mean he couldn't still do something. His dad was looking into who this necromancer was, but that probably wasn't enough. Abaddon needed to figure out how the necromancer was able to do what he had done. Using both demonic and holy magic, not to mention speaking the cursed tongues? Abaddon began to grab every book he could find that looked remotely relevant: the dustier the better. He was also wracking his brains for any information he had read about humans that would give precedence for this. Unfortunately he was most familiar with A.D. humans, and they didn't even know about Hell (at least not definitively), so that probably wouldn't be any help. Once he had collected an armload of books, he sat down at a table illuminated by a small window and got to work.

Abaddon wasn't sure how late it had gotten when he finally stopped reading. He had been so engrossed in his books that he had completely lost track of time. Normally, this would mean that he had found a lot of very useful information, unfortunately that was not the case. The closest to useful information was the stuff he had found on holy magic. A lot of that he had not known about; it honestly surprised him. His dad had made him read extensively about holy magic, and he thought he'd had a good grasp on the subject, but he was discovering a lot that he didn't know. When he thought about it more, he supposed it made sense that the libraries of Hell would be less knowledgeable about matters of Heaven. But despite learning a lot, he hadn't discovered what he wanted. Nothing in the readings told him how the necromancer could have gotten holy magic strong enough to repel Spellbreaker's power.

According to the books on the subject, there were only two types of mortals who could possess holy magic. Those were the templars, and the paladins. Now, it might not be quite fair to classify templars and paladins as different. Both templars and paladins were warriors given divine magic by the divine council. The difference, was that the templars were Terra's enforcers of the divine council: divine soldiers, police and so on. The paladins were the champions of the council. They actually lived in Heaven and were given a much greater amount of divine power. So they were different in the way a dog is different from a wolf: they're both fundamentally the same, one's just bigger and more deadly than the other.

Abaddon remembered his dad talking about paladins. During Armageddon, the paladins had been some of the nastiest enemies Hell fought against. Indeed they were quite strong, and saved near impossible to kill. His dad had mentioned personally watching paladins walk through hellfire without suffering so much as a burn; they didn't run through it; they just walked. Even Soulcleaver (Lucifer's personal sword) was hard pressed to finish them off. All in all, he had described paladins essentially as golden, self-righteous, cockroaches. So could a paladin's magic be powerful enough as to repel Spellbreaker? Well, it was possible. After all, Spellbreaker couldn't destroy all magic, but the magic that resisted it had to be incredibly powerful. So, even amongst paladins, it would be rare to find one who could do it the way the necromancer did. So that could have been an answer. However, there was another thing that templars and paladins shared: they could fall. In essence, falling meant going against the will of the divine council and losing their powers. Basically, they got their powers from another source, so that source could take them away whenever they felt like. It didn't take a genius to piece together that the divine council wouldn't like their chosen champions using demon magic. And beyond even the council, Abaddon couldn't imagine any paladin doing such a thing, ever. As much as Abaddon had a learned hatred for those divine warriors, he still had to respect them for what they were: good. They were devoted to good beyond anything or anyone in creation, possibly even Heaven itself. No, no paladin would willingly use demonic powers, and the divine council would never allow it. So that couldn't be the answer.

Abaddon was back to square one. Hours of research and he had come up empty. At this point he could have given up. A part of him felt like doing just that. But instead of giving up, Abaddon decided to make use of a lesson every child learned very earlier on: if things don't go your way, complain to the nearest authority figure.

Chapter Thirty-Two
The Plot Thickens

Abaddon made his way to the local templar station, not a place he had ever thought he would go. He got various looks as he walked inside and approached the desk with a templar sitting behind it. The templar wore a less than kind expression on his face as he gave Abaddon a once over, stopping for a few extra seconds at the holy binding on his right arm.

"Hey, I recognize you. You were that demon the angel arrested. You turning yourself in for some other crime?"

"No," Abaddon tried his hardest not to snap. He half succeeded. "I came to lodge a complaint and ask some questions."

"Oh, were you treated unfairly by the mean old angel?"

"NO Ass- no, that is not the reason I came here."

"Well spit it out. I ain't got all day."

"Look, a couple weeks ago now, you got a report from the White Pegasus Guild about a necromancer on the loose in New Eden, right?"

"Eh, yeah, I remember something about a necromancer. There's a sick bastard out there perverting the natural order of things. It had everyone at the station on full alert mode. What of it?"

"He was targeting me specifically. And not long after he first showed up and you all got the call about it, he showed up again to try and finish me off. Where were the templars then?"

"Are you saying we ain't doin' our jobs?" the templar sneered at him.

"No, I'm asking you why you didn't. A necromancer should be top priority for you guys, right? But you let him escape. He came after me again. You need to catch him."

"We don't need to do nuthin'."

"What are you talking about? This is your job!"

"Yeah, well it's also our job to follow orders, and orders say we don't got this case anymore."

"What in Heaven's name does that mean?"

"Higher-ups are handling this matter personally. We've been ordered to back off."

"But you must have sent an initial detachment to track him down. They weren't able to catch him or anything?"

"Hey, don't come waltzing in here and telling us how to protect the people. I don't come to wherever it is that you do what you do, and tell you how to do whatever it is you do there. As far as we're concerned, the book is closed on that case. So, if you still wanna gripe at someone, gripe at an angel or somethin'."

Something was definitely going on. Abaddon didn't care for the templar's attitude, but then again he never did. Besides, he was more curious than angry at this point. The divine council was getting involved directly in this matter it seemed. Even if necromancy was the highest on the list of restricted magic, it was still a case of catching a dangerous criminal. The templars should have handled that. Then again, an angel had shown up personally to arrest him when he broke his seal. They must handle restricted magic personally. Hang on. Abaddon couldn't believe this had just occurred to him. When the necromancer had first shown up, he reanimated the hydra. That was clearly necromancy, the worst of all the restricted magics. He had used necromancy, and yet no angel had appeared. Abaddon broke his seal, and within moments, he was attacked by the seraph. This meant one of two things: it was all some big conspiracy where the necromancer and the divine council were working against him, or the necromancer had some way of hiding his magic from the divine council.

Abaddon was back at the library. His initial search had been useless, but now he had a new angle to look from. This time he grabbed every book even remotely connected to the divine council. How had they known the instant he broke his seal? If he could find out how the divine council tracked restricted magic, then maybe he could figure out how the necromancer had eluded them. At least he had something a little more concrete to go on. But now he had a necromancer with a demonic right arm, holy left arm that could repel greater artifacts, who could speak in the damned tongues of demons, and could hide his black magic from the divine council. This man was an impossibility several times over.

"Let's see," Abaddon opened a book entitled *"The Divine Council and the Creation of Terra"* and started to read aloud. "The council of Heaven was remade after Heaven reforged the Earth into Terra. The overall structure of Heaven's system of governance had to be reformatted since Earth was no more. This was done to address the changes between Earth and Terra, such as the influx of entities from other realms, and the restructuring of Earth technology to work with the addition of magic. One of the most notable ways that Earth technology was modified to accommodate magic, was the removal or alteration of any technology using power sources that would interfere with magical energies and leylines, such as electricity or nuclear energy," Abaddon sighed. This was mostly basic information he already knew. But he kept reading for a bit longer just in case. "The changes to military and weapon technology in general, was the most severe. After the non-magic weapons of the humans proved largely ineffective against the invading demon armies during Armageddon, the divine council decided to do away with all modern human weaponry and the knowledge of/ use/manufacture thereof, thus effectively resetting human warfare to a pre-gunpowder state. However, the addition of magic added further dimensions to warfare, so direct parallels to Earth medieval period warfare could not be drawn," After some more reading, and a bit of skipping ahead, Abaddon realized that this book contained no information that wasn't basically common knowledge, or that he did not already know from the libraries in Hell. Aside from answering his curiosity about whether or not Terra still used electricity, it was useless, so he put it down and picked up the next book in his large stack of tomes.

Abaddon spent several more hours poring over books. The silver lining to this whole mess was that he was learning a lot more about the way Heaven's legal system operated. But he wasn't getting the information he needed. He supposed it made a fair degree of sense. Once he stopped to think about it, it would basically be a resource to help criminals get away with forbidden magic, so unsurprising that there wasn't anything about it in the texts. Still, he might have found a hint.

Once Abaddon had exhausted his supply of books about Heaven and the divine council, he went back to looking for books on divine or demonic magic. As with his previous search, he uncovered no useful information. Abaddon was starting to come to the conclusion that this library contained no useful information at all. But he had to remind himself that what he was looking for was very obscure knowledge.

Finally, after he had gone through all of those books, he looked for anything on forbidden or restricted magic. He assumed, from his other two searches that he wouldn't find any books on that subject, but figured he might as well try anyway. On that, he also came up empty. Eventually he had to give up and go home before the library closed on him.

Back in his apartment, Abaddon flopped down on the floor, and Boris came over and began licking most of his face. Abaddon sighed as he pushed Boris off. Boris whined as Abaddon used a little more force than he had intended. He didn't want to start taking his anger out on Boris, but he was in no mood to be affectionate at the moment. And returning to his apartment, he was dangerously close to reverting back to his angry sulking mode, and his wall couldn't take much more of that. To preempt such problems, Abaddon went into his small kitchen in search of food. He passed over the bananas. They just didn't taste right without being hell-roasted, and until he lost the holy bindings on his arm, he was stuck with raw. He settled on some sourdough bread, which despite its name was quite good, and not sour at all, unlike those lemons. He had assumed they must be tasty if they were bright yellow like the bananas, but.... Well, he had come to the conclusion that neither he nor his kitchen sink could take another attempt and had sworn off them after that.

As Abaddon munched absentmindedly on the loaf of bread, he tried to think of what his next move should be. If he just hung around the apartment feeling sorry for himself, well, that was clearly no good. But he didn't know what else he should do. His dad hadn't figured out anything about the necromancer yet, or at least hadn't sended if he had. Both the library and the templar station had been a bust. But then Abaddon remembered what the templar had said to him before he left: *As far as we're concerned, the book is closed on that case. So, if you still wanna gripe at someone, gripe at an angel or somethin'*

"Great. So, all I need to do is talk to an angel. Good thing I have a magic button that just summons them whenever I-" Abaddon stopped as a terrible idea entered his head. "Well, this is one of the dumbest things I've ever done."

Abaddon breathed deeply. He then removed the obsidian gauntlet on his right arm. There was an explosion of light from the holy biding. The next thing he knew he was being slammed against his poor, poor wall, a white gauntleted hand around his throat.

Chapter Thirty-Three

Just Wanting to Talk

"YOU WERE WARNED," Cassandra's eyes glowed with divine fury.

"Ca-calm down," Abaddon managed.

"You break divine law a second time and expect me to calm down?!"

"It-it's not what you think."

"SILENCE," Cassandra's hand clenched tighter around Abaddon's throat.

"I just wanted-"

"To flee your righteous captors!"

"N-no, to t-talk."

"You expect me to believe such lies, demon?"

"I- no lies," Abaddon could barely get the words out. "Just-just talk."

"You're kind offer nothing but deceit. I will not be swayed by silver words."

"G-good heavens you-you're stubborn."

"And you are a criminal. Because you broke the seal, I have the right to bring you before the divine council."

"G-good. Maybe- maybe one of them will- will listen."

"A cheap cover for a pathetic escape attempt. I would have expected a better lie from you, demon."

"That's cus, I-I'm not lying."

"You expect me to believe that?"

"N-no. It's my only chance to- to stop-stop the necromancer."

"You tried to escape to finish your fight with the necromancer?"

"No, bless it. I-I need-" this would have been difficult to say, even without a hand on his throat. "Your help – to stop-"

"What is this?" Cassandra dropped Abaddon. "Speak freely. But make one wrong move and I destroy you," her hand glowed with holy magic.

Abaddon's landlady was standing in his doorway, her hand still raised in a knocking position "What the hell?"

"Hello Ms. Darktooth," Abaddon coughed, rubbing his throat.

"You know this fiend?" Cassandra addressed the landlady.

"Yeah…. He rents this place from me. What is this?" she noticed the wall. "And what the hell did you do to my wall?"

"That- that was me," Abaddon still hadn't fully regained his voice. "I'll pay for that."

"Looks like you already did. Don't tell me you're picking fights with angels now. That *WILL* void your agreement."

"No fights, just talking."

"I can see that," Ms. Darktooth had calmed down enough to absentmindedly pull out a cigarette.

"He speaks the truth for once. This foul pit-dweller has convinced me to stay my hand…. for the time being."

"Fine, but it looks like my tenant can't take much more *TALKING*. If you two are gonna start something, do it where it won't damage my property…. anymore."

"Can do," Abaddon was still on the ground. He waved awkwardly as Ms. Darktooth left.

"So talk," Cassandra had turned her full attention back to Abaddon. "You dare ask for the assistance of an angel?"

"I dare," Abaddon started to move, but Cassandra's hand twitched, and he instantly stopped. "When I was fighting the necromancer, and released my seal, you instantly detected my restricted magic, and arrived within moments. How were you able to do that?"

"As if I would tell the spawn of evil the secrets of my divine powers."

"No, listen. When the necromancer first showed up, after Artemis and I defeated the hydra, he used necromancy to reanimate it. No angel showed up then. You should have been able to detect that too, right?"

"Of course. The eyes of Heaven are all-seeing."

"Yet they missed that."

"I still don't believe your story from the trial. I know you are a liar and deceiver."

"Yeah, yeah, vile demon," Abaddon was trying with every bone in his body not to attack her. "You don't have to believe me. You heard Artemis corroborate my story. There's even a report, from her, back at the White Pegasus Guild, that says the necromancer reanimated the hydra. Somehow, he was able to use restricted magic without the divine council noticing. I need your help to find out how he did that."

"I already told you, such a thing is impossible."

"And yet somehow it happened. Regardless of your thoughts about me, you have to respect a senior member of a heroes guild, right? Artemis has slain dozens of vicious monsters in order to protect this city. Do you really think she'd lie to help me?"

"Perhaps if you poisoned her mind like you are trying to poison mine."

"Good heavens, what is wrong with you?!"

"Watch your tongue filthy-"

"Enough with the filthy demon, and evil spawn of Hell stuff. Look, I don't care if you don't like me. I hate you, so let's call that even. But just because you don't like me, doesn't mean I am automatically wrong about everything. Alright, so maybe you hate me enough to ignore evidence from a hero. But what about your own divine council?"

"You drag them into this?"

"I went to my local templar station today and asked them why they failed to catch the necromancer. The templar there told me that they got a call from their higher-ups saying that they were off the case. YOUR bosses thought this matter was above the templars' paygrade. This is SERIOUS. If you want, I'm fine going to the templar station right now to talk to them. But regardless, this necromancer is a real threat, and I'm trying to figure out how to stop him. I was getting nowhere on my own. I knew I needed help from an angel, or someone else higher up connected to the divine council, and the only way I had to get in contact with one, was…. well, that's why I took off my obsidian bracer," As he said it, Abaddon slowly reached out, grabbed his bracer, wincing as his hand touched the holy binding, and put it back on his arm."

"By the council, you actually look serious."

"Yeah, no shit, I'm serious."

"If the divine council did indeed take over this case personally, then it is something I cannot ignore. Very well, for now I will take you at your word that you wish to stop the necromancer."

"Great. So now you can tell me what I want to know?"

"That I cannot do. But I have another way you might get what you desire."

"Why do I have a bad feeling about that?"

Chapter Thirty-Four

Go to Heaven

Abaddon was right. Bad feeling just about summed up his current situation. Though now the bad feeling was less a sense of foreboding, and more a sense of burning all over his skin. Personally, he blamed the holy magic chains binding his torso. If he weren't in constant pain, he would have taken the time to gape appropriately at the scenery around him. The great temples atop shining clouds, light cascading down like waterfalls, glorious gardens and luscious trees would have all felt much more spectacular if he weren't so distracted by all the burning. Within a minute of there arrival, they were greeted by another seraph. She was noticeably shorter than Cassandra and dressed in a white outfit that looked like it was from the place A.D. humans called ancient Greece. She had white hair like Cassandra's, though hers was in a long braid.

"Hey Cassandra, back already are y- what did you do?" her voice turned to mild horror as she saw Abaddon chained at Cassandra's side.

"He wishes to speak with the divine council," Cassandra jerked the chain as she spoke.

"You do?"

"I guess so," Abaddon said through gritted teeth.

"Well this is most irregular. Why did you bring him here?"

"He was most insistent. This is the one who's mixed up with that necromancer down on Terra."

"Oh, no wonder you brought him."

"I must take him to the council straight away."

"Unchain him first."

"What?!" Both Cassandra and Abaddon exclaimed in unison.

"If this is the demon from that trial you went to, then he is the one the necromancer is targeting. His life is in danger, and he's come all the way here to help us catch the guy. There's no need to treat him like a prisoner," she glanced down at Abaddon's right arm, "well, any more than you were treating him like one already. Besides, he's unarmed, and that binding seals away his magic. What harm can he do?"

"But Sophitia, he's a demon! We can't let him roam free in Heaven."

"*CASSANDRA*," her voice was suddenly very stern. Abaddon was shocked to hear someone talk to Casandra like that. But not as shocked as he was at her response.

"Fine," Cassandra begrudgingly undid her magic.

"Thanks," Abaddon managed, still gritting his teeth from the pain. "Sophitia, right?"

"Yes. Not *ALL* of us angels are ruled by single-minded hatred," she gave Cassandra a pointed look, from which she turned away in a huff. "And what's your name?"

"Abaddon."

"Ooh, scary," Sophitia was smiling. "No wonder my sister doesn't like you."

"Sophitia, can we just get on with-"

"SISTER?" Abaddon almost fell over.

"I know. Aside from the hair, we bear no resemblance to each other."

"Like I said," Cassandra was now the one clenching her teeth, "can we just get on with this?"

"Don't mind her," Sophitia turned to lead the way. "She's just mad at me for 'fraternizing with the enemy'."

Abaddon was led into a large ornate temple. In its center was an equally ornate desk. Behind it sat a male angel, dressed similarly to Sophitia.

"I was wondering something," Abaddon turned to Sophitia.

"Yes?"

"Most things here in Heaven look like they are from a span of time in earth's history known as ancient Greece. Why is that?"

"Oh, throughout human history, there were various people or groups of people who got glimpses of the divine truth of the universe. The Greeks got their architecture, among other things, from us."

"Were there many humans who got to see the truth?"

"Some here and there. The written work of one of them became adapted as the holy scripture for the major dwarven and elven faiths. I have a copy right here," Sophitia snapped her fingers, and in a flash of light, a book appeared in her hands entitled "The Hobbit".

"Sophitia, Cassandra," the angel behind the desk spoke up as they approached. "What can I do for you today?"

"This is Abaddon," Sophitia gestured. "He's wrapped up in the whole necromancer mess down on Terra. He is seeking divine assistance in dealing with the problem."

"Oh don't get me started on that whole necromancer business. It's been all anyone up here could talk about. Let me guess, you want to see Wisdom?"

"Would you mind sending us in Byron?" Sophitia smiled.

"Well, I can definitely check with them right now, but I can't promise anything. All of the divine entities are super busy at the moment."

"Thanks a bunch. We're fine waiting if you need to set up an appointment."

"Speak for yourself," Cassandra wore her usual "not pleased" expression.

Byron said a few words of holy magic, and a glowing portal appeared before his eyes. "Sophitia and Cassandra are here to see you. They brought a demon named Abaddon. They say he's the one involved in the recent necromancer business happening down on Terra."

"Please send them in," the response came from an old, male voice.

"You heard them," Byron stood up, opening a much larger portal as he did. "Right this way."

When the light subsided, all three were on a large, mostly empty cloud. The one shape amidst this vast expanse was a tall old man with long gray hair and beard, and a black eyepatch over his right eye.

"Excuse me, uh…. sir?" Abaddon didn't know what to call…. them?

"Yes?"

"Aren't you the divine aspect of wisdom commonly known as Odin?"

"Indeed I am. Weren't you looking for me?"

"Well yes, it's just- I mean, I thought the divine aspects were just the forms you take when manifesting on Terra. I would have assumed you'd be in your true form up here."

"A common misconception. No, our divine aspects are the forms we take when we interact with non-heavenly beings, no matter which plane of existence we're on. We once tried showing the true form of things to one of the brightest humans on earth. It nearly destroyed his mind. Next thing you know, he was writing about caves and shadow puppets or something. Anyway, taking on these forms is much easier when dealing with people from other planes. And this aspect just so happens to be my favorite one to assume."

"Cool. I mean- Oh wise and great…. Wisdom- I mean- geez, didn't realize it would be this hard to talk to one of you."

"Do not worry. There is no formal speech you must adhere to, no honorifics or anything like that. Just speak to me normally."

"Really? Alright then. I came here to find out more about the necromancer who is after me. Can you help?"

Chapter Thirty-Five

Who is the Necromancer?

"You have a right to know about this necromancer," Odin stroked his beard and sighed.

"Should we really be divulging information to a demon?" Cassandra stepped forward. "Can we trust him?"

"The better question, is can he trust us?"

"What do you mean…. sir?" Abaddon almost felt like he should be kneeling.

"I told you, no honorifics are necessary, not for me anyway. Just call me Odin."

"Very well then, Odin. Why should I not trust you? It may not be an easy peace, but Heaven and Hell have reached an… understanding."

"Uneasy peace sounds about right to describe relations between Heaven and Hell," Odin turned his gaze briefly to Cassandra, who this time looked embarrassed rather than angry. "But that is not why I speak of trust. No, it is us, up in Heaven, who are responsible for sending this necromancer after you."

"WHAT?!" anger suddenly flared up in Abaddon, burning away all his awkwardness.

"You can't mean that?" Sophitia could barely get the words out. Cassandra was just silent.

"It is true that we are responsible, though it was never our intent."

"What in Heaven's name does that mean?! If you sent the necromancer after me-"

"I said it was never our intention, but the blame is ours. The necromancer is from Heaven."

"You can't mean that," Cassandra sounded desperate. Now it was Sophitia's turn to be silent. "Necromancy is the worst kind of black magic from the deepest pits of Hell. No one from Heaven could even-"

"IT WAS YOU," Abaddon rushed forward and grabbed Odin by the front of his robes.

Had there been something solid standing nearby, Abbadon would have slammed Odin into it. Instead, he settled for a cry from the darkest pits. What started out as a scream of rage, quickly became a scream of pain, as twin golden bolts of light slammed into him, sending him to the ground in a steaming heap.

"Ladies, please," Odin held up a hand towards Cassandra and Sophitia, both of whom were still holding theirs at the ready for another shot. "Do not attack him."

"He attacked you first," the sisters spoke in unison.

"He is angry, and attacking him will not help. Let me explain. Abaddon," He turned back to the demon who was picking himself up off the cloud, "the name of the necromancer who attacked you, is Arthur Pendragon."

Complete shock kicked all the rage right out of Abaddon. He just stood, stunned, not even blinking. The two seraphs were in similar states. For a moment, or probably much more than that, silence prevailed over the cloud.

"What," Abaddon managed after a short eternity, "in Heaven's name…."

"What is this crap?!" Cassandra blurted. Sophitia was too shocked to even give her sister a disapproving look.

"I speak the truth. Arthur Pendragon is that necromancer."

"Arthur Pendragon?" Abaddon was barely aware of his surroundings. "The legendary human hero who became a paladin? Arthur Pendragon, Heaven's champion and greatest warrior who fought in Armageddon? *THAT* Arthur Pendragon?"

"The very same. The humans knew him as King Arthur, but that was before he ascended. He was the greatest champion on earth, and so to became the greatest champion in Heaven."

"How is this even possible?" Cassandra spoke up once more. "Aside from everything else that is wrong with that statement, Arthur Pendragon died during Armageddon."

"I do not know how he survived, but it is Arthur Pendragon who is now on Terra, and Arthur Pendragon who hunts you, Abaddon."

"But that was over three centuries ago," Cassandra continued. "No mortal could live that long outside of Heaven. Wait, that's not the point. This is Arthur Pendragon. *THE* Arthur Pendragon. He is not a necromancer!"

"I saw him with my own eyes," Odin's voice was a deep sadness. "It was none other than Arthur Pendragon."

Abaddon cut off Cassandra's next reply, "You saw him? When? How? Where?"

"We beings of the divine can see through the eyes of any who possess our divine blessing. I saw through the eyes of the templars who battled him, and lost to him. Once we knew that it was him, we took matters into our own hands personally."

"Wait," Abaddon turned to Cassandra. "You *KNEW* it was King Arthur turned necromancer and you arrested *ME* instead?"

"Filthy lies from a filthy demon. You know I had no knowledge of this. I was as surprised as you, remember?"

"Few knew of this. And when you broke your seal, we were not aware you were fighting Arthur. We sent Cassandra down to arrest you, completely unaware that a more dangerous threat was present."

"But why would you not tell us angels of this? Surely I could have gone back down and-"

"No, the situation is far more complex than you realize. Believe me, it took a lot of my persuading to get the other beings of the divine to agree to let me tell even you three. And there is still more I cannot tell you."

"Listen Asshole," Abaddon snapped.

"How dare you-"

"No," Abaddon's anger was back, strong enough to repel Cassandra's indignation. "I said listen. Arthur saved Pendragon is back from the what we all thought dead, and has tried to kill me twice now, and you still won't tell me everything that's going on? Not only did I almost die by his hand on two separate occasions, but now you've gone and sealed my magic away, so he can come and kill me whenever he wants."

"You were arrested and had your powers sealed because you used class seven restricted magic," Cassandra retorted.

"I used it because *ARTHUR PENDRAGON* was trying to kill me. OH, I'M SORRY, ARTHUR HALF DEMON PENDRAGON! MAYBE YOU CAN FINALLY GET OF MY SAVED CASE MS. HOLIER THAN EVERYONE ELSE.

"Enough," Odin's voice was not loud, but carried a tone of absolute command.

Abaddon stopped. He was no less angry, but there was no arguing with that voice. Had he not been so incredibly mad, he would have been scared.

"I am very sorry, but this situation is bigger, far bigger, than just you. I wish I could tell you more, but I cannot. For now, you will simply have to rely on Cassandra's protection until we resolve matters with Arthur."

"Bullshit. You know it was self-defense. There's no reason for me to keep wearing this dumb holy binding. Give me back my magic."

"That cannot be done either."

"Why in Heaven's name not?"

"You used class seven restricted magic. Regardless of the reason why, you put Terra in grave danger by doing so. You opened a channel directly to the deepest pits of the abyss and drew power from it. Had you lost control, or drawn forth too much power... Like I said, you put Terra in grave danger. And as long as Arthur is still out there and after you, it is highly likely that you will be put in a situation where you must face him again. Would you not resort to that same magic to try and beat him if you fought next time?"

"I can't beat him without it."

"Then we cannot remove that holy binding, not until he is dealt with."

"So what, I'm just supposed to wait for him to kill me? You think Cassandra here can actually protect me from him? Besides, she'd just as soon do it herself. Do you think I'm okay with my guardian angel being my angel of death?"

"I'll do it," Sophitia spoke up. "Let me protect him in my sister's place."

Chapter Thirty-Six

She's the Seraph in these Parts

"Look," Sophitia continued, "obviously neither my sister nor Abaddon are happy with the arrangement of her protecting him. And I agree we can't take the holy binding off of him until Arthur is dealt with. So I'll do it. I actually haven't been down to Terra in a while. I would enjoy the visit."

"Hey, I don't need an angel to protect me! I'm a proud demon warrior. I can fight my own battles."

"Not while wearing the holy binding," Odin took a step forward. "I am sorry about this, but we need to keep your true power contained. And you said yourself that you cannot best Arthur without it."

"I can't believe this. My life is in danger from your top man, and you won't even let me defend myself?"

"That's enough," Sophitia's tone was stern. "This is happening whether you want it or not. You are in danger yes, which is why I am going to protect you, and proud demon or not, you are going to suck it up and deal with it."

"Why? Because you guys say so? Last I checked I wasn't beholden to the laws of Heaven."

"While you live on Terra, you are beholden to their laws, and they defer to us. But frankly I don't care about the law as much as I care about keeping people safe. And as long as you are willing to use restricted magic, no one in New Eden will be safe. From what I hear, you're a hero. Well, maybe you should start acting like one and think of something other than you and your dumb pride."

Abaddon had been ready to get angry at Sophitia again, but he couldn't bring himself to do it now. He tried to think of a response he could give that wouldn't be admitting defeat, but that wasn't working either. When he tried, he remembered what Angga Bayu had said about why he wasn't a hero. He hadn't felt right calling himself a hero and not living up to what it meant to be one. Well, that's what it had sounded like to Abaddon anyway. Was he doing the same thing? There had to be more to being a hero than just killing monsters. Abaddon couldn't tell what was worse, that he was getting lectured by an angel, or that he was agreeing with her.

"Well?" Sophitia prompted. "Are you gonna accept my generous offer, or are you gonna keep acting like a selfish brat?"

"Fine," the words fought their way through miles of mud to get out of Abaddon's mouth. "You made your point. I suppose it would be better to have you around than your sister."

"If I didn't know any better, I'd say that was your way of complimenting me. So how about it?" Sophitia turned to Odin. "I'll take my sister's place as his guardian angel."

"The decision for Cassandra to watch over Abaddon was not made by me. You have to appeal to the justiciar who made the ruling in the first place. Assuming Cassandra agrees to it."

"Do bear souls shit in the sacred woods?"

Abaddon gave Sophitia a look that said, "Do they do that?" Sophitia nodded. Abaddon would have never thought about such things.

"Well Cassandra seems to have given clear approval," Odin coughed. "All that is left is for the three of you to return to the Terran court and get the change officiated."

"All that's left?" Abaddon turned to Odin again. "You still haven't given me any more information and won't even tell me why? I think I deserve to know a bit more about why Arthur Pendragon is after me."

"You do," Odin sighed, "But I still cannot tell you. Arthur Pendragon has very sensitive and secret information concerning Heaven that must be protected at any cost. And we cannot let anyone know that our greatest champion turned to the dark arts. I know this is unfair, but if we are not careful, we could start an interplanar incident. Worst case scenario, we could start another Armageddon. Please understand, this is bigger than just one life."

"Fine," Abaddon said after a minute. "But I still don't like it. Now let's get this transfer over with."

"Well I see no problem," the justiciar seemed in a better mood than the last time Abaddon had seen her, but it was hard to tell for sure. "I assigned Cassandra as his guardian angel to keep an eye on him, and to help protect him, since he is being targeted by a necromancer. If the angel Sophitia would rather perform these duties, she is more than welcome to."

"Thank you madam justiciar," all three said in relative unison.

"Well now I can finally leave this foul demon's presence," the three were standing outside the courthouse. "But lay a single hand on my sister, pit-spawn, and I shall turn you into ashes."

"Be nice," Sophitia chided.

"Never. He is the enemy. Nice is just another form of weakness."

"Fine, be a jerk then. But either way, you know I can handle myself."

Cassandra paused for a moment, "I'll still keep an eye on you demon," she then hurriedly ascended in a pillar of light.

"Sorry about her," Sophitia looked embarrassed. "I swear she's not as terrible as she seems."

"Only when it comes to demons."

"Well... she's just... traditional."

"That's a more diplomatic term to use than I would have."

"Yeah, well she's not *YOUR* little sister."

"Wait, *LITTLE* sister?"

"Yes, I'm the older one. Do you find that strange?"

"No, I just thought-"

"Is it the height?"

"Well, not just that. I mean, she's much more..."

"Serious?"

"Again, diplomatic."

"Fine. What would you call it?"

"Self-righteous fury?"

Sophita laughed, "I'd never heard that one before. But honestly, is that how you think of angels? I must be the younger one because I haven't grown up and become self-righteous and furious?"

"I mean, that IS the only side of angels we demons really see."

"Okay, point. But demons aren't really ever nice to angels either."

"Hey, was I mean?"

"You were offended at the mere idea of being protected by an angel."

"Yeah...." now it was Abaddon's turn to be embarrassed. "In some ways, I suppose I'm kind of 'traditional' myself."

"Huh, and here I thought traditional was your code word for bitch."

"No! I mean, I don't think like that."

"Only when it comes to my sister?" Sophitia smiled.

"Stop doing that."

"Doing what?"

"Winning the conversation."

"Never," Sophitia did an over the top imitation of her sister. "You are the enemy." They both laughed at that.

"Okay, okay, I admit defeat. But in all seriousness, why did you do this? Why did you decide to be my babysitter? There must be any number of things you'd rather do than look after me."

"I meant what I said about wanting to visit Terra. Besides, unlike my sister, I'm actually interested in learning about demons, not just hating them out of habit. And while I'm here, I'll get to do just that. Well, that, and I want to try this human food I've heard so much about. My angel friends who visited Terra told my about this intriguing thing called 'deep frying' that I have been dying to try."

"From what I've heard, you'll be dying *IF* you try it. But if it's anything like the hell-roasted bananas I've been eating, it will be delicious."

"That settles it. Let's get some now," Sophitia grabbed Abaddon by the hand, and before he could even muster half a stuttered reply, they were off.

Chapter Thirty-Seven

Live and Let Fry

"So you've never tried this before either?" Sophitia asked between bites of her chicken.

"I usually fry my own food actually."

"How do you do that?"

"Hellfire. Works great for roasting stuff."

"Wait, you summon the all-consuming fires of Hell…. to roast your food?"

"All-consuming? If hellfire were really all-consuming, I would have burned down my apartment the first time I hell-roasted a banana."

"But don't the flames of Hell consume all in its way, burning even the very souls of mortals fool enough to cross its path? How does a banana survive that?"

"See, these are the kinds of misconceptions people constantly make about demons," Abaddon paused to swallow another bite. "Sure, when we go into battle and unleash the flames of Hell upon our enemies, it's a roaring blaze that turns their very essence to ash, but that doesn't mean you can't use a small amount of it in a controlled way. We demons are more than just chaotic brutes who only know how to destroy. Look, by lighting a match, or summoning a magical flame, you can light a campfire, but you could also burn down the whole forest you're camping in."

"I didn't know demons went camping?"

"Well, I've read about it. The point is, a regular fire can provide utility, or destroy everything if left uncontrolled. The same is true for hellfire. I mean, granted, it is a bit more dangerous than 'normal' fire, but the basic principal is the same."

"Forgive me for not recognizing the great demon chiefs," Sophitia attempted a sweeping, overdramatic bow, only to be awkwardly stopped by the table.

"To be fair, despite my earlier complaints, most demons are battle-crazed savages. I mean, it varies from circle to circle. But as much as I hate to admit it, I'm one of the extremely rare ones, wanting to live on Terra."

"Well what makes you so special?" Sophitia gesticulated with her drumstick.

"Oh, you know a… different upbringing."

"Really? So what was growing up like for a young demon such as yourself."

"Well, my dad actually made me read a lot. He prioritized it fairly heavily. Knowledge I mean. You know, strength and magic are essentials, but well yeah, he thought being knowledgeable about more than just the circles of Hell was rather important."

"Sorry if I didn't really picture you as the bookish type. I mean, what with being a hero and all. I just kind of assumed you swung a big weapon around and killed monsters."

"Well, I do that too. I mean, Spellbreaker isn't really *THAT* big. It's standard size for a demonic war hammer but-"

"Hang on, Spellbreaker? You possess *THE* Spellbreaker?"

"You know about Spellbreaker?"

"Do I know about it? That's one of the most legendary cursed weapons in the world. I mean, come on, it's a greater artifact. Angels still fear that war hammer."

"Yeah, I guess I got so used to carrying it around I sometimes forget what a big deal it is."

"How in the name of the divine entities did you get your hands on a weapon like that? I mean, Spellbreaker terrorized the angelic armies during Armageddon. Our strongest holy wards were shredded like paper before it."

"I don't think a war hammer can shred stuff."

"You get my point. Spellbreaker is one of the most prized treasures of Hell. Seriously, how'd you get something so valuable?"

"Would you believe it was my coming of age present?"

"So, you were given one of the most legendary weapons in the world.... as a gift? From whom?"

"My... dad?"

"Okay then, HOW DID HE GET IT?" Several other tables looked over in their direction. Sophitia was suitably embarrassed. She repeated in a whisper, "How did he get it?"

"Well you see... my dad..." great, Abaddon needed to think of a way out of this one quick. "See, the thing is... my dad..."

"Yes?"

"He's.... that is to say he was.... one of the demon generals during Armageddon. After Lucifer fell, he got away with Spellbreaker," why in Heaven's name couldn't Abaddon ever sound more convincing? His dad was supposed to be the father of lies.

"So your dad just made off with one of the mightiest weapons ever crafted?" Sophitia was understandably skeptical.

"I mean, made off makes it sound like he swiped it and ran away."

"Then what did he actually do?"

"Well, I guess he did swipe it, but he challenged anyone to take it from him. Most didn't try, and he beat back those who did."

"Well, Spellbreaker or not, he must have been an impressive warrior. Then again he *WAS* one of Lucifer's generals."

You have no idea, Abaddon thought to himself, "Yeah, he sure was. But see, that's the kind of demon he is. There was chaos and uncertainty after the war ended, and rather than get swept up in it, he saw an opportunity and took it. He was always clever and stuff like that. I guess that's why he wanted me to read so much."

"Sorry, but that just makes your dad sound manipulative and power hungry. I can't help but think of him as the do-anything-to-succeed type."

"And is that really so bad?" Abaddon was mildly confused, and mildly offended.

"Well, I mean, it's just, taking something that wasn't his...."

"But it was his."

"No, he stole it."

"Well yeah, but that doesn't make it any less his."

"What are you talking about?" Sophitia looked incredulous. "It wasn't his, and he took it without permission. That's wrong. It belonged to its rightful owner."

"... Until he took it away from them," Abaddon seemed just as confused as Sophitia.

"Are you saying that stealing is considered fine in Hell? Wait, what am I talking about, it's *HELL*. I suppose I shouldn't be surprised that you demons wouldn't think theft is bad."

"Hey, if my dad was able to take such a powerful weapon away from someone, they were just too weak, and didn't deserve it anyway."

"I can't believe you'd think like that. So what, you can just take whatever you want from someone if you're stronger than them?"

"That's basically how it works in Hell, yeah."

"That's horrible," Sophitia was genuinely aghast. "Why would anyone want to live in such a terrible place?"

"Hey," now Abaddon was getting really offended. "Sure, Hell can be a rough place to live, but come on. I mean, is Heaven so great?"

"Of course it is. Heaven is.... well, Heaven. It's a paradise in the clouds. No other place in the cosmos can compare to it."

"Then I got to wonder why in Heaven's name you decided to come here," Abaddon got up, dropped some money on the table, and left.

Chapter Thirty-Eight

The Iniquity of the Father

"Is everything okay?" Lucifer sounded concerned.

"Well, okay as it's going to be. I mean, I'm still under a binding holy seal, still probably going to get fired, and I still have a necromancer trying to kill me. Which is actually what I wanted to talk to you about."

"Oh, well I'm sorry to say, I haven't heard anything new about that. Your aunt Lilith has no idea how a human could have found out about the sigils of pain, much less gotten a hold of them."

"Well, that's the thing. I actually *DID* get some new information."

"What happened?"

"I went to Heaven, if you can believe it."

"Excuse me?" Lucifer didn't sound angry, just completely confounded.

"Yeah, the angel who was watching over me took me there so I could find out more about this necromancer."

"Wait, *WAS* watching you? Does that mean she isn't still keeping tabs on you?"

"I have another angel doing that now, but that's beside the point. I now know who this necromancer is."

"You found out the identity? That means the divine council knew who this was, and they're just now telling you? You would think it only customary for the target to know the identity of the one trying to kill them."

"This whole situation is complicated. There's a lot I still don't know, stuff they wouldn't tell me."

"And why not?"

"The necromancer is Arthur Pendragon."

"Bullshit."

"I spoke to Odin, the divine aspect of wisdom. He told me himself. He wouldn't lie to me about this."

"And how can you be so sure of that?"

"Arthur Pendragon was possibly the greatest paladin to ever live. He was the grand champion of Heaven's armies during Armageddon. Do you honestly think the divine council would want anyone to think he had become a necromancer?"

"A very good point. Now I see why they are keeping matters so close to the chest. If people found out about this, it could be a disaster for them. Talk about scandal. This would be even worse than when your great, great, great grandfather found religion."

"Didn't the resulting war nearly destroy the Ninth Circle?"

"Would have, if your great, great grandfather hadn't slain him publicly and put his head on a pike."

"It's almost a wonder the line of Lucifer was ever able to overcome that shame."

"Oh, your great, great grandfather, after killing *HIS* father, slaughtered several dissenting families singlehandedly, all at the same time mind you. That cleared things up pretty quickly. But anyway, back to the matter at hand. How could Arthur Pendragon still be alive?"

"If he learned the secrets of necromancy, there was probably a way for him to extend his natural life."

"Well yes, but why would a paladin learn necro-" Lucifer abruptly stopped. "Oh no," he actually started laughing, "I can't believe this."

"What is it?"

"Oh, this is too perfect."

"What are you talking about?"

"I broke him," he roared triumphantly, "the mighty Arthur Pendragon. I shattered his will."

"What in Heaven's name is going on Dad?!"

Lucifer forced himself to subside, "I'm sorry Abaddon. This is actually all my fault."

"Wait, you're responsible for Arthur Pendragon trying to kill me?"

"No, that is his choice. But I drove him to this state."

"Okay, you'd better start explaining all of this."

"It was just after the war had ended. Heaven and Hell had agreed to a ceasefire. The Armageddon Accords hadn't been formalized yet, but your grandfather was dead, and I had assumed the throne. It seemed that the great paladin Arthur Pendragon didn't approve of the divine council's decision to make peace. He led a group of paladins to attack Pandemonium, taking advantage of the recent power struggle to try and put an end to the line of Lucifer once and for all."

"And you're telling me he survived that attempt?" Even for Arthur Pendragon, that was impressive.

"Survived is strong word."

"But you weren't able to kill him?"

"I didn't even try. That fool was so convinced of his childish notions of right and wrong, good and evil, black and white. It was a simple matter for me to make him believe that his own paladin allies had turned against him. Arthur Pendragon was the greatest champion of good Heaven had ever seen. He was too great. It left him morally weak, someone I wouldn't waste my blade on. With just my words I convinced him to slaughter the other paladins as I sat upon my throne and watched. He killed them to 'get to me'. I saw him fall, right before my eyes. But to think that he would resort to necromancy to try and bring them back, make amends for his failure! I don't think I've heard anything so beautiful since your mother was alive."

Suddenly Abaddon was reminded of what Arthur had said to him in their last battle, something about the iniquity of the father, "Wait, wait. Because of what you did, Arthur Pendragon is now trying to kill me?"

"I told you he was weak. He must know he cannot defeat me, so he's trying to kill you instead. He's too scared, so he's trying to get revenge on me by killing my spawn."

"So all this bullshit that's happening to me is your fault?" Abaddon snapped.

"The self-righteous bastard attacked me, after the divine council had already agreed to the truce."

"And you expect me to blame him for that? Granddad was the one who *ENDED THE HUMAN WORLD*. I can understand why their greatest champion would have been opposed to the idea of making nice with us."

"Hey, I wasn't the one who started the war. I supported the truce."

"Only after you found out our side was losing. You said it yourself: you were out there slaying the first angel."

"What? I should have felt sorry for a saved paladin trying to kill me?!"

"No, you should have killed them all and had done with it."

"I was given the chance to destroy the very soul of the greatest holy champion. No true demon would have passed up such an opportunity."

"*WOULD HAVE* Dad. Do I need to remind you that one of the agreements in the Armageddon Accords was that we would *STOP* torturing humans? If you were so in favor of this truce, then you wouldn't have turned Heaven's greatest champion into a dark psychotic abomination, right before signing it!"

"FOOLISH SPAWN," Lucifer's voice had risen to apartment shaking levels. "YOU HAVE NO IDEA THE SACRIFICES I MADE FOR THAT TRUCE."

"They don't count if they're human sacrifices!"

"I KILLED YOUR GRANDFATHER IN ORDER TO SECURE THAT PEACE."

Chapter Thirty-Nine

Revelations

"What?" Abaddon was trying to feel about four different things at once, and failed at all of them.

"I was the one who suggested a truce. I told your grandfather that if we continued to fight, we'd end up getting both Heaven and Hell killed. He wouldn't listen. He refused to back down. I killed him so that we wouldn't all die."

"You never told me about any of this."

"No one else knows. I thought it best."

"But why? You felt it was the right call and you made it. It's not like uncle Abaddon or any of the others would have faulted you for that. I mean, if you were able to kill Grandad, then that means you were stronger than him. It's the way things are in Hell. Why would you need to lie?"

"Just killing him wouldn't be enough. It wouldn't make the rest of the demons back down, not enough of them anyway. I needed them to think that the enemy had killed their leader. That was the only way they would believe the threat of their demise was real."

"But the forces of Heaven were really strong enough to defeat us, why did they agree to a truce? Why not just wipe us out?"

"I didn't know for certain that we would lose. We might have actually won the war."

"Then why kill Grandad?"

"I said we could have won, but we couldn't have survived. Even if we beat Heaven, we would have suffered too many causalities. You know what demons are like. I made the Ninth Circle one of the most ordered of the circles, but it's still warlike and dangerous. Had we won, those of us who lived would just tear each other apart. All of the circles would have been too weak to keep the tenuous balance that exists in Hell. But Heaven was not in much of a better position. They were much more united than we were, obviously, but they started the war at too much of a disadvantage.

Our initial assaults had gotten the drop on them, and they lost many of their number before the real fighting even began. Had they fought us to our last, they would have most likely fallen in the process as well. But... well, now that you know about this, I suppose I should tell you the whole story."

"What else is there?"

"Another reason why I had to lie about the death of your grandfather. I saw the error of his ways long before I killed him. I talked to Heaven and proposed the truce. I showed the divine council that we would both be wiped out if the war continued. They were easy to convince. I helped them. We demons respect power. The only way to get the others to back down was to show them just how powerful Heaven was. I worked with Heaven to kill your grandfather and stop the war. Had the armies of Hell found out about that, they wouldn't have stopped fighting."

"They would have just gotten angrier," Abaddon was processing the information as he spoke. "All that would have done was make them fight harder."

"Exactly. I knew this plan was the only way to avoid total annihilation. Still, I didn't feel good about it. I mean, working with the divine council? Your grandfather would have rolled in his grave that I put him in. I felt like I betrayed who I was. When Arthur Pendragon attacked, I saw a chance to get back some of my demonic pride and took it. I never would have imagined it could come back to bite me. A fallen paladin alone in Hell? I basically *HAD* killed him. Well that's what I thought. And now you're cleaning up my mess. I can see why you'd be angry."

"Look, Dad, it was unfair of me. Sure, I'm mad at you for what happened, but it's not just you. I might get fired from my job. I was arrested, and now am being watched by an angel. My magic is sealed away. And worst of all, I can't even fight the guy who's trying to kill me. I have to rely on an angel to fight my battle for me! I'm pissed, really pissed. And I'm pissed about a lot of stuff. I've been snapping at everyone lately. You gave me a reason to be mad at you, so I just kind of let it all out in your direction. I shouldn't have done that."

"No, you shouldn't have. But we are a savage and warlike people. Anger is in your blood. You shouldn't deny your anger, but you should learn to control it, especially if you insist on living with those mortals. They aren't used to people flying into a rage."

"Yeah," Abaddon scratched his head awkwardly. "I might have consumed a few bridges in the blackest flames of Hell in the past few days. And here I thought I might have actually been making friends."

"Well," Lucifer's voice took on a scoff, "you sound like you're giving up. The heir to the line of Lucifer cannot be so weak. I will not let my spawn be a coward!"

"Yeah, yeah, I get the point. I've got some other people to talk to."

"Then I should let you get to it. Just because you aren't slaying monsters at the moment, doesn't mean your trials in New Eden are over."

"Thanks Dad. I love you."

"Love you too."

Abaddon had not been expecting the knock on the door. What was even more unexpected, was the angel who had done the knocking.

"What are you doing here?" Abaddon was unsure of what tone to use.

"Apologizing," Sophitia replied. "Well, assuming you don't shut the door in my face."

"No, uh, come on in, and mind Boris, he gets a bit jumpy around new people."

"You have a pet cerberus?" Sophitia knelt down and held out a hand to Boris as he approached. The three heads briefly sniffed it, whined in unison, and backed off.

"Must not like your stench," this time Abaddon settled on mildly awkward.

"Guess I can't blame the little guy, what with me being an angel and all. Speaking of little, I thought cerberuses? cerberai? Anyway, I thought these guys were supposed to be big, like ten foot plus when on all fours."

"I used a black magic curse to shrink him. You have to if you wanna keep them as pets."

"I suppose that makes sense. But I didn't come to talk about dogs, be they three-headed or not. I guess technically the snake tail gives him four heads, but again, not the point. I wanted to apologize, like I said already. Look, I was insensitive back at the restaurant. I'd thought I was so much better than Cassandra and the less 'enlightened' angels. But I still bought into the whole Heaven/Hell antagonism and rhetoric. I didn't even realize how much I had normalized that behavior."

"I don't get a free pass either," Abaddon realized he hadn't actually shut the door, and hastily did so. "I was very quick to confirm my bias about you self-righteous asshole angels. I'm sure I wouldn't have been so angry if someone else had said those things."

"Or if my sister hadn't arrested you."

"She was just doing her job. And as much as it pisses me off, I get it. When I use my restricted magic, I put lots of lives in danger. It only makes sense that you guys would be willing to risk one life to save many."

"Maybe. But it's still a sucky and unfair situation for you. And until this situation is resolved, you're stuck with me, to an extent, so I figure we might as well try to get along."

"I can't argue with that. Besides, I really need to work on not storming out on people. This is becoming a really bad habit of mine."

"Then it's settled," Sophitia smiled. "Here's my number. Use a sending spell and we can set up another get together. But as for right now, I just sort of suddenly moved here, so I need to get back to apartment hunting."

"Well good luck," Abaddon waved as Sophitia headed out the door.

"Oh, Abaddon," Mary looked very surprised as Abaddon literally bumped into her coming out of the White Pegasus office.

"Wow, you are sturdy," Abaddon pulled himself off the floor.

"Are…. you okay?"

"As far as the hitting the pavement thing goes, yes."

"But otherwise?"

"Can we talk?"

Chapter Forty

Things Start Looking Up

"Look, I would start this with 'I'm sorry' and all that, but I don't think that would be a useful way to go about this. I think I just need to tell you everything about... everything."

"Okay..." Mary was understandably confused looking.

"You tried to talk to me about the whole arrest thing, and I got unjustifiably made at you, and so now I just kind of need to explain that. Assuming of course you want to listen."

"Yeah, you can definitely do that."

"Alright," Abaddon had led Mary into an empty room. "I just need to explain."

"You've been acting very strange. I know that it couldn't be easy getting arrested, but what's going on with you?"

"Do you know what restricted magic is?"

"Well no, but I'm guessing it's illegal magic of some kind. You said you were arrested for using illegal magic while fighting a necromancer. What's so bad about this magic of yours anyway? I mean, what did you do that got you into so much trouble?"

"I drew upon power from the very deepest darkest pits of Hell. I brought the true darkness and cold of the Ninth Circle to Terra. I have a special seal on me that keeps this connection to the blackest pits in check. I was given the key to that seal in case I ever needed this power, like I did when fighting the necromancer. But using this kind of magic on Terra is forbidden by the Armageddon Accords. I actually put the whole city in danger."

"Really? It's that bad?"

"If I had lost control of that power, I could have engulfed the entire city in the darkness of the pits of Hell. That's why it's against the Armageddon

Accords: it has the potential to completely Terraform a city. It would be literal Hell on Terra."

"That is pretty bad," Mary whistled. Abaddon spent several seconds trying to figure out how she'd managed that, but then she continued. "But that still doesn't explain the way you acted when I tried to talk to you about it."

"You told me you weren't afraid of me. You said you were confident I couldn't hurt you. But a diamond body couldn't protect you from something like that."

"So that really is what this is all about!" Now Mary sounded mad. "Do you actually think I would get scared and not want to speak to you again? It's not like you'd just summon the pits of Hell any old time and try to kill me. I mean, give me some credit here. And give yourself some credit while you're at it."

"That's not it," Abaddon tried to shout, but just ended up sounding desperate.

"Oh, well what is it then? Cuz right now it seems like you don't think much of our friendship at all."

"Well I wouldn't know. We've already established that I never had friends."

"I get that, but you can't just use it as an excuse to avoid blame any time you act like a jerk."

"It's more complicated than that."

"I get it, you're a demon. Stop acting like I can't handle that."

"That's not it!"

"Stop saying that."

"I'M THE SPAWN OF LUCIFER."

"Well I don't-" Mary was already starting to respond before he'd even finished, but then she stopped dead, "What?"

"That's why I never had friends. I am the spawn of Lucifer, ruler of the Ninth Circle of Hell. I strike terror into the hearts of those who cross me. And they are right to fear me. I've met very few people I couldn't kill easily. But even when I was being trained, back when I was little, I was still feared by all the other spawn."

"I see," Mary was speaking very slowly, clearly thinking about her words. "So your father is Lucifer. No wonder you..... well, I can see why you'd think what you do. But I stand by what I said when we first met. I mean, you chose to come live here in New Eden. Even if your father *IS* Lucifer, that doesn't change who you are. I mean, I liked you before. Finding out this piece of information doesn't retroactively change all that's happened since you've been here."

"Yeah.... well.... it's not just other people."

"What do you mean?"

"I'm scared too."

"Scared about what?"

"I meant it when I said I could easily kill most everyone I've met. I'm probably the strongest hero at White Pegasus, or at least was, until I got suspended. I can't be fully relaxed around people. I mean, there's always a part of me, somewhere in the back of my mind, that's worried. Even if I don't look like it, I always know somewhere deep down, that if I slip up I could seriously hurt someone. I nearly killed Brad for crying out loud. Sure he's an asshole, and frankly I don't care if he dies, but that's beside the point. That's the sort of thing that happens if I'm not careful. But with you.... well, it seemed like I'd finally found someone I didn't need to worry around. I guess I was kinda terrified of losing that."

"Wow..." Mary just stood there for almost a minute. "I- I can't really- I mean, I don't know what to say to that. And here I thought *I* had it rough as a giant rock."

"Good heavens!" Abaddon spat. "I keep sounding like I feel so sorry for myself. I'm not trying to make shit all about how hard it is for me. But then I go and screw things up like I did. Well, at least I explained myself. That's what I came here to do."

"And that is quite the explanation. Well, if it makes you feel any better, I'd say acting like a jerk is reasonable when you've gone through the stuff you have. I mean, demon or not, being really mad makes sense when you get arrested and suspended, just because someone tried to kill you."

"That's…. not why I was suspended. I didn't tell anyone at White Pegasus that I had forbidden magic. I was afraid I wouldn't get hired if anyone knew. As much as it pisses me off, they had every right to suspend me, or even fire me. I mean, I put the entire guild at risk. I suppose it's just lucky I'm the only one who got hurt by this whole mess."

"Now that's not fair. I mean, I definitely didn't have it as bad as you, but when you get hurt, your friends do too. I still have my job, but I have been worried about you this whole time."

"Wow…. Thanks."

"Isn't the phrase 'freaks need to stick together' or something like that?"

"I don't think you're a freak," Mary gave Abaddon a look, but he persisted. "No, I don't. There are weirder things than a living rock in this city. And where I'm from, the only thing that would be weird about you, is that you're not on fire and trying to destroy me."

"That's a pretty good one," Mary laughed, "if a bit corny."

"I'm serious. The Eighth Circle is ruled by Surtr, a great demon of stone and hellfire. It's probably the most violent of the circles."

"Well then I'll try to avoid it."

"Probably steer clear of Hell all together. I mean, I've been defending it since I got here, but…. well…."

"Hey, everyone's home has some rough places," now it was Abaddon's turn for the look. "Okay, but home is still home. And I can't imagine it's very nice having people badmouthing yours all the time."

"I think I'm starting to get used to it."

"Damn, I should probably get going. I was actually working on helping a lower income neighborhood appeal to the city about breaches in their rental contracts."

"Really?"

"I'm a defender of the people. Not all of the threats the people face are from claws and swords. Anyway. I've got to run, *BUT* when I'm not so busy, we should definitely get back to the whole talking thing. Good friends are hard to come by, right?"

Mary left the room. Abaddon stood for a minute. His mind was mostly blank. Finally he realized his blank brain was accompanied by a big dumb grin. But at the moment, he didn't really care.

Chapter Forty-One

A Suitable Distraction

Abaddon had been getting used to things not really going his way. It was a rather sad thought when he actually stopped to reflect on it. So he was quite surprised when he had a moment of very fortuitous timing. Abaddon had been walking Boris, that and going to the grocery store were about the only outings he went on nowadays. He had just been thinking about his job, and how he should probably start looking for a new one. And his immediate next thought was that he really wanted to do anything but that, which was the exact moment he bumped into Sophitia on the street. Just bumping into her was odd enough, the fact that she was now wearing standard Terran clothes as opposed to her white robes only added to the strangeness of the situation.

"Oh great, I was just coming to stop by your apartment."

"Really? Is something wrong?" Abaddon instinctively looked down at the holy binding on his arm.

"Oh no, I was actually wondering if you were free to… well… *DO* something."

"Do what exactly?"

"Well, I hadn't really gotten that far yet. I mean, we're in New Eden, there's got to be loads of places to explore."

"Wow…."

"What?"

"I just realized. I mean, when I first got here I was so fascinated with everything. Just walking down the street was an adventure. But recently, well I guess I've been in such a bad mood that I kind of lost that sense of wonder."

"Well then, consider it my divine mission to restore it," Sophitia grabbed his arm and started to drag him down a street.

For a while, everything was a happy blur of sights and sounds. Abaddon wasn't quite sure where they had ended up. He had been too distracted by the various food carts and odd sights they had seen along the way. When he really focused hard on it, he recognized a lot of the sights and sounds from his usual walks. They had passed by his local grocery store about ten minutes ago. He tried to figure out why it had all looked so strange and different to him. The answer came to him a moment later.

"Holy shit a carnival!" Sophita almost ascended with excitement when she saw the sign. Abaddon gave her a strange look. "What?"

"I just didn't think an angel would say 'holy shit'. Wouldn't that just kind of mean 'shit' as far as an angel is concerned?"

"Huh, never really thought about it before. That is kind of odd."

"Is this kind of language appropriate for an angel?" Abaddon's voice was a mixture of jokingly smug, and genuinely curious.

"It's not as though we can't swear. I mean, well, I suppose technically we're not *SUPPOSED* to, but it's not like there's a divine law against it or anything."

"Ooh, rebel," this time Abaddon's voice was all smug.

"Yeah, yeah, anyway let's go to the carnival already!"

As Sophitia led Abaddon by the hand, he smiled. He'd actually not been to a mortal carnival yet, and was quite curious about it himself, but he imagined it would not have been nearly as fun if he were alone. A part of him still wanted to be angry, but Sophitia was making that quite difficult. Her joyous mood, much like the great plagues of Resheph, demon lord of the Sixth Circle, was proving quite contagious and impossible to fight off.

"Oooh, look over there," Sophitia raced over to a booth where a three-eyed elf in a purple robe stood.

"Ah, welcome milady and kind sir," he bowed deeply as they approached. "I am Guru. I have been blessed by Athena, the divine aspect of wisdom, with Heaven's sight."

"No way," Sophitia got even more excited. "I'm from Heaven!" she unfurled her silver white wings.

"To be blessed with the presence of an angel," he bowed once again. "I am truly humbled by your magnificence. Though I must admit, even for a miraculous carnival such as this, seeing an angel and a demon together is quite a sight."

"So what do you do?" Abaddon was painfully obvious in his attempt to shift the conversation. "What's your booth?"

"Why my fine demon, like I said, Athena herself blessed me with this divine third eye. With it I can sense the innate magical power that sleeps within you. I will tell you of your magical destiny."

"Oh, me first," Sophitie stepped forward. "How does it work?"

"Just hold out your hand, and I shall begin."

Sophitia did as instructed. Guru grabbed her outstretched hand in both of his and closed his two lower eyes. Sophitia glowed a faint gold for a moment, then Guru pulled back, a bit quickly. His third eye was blinking, and he looked mildly dazed.

"As expected of an angel; you almost blinded me. Few mortals could match the power you wield, but then again that is no surprise. If I had to guess I'd say you were quite high up in the Heavenly ranks: a warrior of great skill. Perhaps a second tier Seraph?"

"Wow, you are the real deal. I'm actually a high third tier in terms of my divine power."

"Yes, truly, truly impressive. And I can only wait to see how your companion compares."

Abaddon held out his hand. Guru took it in both of his and closed his eyes, just like he had done with Sophitia. He focused for several moments. Nothing really seemed to happen. He then let go of Abaddon's hand slowly.

"I am sorry to say that I sense very little magic within you," Guru nodded towards Spellbreaker on Abaddon's back. "I take it you are more of the physical fighter type demon. I don't doubt you know how to use that weapon well. But as far as a magic user…."

"Hang on," Sophitia interjected. She turned to Abaddon. "As your guardian angel, I authorize you this once to remove your holy binding.

Don't worry, it will just be a second, and only I will be alerted when it is removed anyway."

"If you're sure," Abaddon removed his obsidian gauntlet. "Would you mind checking again?"

"Very well. We shall see if this has changed matters, though I doubt it will do much."

"I still feel really bad," Abaddon rubbed the back of his head nervously as they walked away.

"It wasn't your fault," Sophitia glanced back to the booth. Guru was rocking back and forth in the fetal position, muttering unintelligibly. "Let's... go to some other booth... quickly... I say this for unrelated reasons."

The next attraction that Sophitia took Abaddon to was an archery range. Set up at a distance were five targets, several behind various forms of cover. A woman dressed in hunter's furs was standing by a stand with arrows and quivers.

"Care to test your luck? Five arrows, five targets. Shoot them all, win an oversized novelty chimera," she stopped and thought for a moment. "Well I supposed it would actually be *UNDERSIZED* for a chimera, but oversized for a stuffed toy. Anyway, three bucks, and the chimera could be yours."

"I'm quivering with excitement," Abaddon paid the woman and picked up the bow.

"Ooh, three out of five. Sorry, but not enough to win the prize

"Right here," Sophitia pulled out some money and handed it to the woman.

With a blur of motion, Sophitia aimed, fired, and repeated. Abaddon could follow all of the shots, but if it weren't for his extensive martial training he wouldn't have seen a single one. The woman looked down right shocked, even more so, if that were possible, when she looked at the targets, all of which had an arrow in the bullseye.

"I-I guess we have a winner," She snapped her fingers, and a stuffed chimera doll appeared in front of Sophitia.

"Good heavens...." Abaddon was dazed himself.

"Didn't know I was a master archer huh?"

Abaddon was about to reply when he got cut off by a loud voice, "Step right up, step right up. Ten bucks to fight the ogre. No, weapons, no leaving the ring, no death, but otherwise no holds barred. Be the last one standing and win the money from all the other chumps who tried to beat him and failed. Joe the ogre has defeated fifteen would-be fighters so far. Is there anyone else who will take the challenge?"

"Alright," Abaddon had a smile back on his face. "It's my turn to show *YOU* up."

Chapter Forty-Two

Ogre the Toss

"I'll take the challenge," Abaddon stepped up to the ring.

"Well would you look at that folks," the announcer was a goblin on a tall stool. "We have a genuine demon, straight out of Hell. This is sure to be a fight to remember. But like I said, no weapons, so you're gonna have to lose the hammer."

"Hold it for me, would you?" Abaddon passed Spellbreaker to Sophitia before stepping into the ring.

The first thing that greeted him was the stench. Joe the ogre smelled roughly equivalent to garbage mixed with trash, with just a hint of filth. The rough tang jammed its way up his nose with lethal force. Abaddon steadied himself, bracing his mind against further olfactory intrusion, and sized up his opponent: big. That basically summed up Joe: big and green. He must have been about ten feet tall. Frankly, Abaddon was surprised that fifteen others had decided to try their luck against this mass of green warts and protrusions. Then he noticed a refreshment cart out of the corner of his eye that was selling beer, and it all made sense.

"Alright," the goblin addressed Abaddon, but loud enough for the crowd that had gathered to hear, "I'll tell ya the rules one more time sos that ya know what ya getting yourself into, and there ain't no cheating: No weapons, no killing, no going outside the ring. First one to get K.O.'d, leave the ring, or give up loses. Oh, and I shouldn't have to say this, but fist fight means no magic, obviously. So, ya ready to fight the big guy?"

"Let's do this," Abaddon smiled again.

"You heard 'em. Fight!" A cheer accompanied the goblin's words.

Joe barreled forward. His right fist came down in a strange diagonal arc. Abaddon easily slipped under the blow, delivering a few quick punches to Joe's stomach as he did. The ogre barely seemed to notice. Abaddon stepped back as Joe spun around. The ogre roared and delivered another wide swing that Abaddon just as easily avoided. He delivered several more blows to the chest.

"Wimpy demon," Joe roared. "Wimpy demon has wimpy punches."

Joe laughed as Abaddon delivered a few more jabs to his stomach. Again, Abaddon jumped back to a safe distance. As expected, Joe hurtled forwards with another barrage of wild swings. Abaddon ducked and weaved, delivering more light jabs with each dodge.

"Would you look at that," the goblin called out. "It's the immovable object versus the untouchable object. Is this fight even going to end?"

Abaddon had to laugh to himself. The fight had been over the moment it started. Oh well, he didn't expect anyone else to see it. It was only another minute and it was all over. It took a bit longer than he'd thought it would, but then again, Joe was quite large. When the green goliath went down, everyone looked stunned. Abaddon stepped out of the ring.

"I believe you owe me one hundred and fifty bucks?"

"I don't believe it," the goblin's voice got louder as he turned to the crowd. "Folks, Joe the ogre is down! This demon warrior took him out," he handed Abaddon the cash.

"Beats a stuffed chimera, right?" Abaddon took Spellbreaker from Sophitia and slung it over his back.

"I got to admit, I didn't think you'd be able to beat Joe."

"Are you kidding me? a trained demon warrior would never lose to someone like him. I mean, all he's got is size and strength."

"Sure you've got more skill, but how were you even able to hurt him? All you did was jab, and no offense, but I don't think you're the strongest demon out there."

"Yeah, yeah, I'm a real lightweight. My uncle Ab... solutely would have crushed him. One or two blows max," Abaddon laughed awkwardly.

"Your uncle sounds tough. But how'd you do it?"

"Are you kidding? It was easy. He never had a chance of hitting me with those wide swings. I was able to maneuver around him no problem. I just focused all of my punches at the same spot in his chest. I mean, my jabs are pretty hard... when not compared to a ten-foot ogre. They were doing some damage. I just waited for it to build up enough for him to drop."

"Impressive. I didn't know you were so skilled at unarmed fighting."

"Eh, I know how to throw a punch. The rest of it is just basic combat training. I suppose you went through that, though."

"Not like you. I'm a specialist caster and archer, though you saw that first hand. Cassandra's the melee fighter in the family."

"But she packs some mean holy magic. She was able to blast right through my restricted magic. I was not expecting that."

"She's good... when it comes to offensive magic. But she's not that good. The divine council authorized her to use level one divine punishment magic to bring you in. She was getting holy energy directly from the council to fuel her magic."

"A filthy cheater," Abaddon sounded mock offended.

Sophitia gave him a look, "And how is that any different than the magic you were using?"

"Well I... don't have an answer to that. Oh stop looking so smug."

"Did I wound the pride of the great demon warrior?" Sophitia shoved him playfully.

"This coming from an archer? The one who stands in the back and fights from a safe distance?"

"Ah," now it was Sophitia's turn to feign offense. She hit him a bit harder.

"Alright, alright, I was kidding. Archers are just as legitimate as melee fighters. I'm not an idiot. Combat training meant more than just how to swing a big stick."

"Well, glad to see you realize how important I am. So what do we do next?"

"No idea. What's nearby?"

"Oooh, how about the hall of magic mirrors?"

"Lead the way."

"Sorry about that," Sophitia said as they stumbled out of the exit.

"Hey, it isn't your fault they kept saying 'unclean' and making the sign of the cross. It's not like I was expecting to win fairest of them all or anything."

"Well regardless, you pick the next thing."

"Okay, that one," Abaddon pointed to a small red booth laden with tchotchkes.

"Really?" Sophitia gave him a look. "You did that on purpose."

"Hey, you said I pick the next one."

"Fine," Sophitia walked up to the booth. "How much for the halo toss?"

"Three bucks gets you five tries. No using magic, but innate abilities such great eyesight or natural coordination are fine. Just land one on the angel's head and you a win a prize."

Sophitia took her glowing rings, sighed, and threw; five tries, five misses, and five different swearwords. Abaddon took his turn. On the forth shot he managed to get the halo to hover over the angel's head."

"We have a winner!" the carny announced.

He handed Abaddon a figurine. Abaddon recognized it as one of the small Jesus statues that he'd seen on some of the chariots in New Eden. Scholars believed that putting these on one's mode of conveyance was done by A.D. humans as an offering to that divine aspect in order to avoiding accidents and speeding tickets.

"You got lucky," Sophitia huffed as they headed towards the next attraction.

"Are you bitter?"

"No. Besides, that game was wildly inaccurate. Angels don't even have-"

There was a puff of black smoke. Abaddon's hand immediately went for Spellbreaker, and Sophitia's started to glow with divine power. A familiar figure in a black suit stepped out of the smoke pillar.

"Sorry to interrupt your 'outing'," Mephistopheles nodded respectfully to Sophitia, "But we have some important legal matters to discuss."

Chapter Forty-Three

Terms of Payment

"Who is this demon?" Sophitia turned to Abaddon.

"My lawyer."

"And as I said, I am sorry to interrupt you two on such a lovely evening. However, the time has come for me to collect payment for services rendered."

"Calling in your favor now? I would have thought it would be at least half a century before I saw you again."

"Normally yes. Favors are not to be wasted lightly, especially favors owed by such important clientele."

"Important-"

"What's the favor?" Abaddon hurriedly cut off Sophitia's inquiry.

"Simple. I want Spellbreaker."

"You want my war hammer?"

"Oh yes. I can't pass up the chance to get a greater artifact. Treasures like this are very rare."

"Abbadon, you can't actually be thinking of giving such a powerful weapon to a demon you barely know, can you?"

"I'm afraid he doesn't have a choice actually. He agreed to one favor of my choosing, so long as it does not endanger his life or his reputation as a citizen of New Eden. And I would assume an angel such as yourself would know that a demon-forged pact is unbreakable."

"How'd you know I'm an angel?"

"The white hair, breathtaking visage, the fact that I can smell the holy magic on you. Take your pick. Now if we can complete our transaction, I will stop intruding on your precious time together."

Sophitia turned back to Abaddon. "You can't."

"I have to," Abaddon reached for Spellbreaker.

"No, I mean you literally can't."

"What?" both Abaddon and Mephistopheles said in unison.

"You just said that the favor you ask of him cannot endanger his life. Well, right now a powerful necromancer is out to kill Abaddon, and all his magic has been sealed away until such a time as the necromancer is brought to justice. That means Spellbreaker is one of his sole means of defending himself. Taking it away puts his life in danger from the necromancer."

"Hmmm," Mephistopheles stroked his goatee. "A very clever girl you've found yourself Abaddon. Very well, I will not be taking Spellbreaker from you. But the primary reason I wanted it was to break a particularly pesky magic barrier. I shall simply have you come with me and shatter the barrier yourself."

"So that's it? I just have to dispel one magic barrier with Spellbreaker, and then your services have been paid for?"

"Believe me, if I knew another way to destroy this barrier I wouldn't be using up my favor from you to do it. But Spellbreaker is the only thing powerful enough to get rid of the saved thing, so alas I have no choice."

"Alright then, where are we heading?"

"Hell, but not right now. I've taken up too much of your time as it is, and I have other matters to attend to. A near suicidal elf over on 52nd street is wishing at this very moment that there was some way to get revenge on her cheating husband and I really must hurry. I will stop by your apartment tomorrow and we can take care of the matter then."

"You know where I live?"

"I know where most people live; it's good for business. Now I really must go," Mephistopheles bowed again and vanished in a second puff of black smoke.

"Thanks for the save there. I couldn't imagine losing Spellbreaker."

"There was no way I could let that demon get his hands on it, or anyone else for that matter."

"What are you talking about?"

"When you handed me Spellbreaker while you fought Joe, I could feel the dark power in it. I could feel the curse. There was a deep hunger in it. Somehow you are able to withstand the curse's influence, but just thinking what it might do to someone else...."

"I'll admit it was rough at first, but I managed to get it under control."

"Well someone else might not. And Spellbreaker could do a lot of damage. It was seeking out magic to devour, destroy. It even reacted to my own divine magic. You need to be very careful with that weapon."

"Don't worry, I know what I'm doing."

"Yeah, you're letting that demon use it to destroy some powerful barrier, and you don't even know what it is sealing or why."

"I don't have a choice. Like he said, demon-forged pacts are unbreakable."

"But you didn't have to make the pact in the first place."

"It was that or face your sister alone in court after she had just arrested me for using restricted magic. Can you honestly tell me I'd have had a chance without exceptional representation?"

"Good point. I don't like this idea, but I suppose you didn't have another option. Oh well, regardless of what I think, this shouldn't ruin the evening. There's still a lot more carnival to explore."

Both Abaddon and Sophitia did their best to uphold that noble idea. Their next stop was the bumper chariots. Abaddon was very impressed by the magically animated bumper horses they used: very lifelike. After that they grabbed some concessions and sat down at a picnic table, relaxing in the cool breeze of the evening. Abaddon found to his surprise, that while he liked bread, and most of the cheeses he had tried, this combination thereof known as pizza did not agree with him. The pop-unicorn on the other hand was quite delicious, and the little horn made for an excellent toothpick. The elven forest dew was alright. It tasted leafy, but not in a bad way.

"So, what's next?" Abaddon was picking the last of the unicorn bits out of his teeth.

"Hmm, I'm actually fairly stuffed. Definitely shouldn't try anymore rides. I hear there's a great view of the West River just on the other side of the carnival. We could just sit there for a while I suppose.... unless you'd find that boring or anything."

"No, no, that's fine.

The view was quite pleasant. Abaddon had rarely just sat and watched anything before, but it was oddly enjoyable. He hadn't really been expecting to have such a good time. Definitely a pleasant surprise. He was still getting used to grass, and he wished they'd brought a blanket for the little hill they were sitting on, but it didn't matter. After the days he'd been having, a little thing like itchy grass wasn't really important. Besides, he was too distracted by Sophitia. It was odd. He was still trying to figure out the whole angel wanting to hang out with a demon thing. If you'd asked him, he wouldn't have been opposed to the idea; it'd just never crossed his mind before. Well, he had come to New Eden to experience different things after all.

"I should probably be getting back to my apartment," Sophitia said after a while. "Sadly, the night isn't getting any younger."

"Yeah, I suppose I should too. I'd offer to walk you home, but something tells me you don't need an escort."

"That's sweet, but yeah, I think I can take care of myself. Besides, I could probably just unfurl my wings and most people would run away."

"Sounds about right. I don't think many people would be too eager to pick a fight with an angel."

"But hopefully some people might be eager to pick another date with one," Sophitia smiled as she got up to leave.

"Sure, that would- wait, is that what this was?!"

"See you soon," Sophitia waved, and before Abaddon could fully process what had just happened, she was gone.

Chapter Forty-Four

New Developments

"Good heavens you scared the crap out of me!" Abaddon was still holding his yet-to-be-eaten loaf of bread as Mephistopheles appeared in his living room.

"Really, I would have thought you'd be used to this by now."

"This is like the fourth time. It takes more than that to get used to something. Seriously, you could have at least appeared outside my door and knocked."

"A most inefficient way of going about it."

"Not that it matters, you're gonna have to wait for me to eat some breakfast anyway."

"Not going to offer your guest anything?"

"You technically broke into my home, so I'd hardly consider you a guest."

"Details, details."

"But the devil's in the details."

"Touché."

Abaddon took his time and finished his bread. He hadn't tried this garlic variety before and didn't want to rush it. Mephistopheles at least had the manners to wait patiently for Abaddon to finish. Abaddon was realizing that this demon was an odd combination of respectful and inconsiderate.

"Alright, let's get this over with."

"Very well," Mephistopheles put his hand on Abaddon's shoulder and they both vanished in a puff of black smoke.

"Well, here we are."

"And where exactly would that be?"

"Don't tell me you can't recognize your own circle of Hell?"

"Well, a lot of the Ninth Circle is just kind of.... dark. And dark looks the same most places."

"We are in the deepest pits, so I suppose that makes sense. Follow me."

Mephistopheles led the way through the blackness. Like all demons, Abaddon's eyes were better suited to the dark, but this deep down in the Ninth Circle, even he was having trouble finding his way. It felt like they walked for almost an hour. Then suddenly, the darkness was gone, or rather, pushed away by a very bright light. It appeared to be some sort of opening, much like a cave. The opening itself, and the rock wall on either side of it, was protected by a great golden barrier of light. The barrier extended outwards, like a dome that had been put on its side.

"This is incredibly powerful holy magic. What in Heaven's name is a holy magic barrier doing in the deepest pits of Hell?"

"What in Heaven's name indeed. I can't actually tell you anything about this. I just need you to break that barrier. And I would recommend not looking into this either. The less you know about this situation, the better off you are. I mean this in no way to be a threat mind you."

"So I'm meddling in something way above my paygrade in other words?"

"I thought you got suspended."

"It's just a figure of speech. And how in Heaven's name did you know that?"

"Same way I knew where you live. Now if we could get to the matter at hand please."

"You don't like telling people stuff, do you?"

"No, it's bad for business. If you don't mind," Mephistopheles gestured to the barrier.

Abaddon drew Spellbreaker and approached the barrier. He could almost feel the holy magic burning him as he got close. He took a mighty swing with Spellbreaker. For a second he felt pressure, resistance against his hammer, and then the barrier shattered.

"You weren't kidding about this being a tough barrier to break. For a second there I thought Spellbreaker wouldn't be able to do it."

"Honestly I had my doubts. But it all worked out. You've paid your legal fees. Now I can send you back to your apartment, and you can go on with your life as a moderately free demon."

"And you really aren't going to tell me anything about what I just did? Why you had me break this barrier?"

"Of course not. But don't worry, as per our arrangement, your favor to me cannot endanger you at all, or your reputation here on Terra. Frankly, I doubt the effects of what you have just done will be felt during your lifetime. Now, I've had quite enough sharing," Mephistopheles put a hand on Abaddon's shoulder, and in another puff of smoke, they were in the apartment again.

"Wait," Abaddon was still adjusting to the sudden change in environment, "why couldn't you just teleport us directly to the barrier? Why did we have to walk?"

"I said I wasn't going to tell you anything, and I stand by that. Goodbye," Mephistopheles disappeared in yet another puff of smoke.

On the one hand, Abaddon hoped that was the last time he would see Mephistopheles, at the very least for a really long time, but on the other hand, he was mildly concerned about what he had just done. He would have been more concerned about it, if there had been anything he could do now, or could have done at the time. But since that wasn't the case, there was no point to dwelling on it. Besides, Abaddon would have plenty to dwell on soon enough.

Abaddon had not been expecting to get a call from Ms. Weathers. A part of him had been repressing any extended thought having to do with the guild. But as soon as she called, it all came out at once. Abaddon had to fight through all of the different half-formed emotions in order to even answer her.

"Su-sure, I can come in tomorrow. 10 A.M. Yeah, no problem."

"So…" Abaddon was unsure of what to say as he closed Ms. Weathers' door behind him.

"I am going to cut right to the chase. I'm afraid you are being fired."

"Oh… okay."

"I am sorry about this. I did fight for you, though I'm not entirely sure why, but I couldn't win it by myself."

"So, you were the only one who was on my side then?"

"You have to understand, they were only thinking of the good of the guild."

"And my gray skin and horns."

"Don't try to play the demon prejudice card. Of course this is about you being a demon. If you weren't a demon, then you wouldn't have had restricted magic in the first place. Being a demon is a requirement for doing what you did."

"But if Mary or Brad had done something just as bad then-"

"What could they have done that would be as bad as what you did?"

Abaddon tried to respond. He couldn't come up with anything to say. He just stood there for several seconds opening and closing his mouth. Eventually he decided on keeping it closed.

"It is a shame to lose your talent. But there's nothing that can be done about it. If you have any personal effects in the locker room, please retrieve them."

Chapter Forty-Five

Job Hunting

Abaddon was in a surprisingly okay mood. Yes, he was out of a job, but he had been frankly expecting that for several days now. And getting fired meant that he actually had to face the prospect of finding a new job. Before, he had just been ignoring it, but he literally couldn't afford to do that anymore.

Abaddon was trying to figure out what approach to go with in finding a new heroes guild to join. He decided on naïve optimism. He started with the other big-name guilds. Unsurprisingly, Defenders of Terra, the guild Adonis belonged to, rejected his resume. Lionheart also turned him down. New Eden had a few smaller heroes guilds to try, but Abaddon was starting to get worried. It took him several days, but Abaddon finally got an interview with one of the lesser known guilds.

Abaddon wasn't sure he had the right address. The building he was looking at was rather on the small side. It wasn't until he got closer that he saw the sign on it that read, "Knights of New Eden." He wasn't sure what to expect when he got inside. The building wasn't shabby by any means. It was just… well… When he stopped to think about it, Abaddon realized there was nothing wrong with the building. Sure it was small, but that was compared to White Pegasus, which was a major guild.

Abaddon made his way to the front desk. It was nothing impressive, and it looked like a tablecloth was draped over it. Sitting behind the desk, was a woman with short dark hair, an eyepatch, and a cigarette. She gave him a look over. He realized he must be quite the sight, seeing as he was constantly looking around like a lost idiot.

"Can I help you?" the woman's voice was sharp, but softer than he would have expected.

"I had an interview with a Mr. Cain."

"Oh, you must be the new kid. Just head down that way, last door on the left."

"Thanks."

"Hello?" Abaddon knocked on the door.

"Come in."

The office Abaddon stepped into was very small. The desk inside looked nicer than the one out in the main lobby, and there were a few chairs on either side of the room. But just like everything else so far, it felt off. In his head he was contrasting it with Ms. Weathers' office, and all of the differences exuded a surreal quality.

"You must be Abaddon."

The figure behind the desk stood up and walked from out behind it. He was a bald elf, with a face covered in scars. As he stepped forwards, Abaddon saw he was wearing blue jeans, and a white t-shirt. Another very odd contrast with White Pegasus.

"You must be Mr. Cain."

"Please, call me Arthur," the elf held out a hand.

"Sure," Abaddon shook it.

"So, you're looking to become a hero for the Knights of New Eden?"

"That's right."

"All the good guilds turn you down eh?"

"Well no, that's not-"

"Ha!" Arthur laughed. "Don't look so embarrassed kid, I know where we stand. And it says on your resume that you worked for White Pegasus. No one would go from the top four to a bottom-rung guild like ours unless they had no choice."

"Now you're making me feel bad."

"Don't," Arthur gestured to the chairs, and the pair sat down. "I like to be frank about things like this. I don't see a need to pretend that we're anything more than small time. I mean, you'll be the fourth active hero at the guild, assuming you sign on, and the sixth member over all."

"Wait, you mean the woman at the front desk-"

"Is the only other person here? Yup. My wife and I run the place, and we currently have three heroes on active duty."

"She's you're wife?" Abaddon wasn't sure why that surprised him that much.

"I know, I know, this place must seem quite unprofessional compared to White Pegasus."

"Well to be fair, White Pegasus is the only other heroes guild I've ever seen, so I wouldn't really know."

"So you just showed up and got hired to the big time right away?"

"Yeah, I guess so," Abaddon was starting to feel embarrassed.

"Well, your resume is quite impressive, so honestly not that surprising. You have extensive martial training, magical abilities, and are in possession of a major artifact. I'm guessing it's that war hammer on your back?"

"Yup. This is Spellbreaker and-"

"*THE* Spellbreaker?"

"You know about it?" Abaddon was taken aback.

"You bet I do. I've always been a history nerd. My favorite subject was Armageddon. I wrote my doctoral thesis on it."

"You got a doctorate?"

"Yeah, for a while I thought I'd teach history at some university."

"But you ended up running a heroes guild instead."

"Co-running. Sarah, my wife, and I both started out as heroes ourselves first."

"That makes sense."

"Oh?" Arthur gave him an inquisitive look.

"You're in great physical shape, and those scars on your face and arms are clearly battle wounds."

"Ha! That's the eye of a trained warrior for you. Back in the day I was quite the archer and swordsman if I do say so myself. Sarah and I were never big names, so I wouldn't expect you to have heard of us. But enough about that. This is supposed to be a job interview."

"So I guess you should ask me some questions?"

"Let me get the obvious one out of the way. Why did you leave White Pegasus?"

"Well actually…. I was fired."

"Really? I'm guessing that has something to do with the holy binding on your arm?"

"I kinda got arrested and am currently on probation. This binding seals my magic away."

"So you got fired because you got arrested?"

"Not exactly," Abaddon took a deep breath. "I was arrested for using restricted magic. I got fired because I didn't tell White Pegasus that I had restricted magic during my interview. I was hired by them under false pretenses."

"Which line are you?" Arthur's question came out of nowhere.

"What?"

"Which line? You know, line of Surt? Line of Lilith?"

"What makes you think I'm an elder demon?"

"Oh come on. You are in possession of Spellbreaker, a legendary demon weapon, and you possess restricted magic. The focus of my thesis was on the Armageddon Accords. In short, I can put two and two together."

"I- I'm the heir to the line of Lucifer."

Arthur whistled, "To think I've got a real-life legend wanting to join my humble Guild. Consider yourself hired Abaddon."

Chapter Forty-Six

Catching Up with Mary

It had taken Abaddon a long time to actually contact Mary. He'd been meaning to try and get in touch with her for a while now, but it never happened. Every time he thought about doing it he stopped. It just felt weird. He wasn't at White Pegasus anymore, and it was almost as if he didn't have a reason to talk to her anymore. But after his interview he needed to talk to someone, and well…. he didn't really want to talk to anyone else, at least not about that. So finally he got up the courage used a sending spell, and asked to meet with her. To his immense relief, she sounded just the same as always. Well, she sounded the same as the few times he'd talked to her at any rate. When he stopped to think about it, he didn't know her very well, and yet she was the person he knew best in New Eden. So what did that say about him?

On this particular day, the weather had taken a rather wet turn, and so the two had decided to meet inside. They found a nice little restaurant. It had a booth that was actually big enough for Mary to sit down. It was still a tight squeeze, but at least the booth seemed sturdy enough that she could sit without worrying about breaking it.

"So…. uh, thanks for agreeing to meet me again."

"Of course. I was glad you contacted me. I mean we haven't talked since you…"

"Got fired?"

"Yeah, that. I'm really sorry about the whole thing."

"Well, I mean I did have it coming. I broke the law and lied to White Pegasus."

"Still sucks that you're no longer at the guild."

"Yup. How's that going for you?"

"It's going good. I've been keeping busy."

"Get into any fights, or has it all been the social justice work?"

"Social justice mostly. I did foil a mugging, I suppose. I don't know if it really counts though, since all I really did was stand in his way and let him crash into me."

"Hey, whatever works I guess. So I assume you're still liking it at White Pegasus then?"

"Oh yeah. I mean, Brad's been insufferable ever since you got fired, but then again I don't see much of him, thankfully."

"I would have thought he'd be happy that I'm gone."

"Oh, he is. You can practically smell the smug coming off him from at least three rooms away."

"I'm sorry to hear that."

"Well, silver lining for you I suppose. How have things been for you since getting fired?"

"I might have a new job."

"Might? What happened?"

"Well I had an interview at another heroes guild the other day. They want to hire me, but...."

"But what? I mean, you'll need a new job."

"Yeah, but this place is small. I'd be the fourth hero they have, and sixth person in the guild all together."

"So wait, four heroes, and two employees?"

"A couple. They are former heroes. They seem nice enough from what I can tell, but I don't know."

"Did you tell them about the whole arrest thing?"

"Yup, didn't seem too bothered by it. Look, I know I should jump at the chance for a new job, I just-"

"Let me guess, you don't want to go from a top guild like White Pegasus to a small one like this?"

"Yeah, kind of. I feel like I'm acting really spoiled or something."

"It's an adjustment. Going from the top to the bottom like that would be hard for anyone. A lot of people wouldn't be able to handle it. I assume you tried all the other big guilds already."

"Yeah, none of them wanted to hire someone who got fired from White Pegasus."

"I can imagine that that must hurt. The other guilds don't want the reject. I don't mean to imply that you are a reject," Mary added hastily, "just that they... would... all... see... you... that... way... Look, you don't need to take this job."

"I kind of do. I mean, I need money to buy food and pay for rent."

"Do you? Your dad *IS*... well, you know, you could always just ask him."

"No!" Abaddon looked around sheepishly as everyone in the restaurant stared at him. "I- no, I can't do that."

"Can't go back, or can't ask him for money?"

"Both."

"Why not?"

"I came here to experience new things and try stuff on my own. I can't admit defeat now."

"Who said anything about admitting defeat. It's not like this is a battle or anything."

"Of course it is."

"Wait, you're actually thinking of this situation as a battle?"

"Yes. If I give up now and either head home, or go crying to daddy, then I am just weak. I can't be weak."

"Wow, that's really messed up. There's nothing wrong with crying, you know."

"I guess I used a poor choice of words. I am well aware that there is nothing wrong with crying."

"But then what did you mean?"

"It's giving up that I have a problem with."

"What's wrong with giving up then?"

"I chose to come here and make it on my own. I wanted to do this by myself. I mean, at the start I had a little help from Dad, but that was a necessity. I can't give up if there is another option. That would just mean I'm weak. I have to fight to the last."

"This isn't a fight!" Now it was Mary's turn to be embarrassed at her own outburst.

"Not to you. But we demons think of most things in these terms. It is all about winning and losing, strength and weakness."

"Well that's just stupid. Winning and losing isn't everything."

"You're so lucky," Abaddon's words caught Mary completely off guard.

"W-what?"

"On Terra, you're absolutely right, winning and losing aren't everything. In Hell on the other hand…. Hell is a constant battle for survival. Winning and losing are the most important things. In Hell, there are few rules to keep demons from fighting and killing each other. If you aren't strong enough to survive, there aren't laws for you to hide behind. In Hell, you cannot afford to be weak. And I," here Abaddon lowered his voice, "am the spawn of Lucifer. I am the next heir to the line of Lucifer: a line that has gone unbroken to this day. Look, I'm sorry if this sounds crude or barbaric to you, but weakness is not a luxury I have. Even now that I am living here on Terra, I am still heir to the line of Lucifer. I am still bound by that iron-clad rule: I cannot be weak, ever."

For at least a minute, Mary just sat there. It looked as though she was in deep thought, but then again, it usually looked like that. Abaddon was starting to feel a bit tense, unsure if he should say something else, or if he needed to wait for her to speak. Finally, she did.

"Okay then," Mary said, "It looks like you have your answer."

Chapter Forty-Seven

A New Start

"Hello everyone, and welcome our newest guild hero, Abaddon," Arthur clapped briefly as Abaddon stood up, "So why not introduce yourself, tell us about your special skills and talents, and everyone else will do the same."

"Sure. Hi, I'm Abaddon. As you can tell I'm a demon. I have extensive martial training, as well as some demonic magic. This war hammer on my back is known as Spellbreaker. It is a greater artifact capable of destroying all but the strongest of enchantments. At my last guild I was a monster-slayer."

"I guess I'll go next," a young girl in a red cloak and hood stood up as Abaddon sat down. "I'm Lucinde Kurtz. I work alone; don't get in my way."

A fairly muscular man in his late twenties stood up next, scratching his brown shock of hair, "Charming as always Lucinde. Hi, I'm Donny Hanson. I'm actually training as an enchanter/smith. I made the sword and shield on my back and enchanted them both myself. Nothing fancy, the sword can freeze things it cuts, and the shield has greater resistance to both physical and magical attacks than a normal one would. I'm still learning both smithing and enchanting, and always looking to improve my abilities."

Finally there was a dark skinned woman with a black ponytail, wearing a gray hoodie, "I guess I'm last. My name's Nanase Kira. I was born and raised in the East Village. I'm a swordswoman primarily, and my specialty is iajutsu: the art of quick-draw sword techniques."

"Well," Arthur stood up again, "I think I speak for everyone when I say welcome to our newest hero Abaddon. To celebrate us getting a new family member, I brought coffee and doughnuts. So feel free to dig in, and please, don't hesitate to get to know each other."

The doughnuts were quite tasty. For a few minutes Abaddon just stood by the table awkwardly eating. It didn't look like the others were overly sociable. Lucinde left as soon as the introductions were over, without even saying a word. But it was only about another minute before Donny came over to where Abaddon was standing.

"Welcome to the team," he held out a hand. Abaddon shook it. "I'm guessing you're quite the strong fighter aren't you?"

"Yeah. I had to go through really tough training in Hell. I'm guessing you're pretty good with your sword."

"To tell you the truth, I'm actually only an average fighter. I haven't had much real combat experience. I thought an expert warrior like you would be able to tell."

"Well… I didn't really want to say anything."

"Nah, it's cool. I only started as a hero recently. I have to divide my time between working on my smithing and enchanting as well as my fighting, so I haven't had a lot of time to practice. Then again, I suppose you learned fighting and magic, so I don't really have an excuse," Donny looked a bit sheepish.

"To be fair, I have the advantage of living a lot longer than you mor-" Abaddon paused, "humans. I *AM* two hundred and fifty."

"Wow, that means you're even older than Arthur."

"I think demons have a longer lifespan than elves, but I'm not really sure."

"Well congrats. And here I thought Lucinde was the veteran."

"That girl, really?"

"Yeah, she's a total badass, and knows magic and stuff; it's crazy."

"Are you guys talking about Lucinde?" Nanase walked over, a cup of coffee in one hand, a doughnut in the other.

"I really don't know what to think of her.."

"Yeah, I'd just ignore her. She's doesn't like people, so I say leave her alone," Nanase gave Donny a pointed look.

"I was just telling Abaddon here that she's a total badass.."

"And last time you started bombarding her with a bunch of questions about it she got really mad, remember?"

"Remember? She pulled a knife on me."

"Is there something…. wrong with her?" Abaddon quickly gave up on trying to find a nice way to phrase the question.

"Can't say," Nanase replied. "It's her business Besides, Arthur gave her the okay to work here, so she must be alright.."

Donny crossed his arms, "That just makes me more curious. Ah well. Hey," hey turned back to Abaddon, "Can I see that war hammer? You said it was a greater artifact, right? Must be a cursed demon weapon. I've always wanted to study one of those."

"Sure," Abaddon handed it over, then instantly regretted his action.

"Ahh!" Donny dropped Spellbreaker almost instantly. "What the hell? Dude, that war hammer is hungry. It wanted to eat my sword."

"Don't be a moron," Nanase sighed. "How can a hammer be hungry?"

"Sorry," Abaddon hastily picked up Spellbreaker. "I keep forgetting about that."

"Wait, you're telling me that war hammer actually *IS* trying to eat Donny's sword?"

"See, I told you dude."

"Not exactly. Cursed artifacts sort of have wills of their own. I suppose it would be more accurate to say they have strong desires. That's what fuels their powers. The more powerful the artifact, the stronger the desire. In the case of Spellbreaker, it is the desire to devour magic. I've just gotten so used to it that I don't even really think about it."

"How could anyone get used to *THAT*," Donny pointed a shaking hand at Spellbreaker.

"Over a century of exposure?" Abaddon awkwardly shrugged. "Sorry again for this whole thing."

"It's cool. I'm the one who asked to see it. I should have figured what with it being a cursed artifact and all. I-I'll get over it."

"Yeah, don't mind Donny. He's a genius when it comes to enchanting, but otherwise he's an idiot."

"Well I don't know about genius- HEY!"

Nanase gave a smug look, "Anyway, welcome aboard Abaddon. We can use all the help we can get here," she shook his hand. "Is that a holy binding on your arm?"

"Yeah. I uh…. had some…. legal issues a little while ago."

"Dude you're a criminal?!" Donny sounded excited.

"Knock it off," Nanase lightly shoved him.

"Ow, geez. It's not my fault I have an inquisitive nature."

"No, but it's your fault that you keep acting on it without thinking first."

"No, it's fine," Abaddon held up a hand. "Look, I was in a life and death situation and I had to use some illegal magic in order to get out of it, no big deal."

"That's one hell of a big-" Donny stopped at a look from Nanase. "I mean…. you don't…. have to talk about it…. if you don't want…. to?"

"Really, it's fine. I didn't want to say anything in case you guys were uncomfortable."

"And what makes you think we'd be uncomfortable?"

"Because he's a cirmin- ow! Hey, stop that."

"For such a big guy, you really are a pansy. I barely even touched you that time."

"It's not my fault if I'm sensitive either," Donny's voice took on a defensive tone.

Abaddon laughed, "Sorry, sorry. But I kinda have to agree with Nanase. I mean you *ARE* a hero."

"I'm working on it. I told you I'm still fairly new."

"Hey, I *HAVE* offered to do some sword practice with you before."

"Yeah, but you'd just kick my ass."

"What's the matter, are you scared of little old me?"

"Yes."

Both Abaddon and Nanase laughed at this. Even Donny joined in after a few seconds. Well, this place was definitely different. It would take some getting used to, no question. But if nothing else, his first day here had gone a lot better than his first day at White Pegasus.

Chapter Forty-Eight

A New Day, a New Challenge

"Are you sure about this?" Abaddon eyed Nanase warily.

"Don't tell me you're scared of me, too, new guy?"

"I'd say that I don't want to hurt you, but it seems like you would take offense at that."

"Hardly. You think you're some big bad demon, right? I'd love to take you down and show you up."

Abaddon picked up the wooden training sword Nanase had given him, "If you really wanna do this, then alright."

"Bring it tough guy."

Abaddon moved in as quickly as he could. He hadn't held a blade in a while, so the wooden facsimile felt a bit odd and clumsy, but it was much lighter than Spellbreaker. In moments he had closed the distance and was bringing his "blade" down on Nanase's head. His eye barely followed as she drew her weapon. It arced up, catching his sword, knocking it aside. Abaddon retaliated by digging in his heels and standing firm. Pushing back, he stopped her sword dead. The moment the swords stopped moving, Abaddon raised his right foot and kicked Nanase hard in the stomach. She went to the ground in a coughing heap.

"Good heavens you were fast," Abaddon commented as Nanase struggled to her feet. "I almost didn't see your counter."

"Stopped me good all the same," she managed.

"I have superior strength and reflexes, and a lot more training. It's not really fair to compare me to a human when it comes to a fight."

"But just for the sake of the exercise, how did I do?"

"Well I only ever fought one other human. That punk was slightly slower than you are. I was using Spellbreaker against him, so it's hard to judge his abilities against yours. But he was a van Helsing, and that's supposed to be worth something."

"You fought with the next van Helsing?!"

"I almost killed him. It was my first day at White Pegasus," Abaddon had gone from cocky to sheepish.

"Wait, what?"

"He's an ass. No one really likes him. The little shit is full of himself. But, since he's from a long line of monster hunters, I suppose it's not that surprising that he didn't take too kindly to me."

"That would make sense. So…. he attacked you?"

"Well, first he started mouthing off to me and acting like the jerk that he is. He was trying to convince everyone that it was crazy to let a demon be a hero. I rose to his threats and insulted him back. He got super pissed off and attacked me. I responded in kind. Would have killed him most likely if Mary hadn't stopped me."

"Who's Mary?"

"A golem. She was one of the new hires as well. This all happened right after our orientation."

"Well, she would have had to be quite tough to stop you," Nanase rubbed her chest for emphasis.

"She's over seven feet tall, with a body made of solid diamond, I think that qualifies as tough."

"Yeah, not gonna argue with that. Wow, they've got van Helsing's heir, a diamond golem…. makes us look like kids with toy swords."

"Well aren't these toy swords?"

"They're training weapons. I wasn't going to fight you for real. My Nishikaze wouldn't stand a chance against your Spellbreaker."

"Nishikaze?"

"It's the name of my sword. It means west wind. Apparently wind spirits were bound into it when it was forged. It's faster and sharper than any sword I've ever seen, but it's no greater artifact."

"Well, now that we got this settled, are you satisfied?"

"I just wanted to see how the new guy stacks up. I mean, a hotshot demon coming to us from White Pegasus. You only had to settle for us because you got in trouble with the law."

"I didn't settle for-"

"You settled," Nanase gave him a look.

"Well it doesn't sound nice when you put it like that."

"Hey, no one's going to blame you for thinking that. No one here anyway. White Pegasus is one of the big four heroes guilds. You would have been famous, or at least quite well off financially. Sucks that you had to give that up."

"Maybe so, but you all seem very nice. Well, aside from Lucinde. Anyway, I don't want to go into this moping and complaining about not being at White Pegasus anymore. That is a guaranteed way to not enjoy this."

"That's a pretty mature attitude for a…."

"Two hundred and fifty year old?"

"Okay, but that doesn't count. That's like demon years."

"I'm not a dog. That would make the fact that I have one as a pet very strange."

"No, I mean you guys live for hundreds and hundreds of years, so you're still just a kid or young adult by demon standards."

"So? I've still had over two hundred years on you. All that means is that our young adults are just more mature than your adults."

"Really? You almost kill a man cus he insults you and YOU'RE the more mature one?"

"That has nothing to do with maturity. Violence is a go to answer for demons."

"And you wonder why van Helsing didn't like you."

"No I don't actually. It's obvious why he hates me," Abaddon's tone adopted more anger than he'd intended.

"I'm sorry, I didn't mean to-"

"No, I'm sorry. Going on two months and I'm no better at talking to people than when I arrived."

"Ha!" Nanase looked triumphant. "Well, there's something that I'm better at than you."

"Are you kidding? All I'm good for is fighting."

"That's a terrible thing to say. You-"

Nanase was cut off by a swirl of wind and a glowing pillar of light. The shining form of Sophitia descended from the brilliance, silver-white wings vanishing as she touched silently on the ground.

"Sorry if I'm interrupting," she turned to Nanase and held out a hand. "My name's Sophitia."

"Y-y-you're an angel," Nanase could barely get the words out.

"I'm his parole officer," Sophitia smiled at Abaddon.

"Wait," Abaddon looked at his arm. "So this thing lets you track me?"

"Of course. It would be hard for me to do my job otherwise."

"And I'm almost worried to ask, but why did you come here?"

"To see if you were free this evening."

Chapter Forty-Nine

Heaven's Date

Abaddon and Sophitia were sitting at a fancy table with pristine white napkins and a tablecloth to match. Low lights from the ceiling lit the room with a pale green glow. All around them were couples in resplendent attire. When Abaddon and Sophitia had walked in, people had stared at him like he was some sort of monster, but he actually thought it was because of his clothes rather than his horns.

"So, you really wanted to go out on a date with me?" Abaddon spoke between mouthfuls of steak.

"I'm treating you to dinner at the fanciest dwarven restaurant in the city, so I think that's a yes."

"I already told you, you didn't need to bring me here."

"And I already told *YOU* that I have been dying to try dwarven cuisine."

"Well I'd be more than happy to pay my share of the bill."

"Didn't you just recently get fired from your job? I don't think you're in the most financially stable position right now."

"I got a new job," Abaddon was surprised at how defensive he sounded.

"Really? Don't take this the wrong way, but I'm a little surprised that another heroes guild hired you. Weren't you fired from one of the top tier guilds?"

"And I ended up in a bottom tier one. I am the fourth hero they have on active duty."

"Okay that's a bit small, but I don't think most guilds have many active heroes. I mean, it's not the most sought-after job, and few are qualified for it."

"That makes me the sixth employee in the whole guild."

"Okay, small might not cover it. How are there only six people total? I'll admit I don't know much about heroes guilds, but a business shouldn't be able to function like that."

"Mom and pop operation sounds about right, though I'm not sure if Arthur and Sarah actually have kids."

"Husband and wife running the guild?"

"Yup, both retired heroes themselves. Arthur claims they were quite good back in the day, though not big names or anything. He definitely has the look of an experienced warrior, and his scars prove he's been in his fair share of tough fights."

"And the wife, Sarah you said her name was?"

"Well, she's missing her right eye and likes to smoke. I don't really know much else about her."

"What about the other three heroes? Have you met them yet?"

"We had a little introduction with doughnuts and coffee right after I joined. There's Donny. He's actually working at making magic weapons. He forged and enchanted his sword and shield himself. He seems to be the least experienced in the guild. Then there's Nanase. She grew up in the East Village and is quite a skilled swordswoman, for a human anyway. And finally, Lucinde," Abaddon couldn't keep the sigh in.

"What's special about her?"

"Well, she's apparently very skilled in both fighting and magic, despite being basically a kid. She's also just about the least social person I've ever met."

"And this coming from a demon. So what's her deal?"

"I don't know actually. Like I said, she's not very personable. Apparently she threatened Donny with a knife when he got too talkative."

"Yeesh. Can't imagine she'll be fun to work with."

"She only works alone apparently, so that's something at least. Sorry about this. You take me to a nice restaurant and I start talking about my problems."

"That's not fair. I asked, remember? Besides, I like learning stuff about you."

"And here I know almost nothing about you, except that you're good at archery. What have you been doing since you came down to Terra?"

"Everything! I basically binged on all the sights, sounds, smells, you name it, that New Eden has to offer. My being your guardian angel, as it were, is still part of my job. I have lots of free time."

"So you're getting paid to hang around in case I break my parole?"

"And I thank you very much for it. It's the sweetest job I've ever had."

"Well glad some good came from my getting targeted by psycho Arthur Pendragon."

"Yeah, about that; are you okay? I mean, it must be hard getting targeted like that."

"Yeah, I'm fine."

"Really?" Sophitia gave him a look. "A dangerous individual is trying to kill you. You have to look over your shoulder everywhere you go. How can you be fine, knowing that you could die at any moment?"

"I spent that past two hundred and fifty years in Hell. This is normal for me. As a demon, you make peace with that at a young age."

"That sounds awful."

"Are we going to get into this again?"

"I'm sorry, but it does. I don't mean to keep badmouthing your home, but that's just how I feel. I can't imagine living like that. I mean, how do you deal with it?"

"You get strong. I live every day knowing that someone could be coming after me. But I don't live every day knowing that I could die at any moment. Those are two different things."

"So you're saying you get strong enough that you don't have to fear other demons?"

"Exactly."

"But doesn't that just mean that the violence of demons is a vicious cycle? A self-fulfilling prophecy? I mean, you wouldn't be so war-like if you didn't have to learn to fight to protect yourself from the other war-like demons. Now I need to apologize. I'm getting into philosophy. It's not usually a typical date discussion topic."

"Well don't worry. I wouldn't know. I mean, this *IS* my first date, unless you count the carnival, but I don't since I wasn't aware that's what it was until it was over."

"I guess males are clueless no matter what species they are," Sophitia smiled.

"Yeah, just like females are weak and need protecting."

"Wow, that's pretty offensive."

"And your statement wasn't?"

"Okay, point."

"Not to get into a sociological conversation, but I don't see how it's okay to make broad negative generalizations about males, and not females. I mean, it's not that way in Hell."

"Oh? Demons have gender equality?"

"Demons take what they want by force. Those are the rules, so if you are strong enough, you get to do what you want. Think what you will about that way of doing things, but it means that we don't have the illusion of one gender being inferior to another. Since that isn't true, it means we get reminded of that on a daily basis."

"So female demons aren't on average weaker than male demons?" Sophitia was no longer disbelieving, but just curious.

"Unlike many creatures, demons aren't uniform. Some are ten feet tall with massive wings, some have magic, some don't. Comparing all demons would be like comparing all creatures from Terra. Some are big and hairy with claws, others are small and fast, some can fly. They are different enough that it is silly to lump them all in the same category. What?" Abaddon was genuinely confused by Sophitia's laugh.

"I take back my apology. I am very much enjoying this philosophical and sociological conversation."

Chapter Fifty

A Good Night for a Stroll

"Alright," Abaddon laughed as they walked down the street, "Your turn."

"Fallen angels, not real."

"No way."

"It's true. No such thing as fallen angels."

"I just assumed, I mean, fallen paladins and all that."

"Angels can't fall. We have our own divine powers, not granted to us by other entities. We can lose the favor of the divine council, but we can't lose our powers. Alright, you got another one?"

"Hmmm, ah, got one. Demons don't devour mortal souls."

"But that's like a classic demon thing. No soul devouring? I thought it increased your demonic powers or something."

"Felgreth the Pain Bringer started that idea as a fad diet a couple thousand years ago or so. He was debunked as a fraud shortly thereafter."

"Fascinating. Let's see if I can think of another. Oh, angels don't play harps. They're not a divine instrument."

"Huh, I feel like I read that one somewhere."

"Personally, I find them a rather boring instrument. I prefer the piano. What's your favorite instrument."

"Bagpipes."

"Really? Why?"

"Nostalgia. I used to listen to them when I was a young spawn. Also pride I suppose. The first bagpipes were forged by demons."

"Demons invented the bagpipes? Yeah right."

"Don't look so surprised. I mean, they're made by mutilating animals. Bagpipes are an instrument of torture. Not that good for the sheep either."

At that, Sophitia burst out laughing, "Wow."

"What?"

"I didn't take you for the corny joke type."

"It's in my blood."

"Oh really?"

"Yeah, really. Demons were the first to make puns you know."

"So you invented the bagpipes and puns?" Sophitia sounded half skeptical, and half amused.

"Yup. That's why there is an irrational hatred of puns by most people. The puns themselves aren't bad, but back in the day they had an association with demons, so people thought they must be an evil art. Now there's a learned societal dislike of them, even though no one remembers the original reason why."

"I can't tell if you're screwing with me or not," Sophitia smiled.

"It's all true. We created bagpipes and puns. Ask any demon, they'll tell you the same."

"But you are a creature of lies," Sophitia put on her best Cassandra impression, "I must not believe anything you say!" both Abaddon and Sophitia got a good laugh out of that.

"No offense, but I'm really glad your sister isn't my guardian angel anymore."

"Why would I be offended? She's my sister and I love her, but I completely understand why someone would not like her, especially you of all people. Wow, I wonder what she would say if she knew that I was on a date with you," Sophitia chuckled at the thought.

"Ah shit!" Abaddon stopped in his tracks.

"What? What's wrong?"

"I didn't even think about how pissed my dad would be if he found out about this."

"Well, I suppose a demon general from Armageddon wouldn't like angels that much."

"That's not…. entirely true."

"What's that supposed to mean?"

"He supported the Armageddon Accords. He was actually one of the first to support an end to the war. It's just that he's a little…. well…. ah, good heavens!"

"What?"

"I can't think of a word to use other than traditional."

Sophitia laughed again, this time it was accompanied by a smug smile, "I understand what you mean. Even if he is one of the more progressive ones, he still is of those generations. Look, tell you what, I won't tell my sister about this, if you don't tell your dad. Deal?"

"Alright, deal. But wait, didn't your sister say that she was going to be watching me carefully to make sure I didn't do anything to you?"

"Tough talk. She actually can't. Now that I'm your guardian angel officially, she can't keep tabs on you with the holy binding anymore. She'd have to come down here in person and stalk you if she wanted to 'keep an eye on you'. And angels descending to Terra is a rare thing. Our travel to other planes is carefully regulated."

"But don't some angels live on other planes of existence?"

"No, actually. The hierarchy in Heaven is strictly regimented. Every angel knows their place, and follows the rules. One of those rules is that we live in Heaven, watching over the other planes. "

"So angels don't have any freedom is what you're saying."

"That's a gross over-generalization. We just have a strict structure of rules and laws, unlike Hell."

"Yeah, well, I'd take the freedom over the rules any day."

"But you ended up living here. Terra has lots of rules."

"I wanted to try something different. I mean, not to badmouth your home plane or anything, but what's so great about all those rules anyway?"

"Security, stability, safety. You may find it boring and restrictive, and I can sort of see where you might get that idea. But I'd much rather have that level of restriction than have to worry about danger lurking behind every cloud."

"Hey, you're a tough fighter."

"Yeah, but that's because I'm a seraph, a heavenly enforcer. Not all angels are bred for battle. Some learn to sing, rather than fight. It's nice when swinging a sword better than the other guy is not a basic survival skill."

"I…. I guess."

"You seem thoroughly unconvinced."

"It's just, needing to rely on a set of rules to keep you safe, not being able to protect yourself…. Forget the restrictive rules, I can't imagine being less in control."

"Well I guess that just shows how different we are."

"Good heavens, sorry about this," Abaddon rubbed the back of his head, "I didn't mean to get into all of this. We were really having a nice time and-"

"Still are," Sophitia smiled. "It would be boring if we were identical. And besides, I think I might like you."

Before Abaddon had a chance to process her words, Sophitia gave him a kiss. When she pulled away, her smile was bigger than ever. She waved as she turned to leave.

"Well I should probably get going. See you soon, 'kay?"

"Uhhhhhhhhhhhh," Abaddon didn't even try to form words, instead giving in to standing at the street corner and staring into space like an idiot.

Chapter Fifty-One

Moving Forward

"It's been a while since we talked. How's my favorite spawn?"

"Dad, I'm your only spawn."

"That just means you have to be my favorite."

"But I also have to be your least favorite."

"Alright, let's stop before we turn this into a logic loop. How are you doing?"

"Better…. than I was. I have a new job now. Not as good as my old one, but at least it's a step forward."

"And you still have Arthur Pendragon after you."

"You know I'm a tough warrior. And besides, I haven't seen a trace of him since our last encounter."

"You mean when you used your ace in the hole, and promptly got your ace and your hole taken away by divine magic?"

"I'm not saying he's gone for good. Look, just before he vanished I saw it in his eyes. He didn't know about the restricted magic. He was scared, and overwhelmed. If Cassandra, the angel who arrested me, hadn't shown up right when she did, I would have killed him. I sent him running scared."

"You mean you tipped your hand to the enemy, showing him your secret weapon, a secret weapon which you cannot currently use, and then let him get away?"

"Well when you put it like that…."

"You realize he hasn't made a move all this time because he has been making counter measures against the restricted magic."

"How could he counter the powers of the darkest pits?"

"He countered Spellbreaker. You told me his holy left arm was able to deflect it. Despite what I may have said about him, Arthur Pendragon was the greatest fighter in Heaven's army. I wouldn't put anything past him."

"Yeah, well for the time being, there's nothing I can do about it. Like you said, I don't have my ace in the hole. That was the only thing I could beat him with before. Right now all I can do on the Arthur Pendragon front is sit back and let Heaven handle the matter."

"So you're just going let the angels fight your battles for you?"

"Do you think I want to do that?" Abaddon snapped. "I don't have a choice right now. You just reminded me I'm not strong enough to beat him at the moment. I wouldn't know where to find him even if I had the strength to take him on. I don't have other options."

"My favorite spawn disappoints me. I thought I taught you that strength isn't all there is. Arthur Pendragon planned and prepared to fight you. He almost beat you twice because he was ready before hand; he had the initiative. There's no reason you can't do that too."

"And how do I study this enemy? He fell. He lost his old powers and gained new ones. Where do I even begin?"

"You said he can speak the demon tongues and has a right arm forged of obsidian and engraved with your Aunt Lilith's sigils of pain. I've been looking into that here, but you can do the same. If nothing else you can research his new demon half. And if you have to be chaperoned by saved angels, you can at least get some use out of it. They might know of divine magic that could repel Spellbreaker."

"Good point. If nothing else, it beats sitting on my hands waiting for him to make a move."

"Look, I can't imagine how hard it would be to not have your full powers and not be in control. Having to rely on someone else for your own protection…. I'm here for you. You know that right?"

"Of course. Thank you for everything."

"Well, nasty business with Arthur Pendragon aside, you said you have a new job?"

"Yeah. The firing from White Pegasus was official as of a few days ago. But I managed to land a gig with a small-time heroes guild. It's not as good of a job as the one with White Pegasus obviously, but the people are nice…. for the most part."

"Hopefully that will all work out."

"I just keep telling myself that it will only be as bad as I let it be."

"You know I know demons twice your age who could benefit from your wisdom."

"You're gonna make me blush dad…. Well, most demons are physically incapable of blushing, but you know what I mean."

"Hey, I mean it. You are showing incredible strength through adversity."

"I'm from Hell; adversity is just another name for Tuesday."

"But this is a special kind of adversity. You chose to put yourself in a situation you can't just fight your way out of. Most any demon would be way out of their element. I am impressed that you dove into this so readily."

"Well it means a lot to hear you say that. That's my life as it stands. How are things back in the good ol' Ninth Circle?"

"Quiet…. for the moment. Actually, your uncle's been getting really bored. He's threatening to come visit you if something doesn't happen soon."

"Maybe you can put in a word with Surt to have the Eighth Circle invade?"

"Ha! You're that worried about your uncle coming to Terra?"

"If he did, it might fall under my job description to slay him. I'm only half joking here."

"Oh believe me, I know. He has the title of Demon Lord of Destruction for a reason. And during Armageddon I watched him earn that title first hand. Good heavens, he almost scared me at times."

"Now that's something I could never imagine."

"Your dad getting scared?"

"Two hundred and fifty years and I've never seen it once."

"That's just because when I'm scared, I don't show it."

"So, you're saying you hide your fear?"

"No. Hiding fear is just another form of weakness. What I'm saying, is that my response to fear, is not to be afraid, not in the traditional sense anyway."

"That doesn't make much sense."

"Do you remember when your uncle discovered that you had a secret stash of holy water when he found Nidhogg dead in the back yard?"

"How could I forget? You gave me a thousand lashes for that."

"And *THAT* was my reaction to being afraid."

"Afraid? You were more pissed than I had ever seen you before, or since."

"Anger and fear are very good friends. Nidhogg died. Your uncle's pet died, and it could have just as easily been you. How could I not be afraid?"

"But I always thought fear was a weakness?"

"Oh, it is. But thinking that you will never feel fear? That's just foolishness. To feel fear is to be weak, but it is one weakness that is unavoidable. So it must be met head on and overcome. Just like any other challenge it must be conquered."

"And how do you conquer fear?"

"In theory, it's easy. All you need to do is react to that fear in a productive way."

"Giving me a thousand lashes was productive?"

"Did you ever do anything that stupid or dangerous again?"

"No."

"Well there you go. I achieved my goal. And just now I achieved my goal of being a helpful parent. Hopefully anyway."

"You definitely did. Thanks Dad."

"Of course: it's what a parent does. Now I should probably let you go put this help into practice."

"Yeah, thanks again Dad."

"I love you."

"Love you too Dad."

Chapter Fifty-Two
The Old Man and the Tree

Abaddon was out on the streets. There was a rush of activity, sights and sounds and smells of all kinds. Abaddon was barely registering them. He'd almost walked into traffic twice already. He knew he needed to pay more attention, but his mind was not cooperating on that front. He was actually out and about looking for acts of heroism to perform. He had to start trying to get back into the swing of things. For several days he'd been putting it off. He made excuses: he didn't feel quite right, he didn't want to fight without his magic, there were more important things to do. He'd finally convinced himself to go out and look for something, but he was still fighting it.

Abaddon was so lost in thought, that by the time he realized what he was doing, he had left his neighborhood, and ended up in a part of the city he'd never seen before. He would have missed it entirely and kept walking, but he crashed headlong into a massive tree, and that snapped him out of it. Abaddon shook his head and looked around. He found himself at the edge of what appeared to be a large forest. Abaddon hadn't been aware of there being any forests in the middle of New Eden. It seemed odd in the middle of a city. Then Abaddon remembered walking through customs and seeing the treefolk. When he stopped to think about it, it seemed rather silly to think of them living in apartments. He supposed there must be a lot of citizens who needed special living environments like this. Abaddon was suddenly intrigued. He'd never actually seen a forest that wasn't cursed before.

Walking into the woods was a very surreal experience. He was surrounded by green everywhere he looked, greens and rich browns. It was so.... so.... vibrant, like it was full of life. And there was the gentle sound of his boots stepping on twigs. To be surrounded by trees on all sides without the wailing of lost souls to accompany them was just bizarre. Abaddon took his time, walking very slowly, making sure to take everything in. As he was turning his head to gaze at the nature all around him, he walked right into another tree.

Once again, Abaddon picked himself up, this time brushing leaves and twigs off of his jacket. He then heard a noise that sounded like footsteps.

He turned in the direction of the sound. For a second, nothing, then out from one of the thicker sections of the forest he saw, a wizened figure stumble out into the open.

"Feh, to hell with all of you, you bums."

"Sorry," Abaddon quickly made his way over to the man. "Is someone causing you trouble?"

"Oy, fae."

"Excuse me?"

"The fae. You know, faeries? I swear, moving in next to this forest was the biggest mistake I ever made."

"I've never actually met a faerie before."

"And that you never will. Always with the celebrating those fae. With the drinking, and the dancing, and the playing their flutes."

"Well, what's wrong with celebrating?"

"What's wrong? I can't get a moments peace is what's wrong. Every day there's something new in this farkakteh forest that they need to honor with a feast. And don't even get me started on the solstice. Longest night of the year, but do I get any sleep?"

"Well I didn't hear any sounds of partying going on or anything."

"So I exaggerate a little, but not by much. This is one of the rare days you don't hear a ruckus from this place. I figured now was one of the few times I could come here to complain. Enough is enough I say, but will they listen?"

"Sounds like it didn't go too well."

"I tell ya there's no reasoning with these people. You step on the wrong twig and suddenly you're destroying the forest. They practically threw me out of the glade they did. And for what? Trying to get them to keep it down once in a while?"

"They really behave like that? What I'd heard about the fae was that they were noble protectors of their ancient forests."

"Ancient nothin'. They moved in here five years ago, and they act like it's sacred. I tell ya, I never met anyone so high and mighty. They'll piss in your face and act like it's elderberry wine."

"If it's that bad, then you should move?"

"And with what money will I move? I'm not some fancy cleric like my brother Irving. The reason I even took this place was the rent is so cheap. Had I only known why. Oh, but listen to me go on and on. I barely know you five minutes and it's just complain, complain, complain. I must be driving you sick."

"Oh no, I-"

"I'm Sam, Sam Adelman," he held out a hand.

"Abaddon," he shook it.

"What? No last name?"

"Demons don't have last names."

"Right, right, you're a demon, what with the horns and everything."

"You don't seem that surprised to find a demon in a faerie forest."

"Surprised? In this city? When I was ten I saw a nine-foot-tall rock tapdancing on a street corner while a wolf man rode circles around him on a unicycle. I gave them five bucks I was so impressed. But trust me, you want nuthin' to do with these fae. There isn't anything worth seeing in this forest."

"Yeah well, I should probably get going anyway. I need to find a monster to slay, or a mugging to stop, or something. I'd settle for any heroic deed at this point."

"You wanna be a hero? Get these farkakteh fae to shut up for three seconds."

"Well I-" Abaddon paused for a moment. "You know what? That's actually a good idea."

"You're wasting your time," Sam called after Abaddon as he walked towards the glade. "They don't listen to nuthin' from nobody."

It was even more breathtaking inside the glade. And Abaddon could barely believe it, but it seemed more silent too. He had taken one step inside the circle of trees and Sam's voice had instantly cut off. Now he was just left with the dappled sunlight and silent swaying of the leaves. Then seemingly out of nowhere, figures appeared. He hadn't even heard them approach. Abaddon's hand instinctively reached for Spellbreaker, but he stopped himself. The figures were tall, thin, and pale. They had an eerie beauty about them. It was especially eerie given that demons tended to not find things beautiful. One of the figures stepped forward directly in front of Abaddon.

"Outsider, what brings you to the home of the summer court?"

"Summer court? Isn't it still only March?"

"I'll ask you again. What brings you to our home?"

"Well I uh-"

"Speak, outsider."

"I come on behalf of the human Sam Adelman."

"You mean the outsider who barged into our glade?"

"Yes. He said you were constantly disrupting him with your nose and-"

"He complained about our feast of the glade."

"And our feast of the glen," another chimed in.

"And our feast of the grove."

"Yes," the lead fae nodded. "That outsider does not understand our ways."

"Well look, I don't really think that's fair. I mean, he lives right next to your forest and-"

"Where the outsiders live is no concern of ours. Leave now, we do not wish to speak to you further."

"But you haven't even let me say anything yet and-"

"I said leave."

"But if you just-"

"You are not wanted here."

"GOOD HEAVENS JUST SHUP AND LISTEN, YOU ASSHOLE."

Chapter Fifty-Three

A Faerie Fight

"Mind your tongue outsider."

"What is your problem? I'm just trying to make peace between you and Mr. Adelman."

"And why would we want peace with him? He knows nothing of us and our ways, yet he comes here to tell us how to behave in *OUR* forest."

"He's your neighbor! He was just asking you to keep it down once in a while."

"We do not care for neighbors."

"Well you have one. You need to care."

"We have secluded ourselves from your world. This glade blocks out all outside contact. We are completely removed from you outsiders."

"No, you are not. You may not be able to hear him, but he hears you. Your constant feasting and celebrating is bothering him."

"And what concern of yours is this?"

"I'm a hero; helping people is what I do."

"The fae do not recognize your institutions. You may leave now."

"Look, I'm just trying to do my job and help a person in need."

"We have no need of you, and our patience runs thin. Leave now."

"Good heavens this is not about you! Is it really so much to ask that you pay a little respect to those around you?"

"You simply do not understand. You are like the other outsider. Now if I must tell you to leave again, we will treat you as a threat to our forest."

"Oh, so now you're going to attack me because I tried to talk to you?"

"Enough, the court of summer recognizes the outsider as a threat."

All around Abaddon, the tall pale figures of the fae drew blades and bows. Abaddon was already angry enough that he didn't even try to hold himself back. Spellbreaker was drawn and he was charging the leader of the fae before he even fully realized what he was doing. An arrow caught him in the left shoulder as he brought Spellbreaker down on his foe. The lead fae raised their sword to block. The blade shattered, and Spellbreaker continued undaunted, striking the fae on the crown of the head. Abaddon knew the blow was not fatal; he had enough self-control to refrain from killing. He dodged another two arrows as he launched himself at the next enemy.

Within moments Abaddaon had rampaged through most of their number. He was sporting several slashes on his back and two more arrows sticking out of him, but there were just three more fae left. He was already in the process of taking down the next one when the other two started to chant. Their tone was at once a deep sound of the earth, and a gentle lilt, like wind through the leaves. Massive roots rose out of the ground, trapping Abaddon in a wooden cage. They tightened, wrapping around Abaddon's arms and legs, locking him in place. He struggled, but to no avail.

The fae approached him, "Now you must pay for your crimes."

"That's my line," a great pillar of light crashed down in between Abaddon and the advancing fae, and Sophitia stepped out of it.

"This matter does not concern you angel."

"Actually it does. I am in charge of this one. I am his guardian angel."

"Then you are responsible for what he has done."

"What he has done? Thanks to that glowing mark on his arm, I can watch his every move. I saw everything. What he did was defend himself, maybe a little overzealously but-"

"He has proven himself a threat to our forest."

"How?"

"He attacked the leader of the summer court."

"After you all drew weapons on him. We call that self-defense."

"We have been wronged. If you are truly in charge of this one, then it falls to you to pay for what was done to us."

"Sorry, but in New Eden, the aggressor does not get to press charges against the aggressee."

"The summer court does not obey the laws of New Eden."

"You live in New Eden, so yes, you do. Despite what you might think, this forest is not a sovereign nation that lets you do whatever you want. It is part of New Eden and obeys its laws. Now I am feeling nice, so I will take Abaddon and leave, *WITHOUT* pressing charges against you. So you can either undo the spell that is holding him, or I can destroy those roots with holy magic."

"If you would stand with the outsider then you must-"

Sophitia did not let the fae finish. They were cut off by twin beams of holy light that shot from her hands, striking both fae in the chest. She then turned her attention to Abaddon, firing more beams at the thick roots surrounding him.

"Hey, watch it!" Abbadon jumped free as soon as he was able.

"I believe the appropriate phrase is thank you."

"Yeah thanks, but sorry if beams of holy light right next to my skin make me a bit nervous. So what, do you just watch me all the time? I honestly wasn't expecting you to come to my rescue."

"I have a passive awareness of you all the time. I have to focus in order to watch you directly. I decided to 'tune in' as it were, when I noticed you going into an area soaked in powerful magic."

"Well you got to see me fail spectacularly at my first attempt to get back in the saddle."

"Fail spectacularly? Don't you think you're being a bit hard on yourself? I mean, you complain about angels being self-righteous, but these guys. I wonder if all fae act like they can just do whatever they want, or if it is just this summer court?"

"You're guess is as good as mine; today is the first I've seen one. I guess neither one of us left a very good impression."

"Nonsense, you left a very nice impression on that one's forehead."

"I'm being serious."

"And so was I. You were in the right, they were in the wrong. You came in here to try and make peace between them and the old man. They wouldn't even so much as hear you out, and then proceeded to attack you once they deemed the 'conversation' had gone on too long. You have grounds for assault charges, for crying out loud."

"I don't care about that. I just- oh, never mind."

"What? Why are these pricks bothering you? I mean, I wouldn't think you'd feel bad about smacking them around, especially when they asked for it like that."

"No, this sounds dumb."

"Come on, tell me."

"I've been in a slump the past several days, and couldn't motivate myself to try and do heroic deeds. When I talked to Mr. Adelman, it was different; I was ready to do this one. I think I was finally motivated because this was a chance to try something new, to try solving a problem without resorting to violence. Well, so much for thinking I'm capable of that."

"Aw hell no!" Sophitia pointed her finger aggressively at Abaddon.

"Did you just say-"

"Not the point. Don't you dare try and play the sad mopey 'I'm just a monster' card. I am not letting you do that to yourself. Get that crap out of your head right now. I don't even know where to begin trying to tell you all the things wrong with that line of thinking. Now come on," Sophitia grabbed his arm.

"Wait-wha- where are we going."

"Lunch, I'm buying, you're feeling better."

Chapter Fifty-Four

Third Date's the Charm

This was the first time that Abaddon had tried this pie thing. He didn't quite know what to make of it. Before he could figure it out, he'd already made his way through four slices. He supposed that meant he liked it. Then again it could just be how easily it went down. He could practically inhale it. He'd learned to eat more slowly as a rule when he was in public. The people of New Eden seemed to think it bad manners to eat really fast. But Sophitia was laughing.

"So you like pie then?"

"I guess so."

"You guess so?"

"I can't really tell. I'm eating a lot of it, but I can't quite figure it out. Maybe it's the harder crust combined with the weird center, I don't really know."

"Well, you feel better at any rate?"

"Yeah, thanks. Sorry you saw me acting all mopey."

"What are you apologizing for? You were depressed; that's not a bad thing. I mean, okay, it is, but you shouldn't feel *GUILTY* about it. I gotta imagine it's hard to get back into the swing of things. The transition can't be easy. And while it was definitely *NOT* your fault, the fact that your first attempt at a heroic deed didn't go so well couldn't help. It's understandable."

"Well thanks, for that, and all of this."

"No problem."

"So… is this a date?"

"I suppose it is."

"Oh…. well I was kind of hoping it wasn't."

"And what's that mean?" it was hard to tell if Sophitia was actually offended, or just pretending.

"Well the last two times we went out on a date, you abandoned me unexpectedly."

"Oh right, sorry about that. I was just kinda messing with you."

"Really?"

"The way you got all flustered the first time, it was kind of cute."

"You think I'm cute?" Abaddon would have probably fallen backwards if the booth they were in had allowed it.

"That's exactly what I'm talking about," Sophitia tried to speak through her chuckling. "You're acting like no one's ever called you cute before."

"Well yeah, no one has."

"Wait, really?" Sophitia's laughing instantly stopped.

"Of course. Demon's aren't cute."

"Don't talk like that. Just because a lot of people think of you as monsters-"

"No, that's not what I mean. We don't think of each other in that way. A demon can be hot, sure, but not cute."

"And why can't a demon be cute?"

"Being cute is a defense mechanism developed by baby animals in order to get their parents to protect them because they are too weak to do it themselves."

"So, what, are you saying that being cute is associated with being weak?"

"Exactly."

"Wow, I guess male bravado transcends all species."

"This has nothing to do with that. In nature, cuteness is literally associated with weakness."

"Alright, maybe in nature, but we're not in nature. Here it's okay to be cute."

"I never said it wasn't okay, it's just not a demon thing."

"Because it makes you seem weak?"

"Yes."

"And you're trying to tell me that it's not a bravado thing?"

"No, it isn't. Look, demons prize strength, and demons associate being cute with being weak, so calling someone cute is basically the same as calling them weak, as far as demons are concerned. So to a demon, being cute is a negative thing, not a positive thing. It would be like…. hm, like if I tried to compliment you by calling you smelly."

"Well being called smelly isn't a compliment, who wants to be smelly?"

"Exactly. That's how demons feel about being cute."

"Huh, you make an interesting point. Well, you know that's not how I meant it, right?"

"Yeah, that was kind of the reason for the whole flustered thing I suppose."

Sophitia laughed again, "Well don't stop, please. I like it when you're cute, by my definition anyway."

"Oh, well uh, thanks, I guess…."

"Wow, sorry, I just can't get over this."

"What?"

"I just thought you would have had some experience with romance by now. You're two and a half centuries old, aren't you?"

"I never really… had a relationship before."

"Really? What were you doing for two hundred and fifty years that kept you so busy?"

"It's not so much what I was doing but… look, I just wasn't really in a set up that was too conducive to having a partner."

"I mean, demons *DO* that kind of stuff, right?"

"Yeah, I suppose, in a manner of speaking. Just, you know, not me, really…."

"Wow, that's pretty sad, in both senses of the word."

"Look, it just never really happened okay?" Abaddon was forcing himself not to get defensive.

"It's fine. If you don't wanna talk about it that's okay. I didn't mean to pry or anything."

"It's alright. I wouldn't have expected you to be experienced in dating though."

"Oh for the love of- Where do people get the idea that Heaven is against dating and sex? No, I know exactly where they got the idea from: damn Puritans, ruining it for everyone. I mean seriously, who outlaws dancing?"

"So wait, angels are totally cool with sex?"

"Yes, why wouldn't we be?"

"Sorry, I guess I just kind of pictured you all as wet blankets."

"Freaking Puritans! And they were just one denomination of one faith of one species, and they have everyone thinking that Heaven is nothing but piety and rules. Well we're not, okay?"

"Okay, okay, again, sorry."

"Me too. Didn't mean to blow up like that. I just get tired of all of this."

"Hey, at least you get the good stereotypes. People around here show you deference, they don't assume you want to kill them."

"Alright, point. But even good stereotypes can be bad."

"Oh no," Abaddon laughed, "Looks like we're getting into another sociology and philosophy discussion."

"The horror."

Chapter Fifty-Five

The Devil's in the Details

"Alright," Sophitia asked Abaddon, "name your favorite thing to do that is not a 'demon' thing."

"Let's see, hmm, I think I'd have to say, reading, definitely reading."

"Yeah, that's not very demon-like. What's your favorite book?"

"Hmm, that's a really tough one. I'm not trying to avoid the question, but I really can't think of a favorite."

"Okay, favorite subject then."

"Definitely A.D. humanity."

"That's still a fairly large subject area."

"I had a lot of time to read. How about you?"

"I don't read that much. I really like my Tolkien book, but that's probably more because it's a rare collector's item."

"So, you like to collect things?"

"Oh yeah, it's my favorite hobby.

"I never really understood it myself. What's the point of having things just so that you can say you have them?"

"That's a very shallow interpretation of the hobby," Sophitia's tone implied she'd put her hands on her hips if she weren't sitting down. Then she calmed herself. "Look, think of it like this: treasure hunting has been a thing for centuries, right? Millenia actually, but that's not the point. People from all different planes of existence have always sought after rare treasures. Okay, maybe a few wanted them so that they could feel important and show them off, but a true treasure hunter isn't trying to impress people. A true treasure hunter enjoys the hunt as much or more than the prize. They know that they earned the right to experience something that few others can. That book of mine; there are only a few in all the planes of existence. To think that I was able to acquire something so rare, so special, I feel truly blessed."

Abaddon gave her a look. "Says the angel."

"You know what I mean. Okay, how about this, don't you feel pride when you defeat a particularly powerful opponent?"

"Of course. My victory is a testament to my abilities in battle."

"And do you need to brag to other people about that victory in order to feel proud of your accomplishments?"

"No. I proved to myself that I am a strong warrior, I don't need the validation of others."

"Well in its way, finding and acquiring a rare treasure is just as impressive an accomplishment and says just as much about the abilities of the treasure hunter as the victory says about the warrior. I mean, people can display impressive feats of ability and skill that don't involve injuring someone else."

"Alright, fair point. But you really think of yourself as a treasure hunter?"

"Do you know what it took me to finally get that copy of *The Hobbit*? I had to visit four different planes of existence tracking down that seller. There was no record anywhere of who they were. All I had to go on was vague rumors here and there. I didn't even know if they were an elf or a human or what. Took me almost a whole year."

"Well that is pretty impressive. But what kind of book seller makes it so hard to find them? That sounds like a very bad business plan."

"He turned out to be a very old demon, I think a bit touched in the head. He told me he'd been waiting for someone he could pass the book down to. He'd let just enough rumor out to bait the hook as it were. According to him, the only one who would be worthy of inheriting the book was someone willing to track him down and find it."

"And what did you give him in return for the book?" Abaddon suddenly sounded worried.

"Nothing, just my word that I wouldn't let anyone else have the book unless they were truly worthy."

"How exactly did you word that?"

"What?"

"The deal, how was it worded."

"I don't know; does it matter?"

"You don't get it, do you?"

"What are you talking about?"

"You made a demonic bargain for that book. Whoever the demon who gave it to you was, he went through the trouble of making sure no one could get their hands on it. Were his exact words, "won't let anyone else have the book'?"

"I think so. Would it be important?"

"Come on, you should know exact wording matters more than anything when it comes to a demonic bargain."

"Alright, so what's so special about the deal I made?"

"You can't let anyone have the book who isn't truly worthy. Not give, but let. You are bound by the strongest magic in existence so that you can never do anything that would allow that book to go to an unworthy person. I can't even begin to think of what the implications of that deal might be."

"So? I just won't let anyone else have it. I wasn't planning on selling it anyway."

"It's not that simple. A deal worded that vaguely could mean any number of things. It might be the case that by ever being in a position where someone could take the book, you would be violating the terms of the deal. Who knows?"

"Well now that you mention it, I always carry the book on me, and never questioned why until now."

"There you go, that's the power of a demonic bargain."

"So, does that mean that every demon possesses this bargaining power for lack of a better term?"

"If a demon makes a bargain with any other creature, it is unbreakable, but both sides have to recognize it as a bargain. Whether or not you intend to keep your end is irrelevant, but you have to understand that a deal is being made. So, for example, when young kids promise to be best friends forever, they are not actually bound to it, but if an adult demon were to make a similar deal with someone who recognized it as such, then it would be binding. It also has to be an actual deal. That means both sides have to give or promise something, and both sides must recognize it as an even trade and then agree to make it."

"And where do demons get this power from? I mean, I'd always known about Faustian bargains and whatnot, but I just assumed that demons used their superior abilities to force mortals to follow through on the deals. I wasn't aware of any specific magic in the deal itself."

"No idea actually."

"Really? And here you are the big bad bookworm, and you don't even know that fact about your own kind?"

"No one does. There are some secrets lost to the ages. The restricted magics for example are all either forgotten or incredibly well guarded. And the demonic bargain is the most powerful known magic in all existence."

"And here I thought it was rather limited in use. I mean the other person has to accept the deal after all."

"When I say most powerful, I don't mean the best to have. I mean that if used, it trumps anything else. Nothing can stop a demonic bargain."

"Well I guess that I'll just chalk that up to one more thing that makes you tall, dark, and mysterious," Sophitia smiled as Abaddon sputtered.

Chapter Fifty-Six
Making it Official

"Wait, are you serious?" Sophitia laughed.

"This-this isn't funny."

"You'd be bright red if you could blush."

"Plenty of demons are bright red."

"You know what I mean. It's like you've never been complimented before. Wait, you *HAVE* been complimented before…. right?"

"Hey, ouch. I'm not that pathetic."

"I didn't mean it like that. It's just, with some of the stuff you've said…"

"I'm a mighty demon warrior, I wield the legendary war hammer Spellbreaker. It's not like I have no self-confidence or anything. You're acting like no one has ever been nice to me."

"I'm sorry. I guess I still think of Hell as nothing but a harsh, violent place where everyone hates each other. When I say it out loud, I sound like a bigot. I just wouldn't dismiss the idea that no one would have ever complimented you. I swear I didn't mean anything personal."

"Well, okay then. There's still a lot we don't know about each other, and we're both going to keep messing up like this. And, I mean, I can't get mad at you every time you say something I don't like, not if I want to keep being your friend at any rate."

"I was kinda hoping we could be more than friends," Sophitia broke out into laughter again as Abaddon nearly spit out his food. "You can't be serious. I mean, come on, we've already been on two dates."

"Yeah, but I didn't think that meant-"

"We were dating? It's not that complicated. And it shouldn't be spit-take levels of surprising."

"Hey, dating's a relatively new concept."

"So, you've never been on a date before?"

"No, dating isn't a thing in the demon world."

"Well then what do you do when you like someone?"

"Screw 'em."

"You sound like a little kid pulling a girl's pigtails."

"No, I mean literally screw them. There aren't any candlelight dinners or romantic evenings out, you just cut to the chase."

"Well there's more to a relationship than just sex," Sophitia sounded mildly offended.

"But sex is the most important part of a relationship."

"That's not true. The feelings you have for the other person go way deeper than mere physical pleasure."

"But it ain't a relationship without sex or sexual interest at the least."

"What? That cheapens the whole thing."

"Really? Tell me, what sorts of things do you do with a boyfriend or girlfriend. I mean in general, not you specifically."

"You go to shows, take long walks, have dinners, just the two of you. Sometimes you stay up all night just talking, and you're not even tired. You get each other thoughtful gifts. Stuff like that."

"Now I'm not that familiar with this sort of thing, but what about friends?"

"What do you mean?"

"Well, I don't really know, but if I really liked someone, you know, as a friend, I would want to let them know. I'd like to spend time with them, see shows. I'd probably buy them gifts, you know, if it wasn't weird or something...." Abaddon trailed off, suddenly feeling very awkward.

"Wow...." Sophitia was silent for almost a minute.

"What?" Abaddon was really feeling embarrassed, and painfully aware that he was showing it.

"That was simultaneously the sweetest, and saddest thing I've ever heard."

"What do you mean, sad? What was sad about that? Am I a loser for wanting to buy friends gifts or something?"

"Wha-no, no, that's not what I meant at all! No, I-you- you've never really had friends... have you?"

"Hey! I've had... two... since I came to New Eden."

"Well, you were right."

"About what?"

"Good friends do do things like see shows and get each other gifts," Abaddon could tell Sophitia was intentionally avoiding broaching the subject any further, and he was eternally grateful for it.

"Well, uh, yeah, that was my point," Abaddon was starting to feel the awkwardness ebb. "See, everything that couples do, friends do, you know, except for each other. If they don't have any form of sexual interest in each other, then it's just a friendship."

"Well that's just- I mean you're really over simplifying-"

"Then tell me what else couples do besides have sex that really good friends wouldn't do."

"Well they.... uh..... Aha! They get married," Sophitia pointed triumphantly.

"Some do, definitely not all do. And so what, are you not in a relationship until you're married? That isn't a requirement for being in a relationship."

"Okay, it's not a *REQUIREMENT* or anything."

"So once again we're back down to sex being the determining factor for whether it is a relationship or a really close friendship. Sex is what defines a relationship, literally."

"Well I suppose *TECHNICALLY.*"

"Why do you have such a problem with this?"

"I just think making it all about sex belittles a true relationship with someone you love."

"Why in Heaven's name would a relationship be all about sex? Sex barely means anything as far as a relationship goes."

"But you just said-"

"It ain't a relationship without sex being involved somehow, but it's not like people who aren't in a relationship don't have sex all the time. I know at one point the A.D. humans were really uptight about sex, but most species don't care."

"You know I have no problems with sex. I mean, you heard my Puritan rant. But in Heaven, casual sex is still not super common."

"Happens all the time down in Hell. Oh, and then of course there are the harems."

"You have harems?!" Sophitia glanced around awkwardly as people stared.

"The ruling demons tend to, or some of the other really powerful ones, yeah. And before you get all sociological on me, there are just as many she-demons with harems, probably more actually."

"Well, I'm a bit more partial to the Terra approach. And I believe the saying is 'when in New Eden' or something like that. So how about just being boyfriend and girlfriend for a while. Forget all the harems and stuff for now."

"Yeah, I'd like that," damn, Abaddon was right back to being awkward again. "But so what should we do about-"

"Eh, we'll have sex under that bridge when we come to it," That got a laugh out of Abaddon. "For now, how about this?" Sophitia leaned over the table and kissed him.

Chapter Fifty-Seven

Fallen Angel

"I still can't believe this," Abaddon felt as though he was in a daze as he walked down the street. "I mean, this is real, right?"

"Yes, for the hundredth time, we are boyfriend and girlfriend now. It was our third date, and we decided to make it official. What's so hard to get about this?"

"I-I just never would have expected it, that's all. I'd never thought about being involved with anyone before. And it never would have even occurred to me that I might be with an angel."

"Okay," Sophitia conceded, "That part is pretty odd, but hey, we both like each other, so what does it matter?"

"Your sister, and my father," Abaddon voice sunk as he said the word father.

"Seriously," Sophitia stopped in her tracks, Abaddon almost crashed into her, "you've got to stop thinking about stuff like that. I mean, who cares if they wouldn't approve. It's not like you're the first person to disobey their father. Geez, I wouldn't have thought a 'proud demon warrior' like you would be so self-conscious of what other people think about you."

"I'm not! Well not usually. What I mean is, my dad's…. well, he's different."

"Come on, I'm sure you've made your dad angry before. He can't be that scary, can he?"

"Yes and no respectively," Abaddon gave the faintest hint of a shudder.

"Ohhhhh?" Sophitia's voice changed from mild exasperation to wicked joy. "I sense a story. Tell, tell."

"It was just stupid teenage rebellion."

"Come on, I have to hear it now."

"Alright. My dad found my hidden stash of holy water."

"No way!" Abaddon couldn't tell if the scandalous tone was real or faked. "Holy water is deadly to demons. What were you doing with it?"

"I wasn't going to use it to kill anyone, if that's what you're thinking. If I wanted to do that, I'd just use Spellbreaker. No, spawns would prove how tough they were by seeing who could drink the most holy water. It was a dumb immature game. I hadn't actually drunk any of it. But Nid- my uncle's pet dragon got into it and died."

"You had enough holy water to kill a devil dragon? And you were going to drink the stuff?!"

"Well I am the son of.... an exceptionally strong demon. I thought I could handle it. Anyway, my dad found out and flipped his cursed shit. I got a thousand lashes for that one. That put an end to my rebellious phase right quick."

"Wait," Sophitia sounded even more concerned. "A thousand lashes? You mean with a whip?"

"Yeah?"

"That's crazy. That's- that's abuse is what that is."

"No, that's punishment. Parents punish their kids when they disobey certain rules. I thought that was normal."

"A thousand lashes with a whip isn't normal. Do you know what he could have done to you?"

"It hurt like heaven, sure, but it wouldn't have killed me. Besides, physical punishment is common in Hell. We don't have much in the form of rules or laws, so things like timeouts or bedtimes don't really exist. If you wanted to ground your spawn, you would need to chain them up or forcibly bind them some other way. So normally we just beat them until they get the lesson. I suppose that might have been a bit excessive but-"

"A bit? Are you seriously-" Sophitia stopped herself. "Look, I'm sorry this sort of thing keeps coming up, but there's just a lot to get used to. I mean, talk about cultural differences."

"Yeah, but I mean my dad was just worried about me."

"He was worried?" Sophitia looked completely taken aback.

"You said it yourself, that holy water could have killed me. He wanted to make sure I never did anything that stupid again."

"So he whipped you to within an inch of your life?"

"Not quite that bad but, but yeah, basically."

"That's what passes for worried in Hell, huh? I just thought your dad would love you enough to-" Sophitia stopped as soon as realized what she had said.

For several seconds, both just stood there. The dark air was still. The only motion, the blinking of a street light. The awkward silence was broken by a strange sound. Both turned, equally eager to have a distraction. They were just in time to see a figure crash into the ground in front of them. He was an angel, dressed in white armor like Cassandra had been, however he only had one wing.

"Ralis!" Sophitia rushed over to the angel and grabbed him in her arms.

"S-Sophitia, is that you?"

"Are you alright? What the hell happened to you?"

"N-no time, we have to get somewhere safe."

"You have to tell me-"

"THERE'S NO TIME."

"Alright, we can go to my apartment. It's not far from here," Sophitia turned to Abaddon. "Help me with him."

Abaddon would have marveled at the size of Sophitia's "apartment" if he hadn't been too busy helping a near unconscious angel onto her couch. It looked more like a townhouse if anything. Apparently being a Seraph paid well. Abaddon's thoughts quickly turned back to the matter at hand as Sophitia spoke.

"Alright Ralis, now can you tell us what in the hell is going on?"

Ralis didn't look nearly as panicked as he had on the street. And on further inspection, Abaddon noticed that aside from his crash into the sidewalk, he seemed to have no visible injuries. So how come he couldn't muster enough divine energy to manifest his wings? Something really serious must have happened; he was breathing heavier than Abaddon had after his first sparring session with Moloch.

"So that's the demon," Ralis said after a minute, turning to look at Abaddon, "the one Arthur Pendragon is after?"

"That's me alright."

"How do you know about that, Ralis?"

"We tracked him down. I was one of six seraphs who were sent to eliminate Arthur Pendragon. We were given the use of level one divine punishment magic. We came at him all at once. We couldn't beat him. Only I survived-"

"Bullshit!" Abaddon didn't care that he was shouting. "I got a firsthand dose of that stuff. There is no way that six of you using that couldn't bring down Arthur Pendragon."

"You don't understand," Ralis coughed. "It didn't work on him. He absorbed it."

"What?!" Both Abaddon and Sophitia cried in unison.

"Somehow Arthur Pendragon can absorb divine energy. I barely retained enough to get to where you guys found me."

"Well that would explain what happened when I fought him," Abaddon had calmed down considerably. "His left arm was covered in divine seals. He had enough holy power there to repel Spellbreaker."

"He must have taken that from the templars who were chasing him before we were assigned to the case."

"I still can't believe this," Sophitia had now sat down in a chair, her face in her hands. "It shouldn't be possible to steal someone's divine energy."

"He can also speak the tongues of the abyss, and has a demonic right arm," Abaddon interjected. "I don't think anything is impossible anymore."

"But then what do we do?" Sophitia slowly stood. "How do we fight him?"

"We can't," Ralis's voice had lost all hope.

"No," Abaddon's entire will was forcing his body not to shake as his right hand clenched Spellbreaker with all the force he could muster, "*YOU* can't."

Chapter Fifty-Eight

A Plan

"Well you can't beat him either," Sophitia was half exasperated, half desperate.

"I could without this magic seal on my arm."

"You know you can't do that. We can't let you use forbidden magic, even in this situation."

"I could just break the seal with Spellbreaker you know."

"Then you would have to fight me as well as Arthur Pendragon."

"Yeah, I figured you say that. Don't worry; I have no intention of doing that. Believe me, I want to crush him myself, but I know that's not an option."

"Then what do we do?" Ralis said from the couch. "We need to stop him, but-"

"No," Abaddon cut in, "We aren't the ones who need to do it."

"Well, if he can steal divine energy, then no one from Heaven can face him. Wait!" Abaddon got the distinct impression Ralis would have jumped up if he could. "You're a hero, right? From the White Pegasus Guild? We could get them to-"

"I don't work there anymore. I got fired because of this whole incident," Abaddon raised his right hand.

"But we could still make a request to them, or one of the other big heroes guilds. Surely they would be able to-"

"We can't do that either," this time it was Sophitia who interjected. "We can't let anyone find out about this. What would happen if people knew that Arthur Pendragon, *THE* Arthur Pendragon had turned into a half-demon necromancer who is out to murder a citizen of New Eden. Everyone thinks he died heroically during Armageddon. Hell, I did too until recently. Besides, Wisdom said that Arthur Pendragon has very sensitive information about Heaven that cannot get out under any circumstances. So using heroes guilds is not an option."

"Well we've exhausted all the options we don't have," Ralis snapped. "How about the ones we *DO* have hmm? Would someone care to tell me those? Because I'm not seeing anything, and we can't let him run around with all that power. I mean, who knows what he could do to New Eden, not to mention anywhere else he felt like, with the power of six seraphs trapped in his damned left arm."

"Wait," Abaddon looked quizzical, "If it has the power of six seraphs in it then how could it be damned?"

"NOT WHAT I MEANT," Ralis started coughing again at that outburst.

"Calm down," Sophitia put an arm on Ralis' shoulder. "We'll think of something."

"We don't need to," Abaddon let out a long sigh. "I know exactly what we need to do."

"Well please enlighten us foolish angels," Ralis had gone from panicked to snippy. Sophitia slapped him on the shoulder. "Ouch. I mean, what's the plan?"

"No one with divine powers can stop him, they'll only make him stronger, and we can't rely on heroes guilds to help. Obviously we need a demon to take him out."

"Okay," Sophitia was clearly thinking this over. "Demonic power *IS* what we need to stop him, but that still doesn't work. First we'd need to get a demon strong enough to stand a chance against him. *THEN* we'd need to get them to agree help. And that still doesn't solve the problem of not letting secret information about Heaven get leaked."

"Yeah," Ralis sounded thoroughly unconvinced. "So all we need is to convince a really powerful demon, and I mean *REALLY* powerful, to kill Arthur Pendragon for us, *AND* he needs to be nice enough to not spill any heavenly secrets he might learn. Who can we get to do that?"

"Lucifer," Abaddon didn't sound any more thrilled as he explained.

"Lucifer? The ruler of the Ninth Circle of Hell? He's just gonna do a favor for two angels and a random demon?"

"He's the one who's responsible for this whole mess."

"Ah so he's just going to go out of his way to do us a solid because it's his fault this happened? That seems believable."

Sophitia shot Ralis a look, "I may not agree with his underlying sentiment, but Ralis makes a good point. I mean, why would Lucifer do us any favors?"

"Because... I'm his one and only son?" Abaddon shrugged awkwardly.

"WHAT?!" Both cried in unison.

"Yeah... so, uh, I'm the spawn of Lucifer, heir to the Ninth Circle of Hell. Sophitia.... I may have lied to you a bit when I told you about my dad."

"A *BIT?*" Abaddon had to actually dodge some spit as she spoke. "You told me he was a general in Lucifer's army."

"Well he *WAS*..."

"Damnit Abaddon- Wait. He's your uncle. By the divine entities your uncle is the Demon Lord of Destruction and you're named after him."

"Yeah....." Abaddon rubbed the back of his head.

"Hang on, when you were a teenager you accidentally killed Nidhogg with some holy water?"

"Hey! I don't really see how that is relevant."

"I can't- I mean you- I mean you're-"

"The spawn of Lucifer, yes. But that's not important right now. I mean, it's the most important thing right now, but stop freaking out about it. Hey Ralis," Abaddon turned to Ralis, but the angel was just lying there, a look of frozen fear on his face. "Angels bless it, not you too. Look, I'm not suddenly going to try and devour your souls or anything. Seriously, this is why I don't tell people about my dad. Can we just focus on the fact that Arthur Pendragon is a crazed half demon and trying to kill me with angel powers? Please?"

"You're right," Sophitia forcibly calmed herself down. "It's rather shocking to say the least, but yes, we need to focus. So, you're saying you can get your dad to kill Arthur Pendragon for us?"

"He *IS* responsible for all of this, so he should be willing to help," Abaddon clenched his fists. Yes he was running to his dad for help, but they didn't have a choice.

"What's he got to do with all this?" Ralis could barely get the words out.

"After Heaven agreed to my dad's idea of peace-"

"*HIS* Idea?!" Ralis cut in in an outraged tone.

"Yes, yes, I'm sure Heaven taught you that you guys were the ones who proposed peace. That's not the point. Anyway, Heaven agreed to peace, but Arthur Pendragon didn't. He thought that all the demons had to be wiped out, and would not stand for Lucifer to live. He led a group of paladins into Hell to storm Pandemonium and confront Dad. But he spared Arthur Pendragon, so now the greatest champion of Heaven is after me."

"That doesn't sound like something a demon would do," Ralis was back into his snippy mode.

"Well *TECHNICALLY* my dad used his silver words to convince Arthur Pendragon that his fellow paladins had been corrupted, thus getting Arthur to kill them all himself. This caused him to fall, losing all of his paladin powers. And after my dad broke Heaven's greatest champion, he left him for dead in the Ninth Circle of Hell so that any old demon who had half a mind to could rip him apart as they pleased."

"Oh…."

"We're getting off track again," Sophitia was making a noticeable effort to hide the horror from her face. Ralis was making no such effort. "Point is, you can send your dad and get him to deal with Arthur Pendragon for us."

"I should be able to. But you guys need to do your part too."

"What do you mean?"

"You have to convince Heaven to go along with this plan. They are the ones going to great lengths to keep this matter internal. If my dad just steps in and kills Arthur Pendragon without us getting the okay from your bosses, then forget my using restricted magic, we might be looking at Armageddon Two here."

"Okay, fair point. I will take Ralis back to Heaven at once, he needs to get healed anyway, while you talk to your dad."

Sophitia stood up. She grabbed Ralis, propping him up against her shoulder so that he could stand. She then waved her hand, and a glowing golden pillar of light appeared around them.

"Give me a sending as soon as you get an update," She said as she ascended.

"Sure, you too."

Chapter Fifty-Nine

Asking Dad for Help

Abaddon stared into the black abyss that was the portal into Hell. He summoned all of the dark powers he could muster and steeled himself for the conversation he was about to have. He then called out in the dark language of demons, and before him was the great visage of his father, sitting atop his throne of bones.

"Hey Dad."

"Hey kiddo, I was meaning to get in touch with you. It's been a while since we last talked."

"Did you just call me kiddo?"

"That's a way people address their kids on Terra right?"

"Never call me that again Dad."

"Alright, alright, I was just trying to be-"

"If you say 'hip' then I will punch you through the sending spell."

"I was going to say cool, but whatever. You look worried. Is something wrong?"

"I-I well- well I need to ask you for something."

"Of course, my spawn. You know I will help you with whatever you need."

"ArthurPendragongotevenstrongerandIcan'tbeathimwithoutyourhelpsoInee dyoutokillhimforus!"

"Whoa, whoa, slow down. Seriously, what in Heaven's name's gotten into you?"

Abaddon let out a tremendous sigh that felt like it would shake the room, "Sorry dad, I just had to force myself to say that or I was never going to. So I was with my guardian angel-"

"What were you doing with her? Are you in trouble again?"

"No Dad, it's- it's not important right now. Anyway, we ran into another angel she knew. Turns out he had had his divine energy drained from him. He and five other seraphs had found Arthur Pendragon and were sent to kill him. Arthur Pendragon stole all of their divine energy. That is a thing he can do apparently. So now he is even stronger. And to make matters worse it means-"

"No one from Heaven can fight him. They will just get their energy drained."

"Yeah, and I can't do it because my magic is still sealed away. And even if it weren't, Heaven would come down on my ass the moment I undid the seal, Pendragon or no Pendragon. So what I have to ask you is- well I need you to…"

"Kill Arthur Pendragon for you?"

"Yeah," Abaddon slumped as he said the word.

"Let me guess, you didn't want to ask my help because you feel ashamed at not being able to take him on yourself?"

"I'm a proud demon warrior. I was trained by Moloch. I'm your spawn for crying out loud!"

"None of that makes you invincible. You are strong, yes. In fact, you are one of the strongest demons alive, but there will always be someone stronger than you. Besides, you said yourself that you can't fight him because your powers are being sealed. You are outmatched, so you are turning to your dad for help, that doesn't make you any less of a demon."

"But I'm admitting my weakness."

"No, no you are not. Sometimes we need the help of others. It is just foolish to think you will always be able to handle everything yourself. And don't forget, you fought Arthur Pendragon twice, and you would have killed him the second time had a saved angel not gotten in your way. I'm proud of you."

"Thanks Dad. So that means you'll fight Arthur Pendragon for us?"

"No."

"What?! But you just said-"

"I have something really important I need to take care of. I can't do it right now."

"More important than stopping the crazy ex-paladin trying to murder your own spawn?"

"Yes actually. Besides, I have a better idea for you anyway," Lucifer turned his head to the side of the portal and called out, "Hey!"

"What?" a voice called back from off portal.

"It's your nephew."

"What?"

"Your nephew. He's sending us. He wants to talk to you."

Abaddon could hear a deep thundering and could practically feel the ground shuddering through the portal. Then he saw the great shadow descend upon his vision. Moments later, a massive torso clad in obsidian armor was before him.

"Junior, is that you?"

"Sit down you saved idiot," Lucifer chastised the figure, "Your head's not in view."

"I'm getting to that," the figured waved a pair of great red hands at Lucifer. "I know how a sending spell works you deviled egghead."

There was another deep rumbling, followed by a crash, as the demon knelt, his big crimson grin and horns appearing in the portal.

"Junior! How in Heaven's name are you? I haven't talked to you since you left for Terra. You'll send your dad, but not me, your dear uncle?"

"Sorry, I've just been really busy."

"Well you've got to tell me everything that's happened. I heard about how some saved angel put you on a chain for breaking your seal. Do you want I should destroy them for you?"

"No just- just please no. And I'm sorry for not sending you sooner, but there's no time for that now," Abaddon quickly filled his uncle in on what was going on.

"HA!" his uncle boomed. "So not only is Arthur Pendragon still alive, but he's now part demon? And your dad is too scared to face him?" his uncle clapped Lucifer on the shoulder with a massive hand, and the heavily armored ruler of the Ninth Circle almost fell out of his throne.

"I'm not scared," Lucifer straightened himself up, looking annoyed at his brother, "I just have something really important to take care of."

"Sure you do," the Demon Lord of Destruction barked a laugh, then turned conspiratorially to his nephew. "Your dad was always more of a scrawny bookworm than a fighter. Your Aunt Lilith will say the same thing."

"Hey, I fought in Armageddon right alongside you and Dad, remember?"

"And killed half as many angels as I did!"

"You've got twice as many arms; I hardly call that fair."

"Once a sore loser, always a sore loser."

"I am not a-"

"Please," Abaddon tried his best not to snap, "both of you quit it. We don't have time for this."

"Right," his uncle's face suddenly looked serious, though there was still a smile, "so where is Pendragon now?" he cracked two sets of knuckles.

"So, you'll fight him?" Abaddon almost didn't want to believe his good luck.

"Are you kidding? A chance to destroy Arthur Pendragon, and now when he's even stronger than ever? Just point me at him so I can rip his soul into pieces."

"I don't actually know where he is just yet."

"But I thought that angel you mentioned had just fought the bastard."

"Yeah, but he's currently up in Heaven with my guardian angel convincing them to go along with this plan.

"Those saved angels with all their rules. It could take forever for them to reach a decision. I'm just going to-"

"No," Lucifer put a hand forcefully on his brother's shoulder as the Demon Lord of Destruction started to rise. "If you go to Terra now, without proper papers or Heaven's approval, it will probably be viewed as a war crime. Do you want to start another Armageddon?" Lucifer cut off his older brother as he started to raise a hand. "You're staying here. Don't make me bind you in the stygian chains of eternal torment again."

"Fine," the Demon Lord of Destruction sat back down with another thunderous crash, crossing both sets of arms, "but you promised me a fight with Pendragon, Junior. If I don't get to kill him then-"

"You are *NOT* going up there."

Chapter Sixty
The Plan is Set in Motion

"Okay, good news and bad news," Abaddon said to Sophitia through the sending portal.

"Great, we need some good news. What is it?"

"My Dad isn't going to fight Arthur Pendragon for us."

"Fantastic, we can't beat him without your dad. We're sunk now. How is that good news?"

"Cause my uncle's going to do it instead."

"I-wait, your uncle? You mean Abaddon, Demon Lord of Destruction?"

"Yup."

"Holy shit!" Sophitia immediately looked around, blushing. "Anyway, yes! We can definitely stop him now, or your uncle can anyway. So wait, what's the bad news?"

"If Heaven says no to our plan, my uncle's probably gonna come up to Terra and try it anyway."

"Oh… yeah, that would be very bad news indeed. Well hopefully that shouldn't be an issue."

"Have they reached a decision yet?"

"No, the divine entities are currently deliberating. But it looks really good for us. Wisdom is on our side, and the others usually listen to them."

"Big surprise."

"Pretty much but still-" Sophitia paused and turned around. "Wait a minute," Abaddon saw her run over to talk to an angel that had just come out of a portal. They stood chatting for a minute, then the other angel opened a sending of their own. "Okay," she ran back, several minutes later. "My turn for good news and bad news. Good news is, that they just agreed to let your uncle Abaddon (oh divine entities that is so weird to say) fight Arthur Pendragon on their behalf. The whole, he-can-absorb-someone's-divine-energy thing kind of sealed that deal. But the bad news is, they unanimously agreed that they will not allow a fight between those two to happen in New Eden. I can totally understand why they would say that, but it sucks for our plan."

"Shit, that does complicate things. Great, now what will we do? It's not like we can just convince Arthur Pendragon to go down into Hell and fight my uncle. And if we could have trapped him then we would have done it alrea- wait!"

"What is it?"

"Do we still know where Arthur Pendragon is currently?"

"I believe we still have a rough idea. I mean he shouldn't have been able to get too far by now, so yeah, I think so."

"Great, then I know how we get him. I need to send my Dad real quick. I'll send you again once I get everything settled."

Abaddon strode down the street, decked out in full obsidian armor. It was cold, and it was raining, but for once he didn't mind the weather. He was too focused, too scared. He did not want to admit it to himself, but he was scared. He was about to go into the only fight he could ever remember where he knew he couldn't win. If all went according to plan, he wouldn't need to win, but still. He could see the image of the cloaked Arthur Pendragon before his eyes, the holy left hand reaching out…. No! He wasn't going to give into fear. He was a proud demon warrior. Abaddon slammed his fist into the ground. The more scared he got, the more it pissed him off. He took a deep breath. He forced himself to calm down.

Abaddon looked around. He knew the area he was in. He recognized a few of the shops, though they were all closed by now. Arthur Pendragon had been seen in an abandoned building over on Luke and 31st. Abaddon glanced up at the sign for Martin Luther King Boulevard as he passed it. The world reforged a new, and still that street was in every major city. He slapped himself and returned to focusing on the task at hand.

The next street over was Luke. Abaddon quickly found the abandoned building he was looking for. He hurled a small spherical object through one of the windows. A few seconds later there was an explosion of hellfire, hurling wood and glass outwards from the building. Not nearly as satisfying as getting to use his own hellfire, but those weapons still did the trick. Abaddon wasn't expecting Arthur Pendragon to still be there, but it couldn't hurt to check.

"Yeah, I guess that was too much to hope f-" Abaddon was cut off as something hit him hard in the back.

Abaddon crashed into the sidewalk. He leapt to his feet, turning to meet his attacker, drawing Spellbreaker as he did so. There he saw the figure of Arthur Pendragon, only this time he wasn't wearing a cloak. He was dressed in armor almost identical to Abaddon's.

"Now you're even wearing our armor?" Abaddon held Spellbreaker at the ready, but didn't make a move to attack.

"I had been waiting for Heaven to send its angels after me," Arthur Pendragon ignored Abaddon's question. "Now I am finally powerful enough to stop whatever pesky magic you have to throw at me. I was planning on hunting you down, but you came to me. This will make things so much easier."

"I don't need that dark power to beat you," Abaddon raised his left arm, still bearing the holy seal.

"Then you haven't learned your lesson from our last fight. Where's your three-headed devil mutt?"

"I don't need Boris for this either. It's just you and me Pendragon."

"WRONG!"

A blade flew through the air towards Abaddon. He raised Spellbreaker to block just in time. However, the second blade caught him through a chink in his armor and he leapt back, blood leaking from a shallow wound. It took him a second to realize what was happing. Five angels were charging him, each armed with a sword.

"You saved lunatic," Abaddon hissed angrily as he fended off the five attackers. "Now you've gone and resurrected the angels who attacked you? I know you hate me and my dad, but I thought a paladin would rather die than use necromancy to revive the corpse of an angel."

"I did die!" Arthur Pendragon roared as he charged to join his fellow attackers. "Your father destroyed Arthur Pendragon the paladin three centuries ago!"

With a few deft swings, Abaddon was able to strike three of the angels, Spellbreaker shattering the magic on them instantly. The fourth angel managed to graze his cheek with their sword, and he caught the fifth one's attack with his left gauntlet. The binding seal crackled as the blade struck it. Abaddon smiled and was about to say something to his opponent, when Arthur Pendragon stretched out his right hand, hurling the all too familiar red lighting at him. Abaddon was able to raise Spellbreaker to block, but was still hurled to the ground as waves of pain shot through him. Luckily it only lasted a few moments as Spellbreaker defused the effect.

Abaddon started to get to his feet, but the two remaining angels tackled him, pinning him to the ground. Before he could throw them off, Arthur Pendragon was standing over him. He held out his right hand and the sigils of pain glowed, hurling more red lighting down on Abaddon. He screamed as pain shot through every nerve in his body.

"Just like I intended the first time we met, I will wrack your body with pain until it kills you. You will die, writhing in agony like the foul monster you are!" Arthur Pendragon was so busy gloating, he didn't notice the dark portal open up behind him. "And this time, no one will get in my-"

A massive red arm wearing an obsidian gauntlet came out of the portal and grabbed Arthur Pendragon, pulling him in, the portal closing behind.

Arthur was flung through the air, crashing into the ground with extreme force. The former paladin jumped to his feet, whirling his head from side to side. He noticed the dark walls of pandemonium, and to his left, the great throne of bones. Then his eyes landed on the sixteen-foot crimson figure standing before him in full demonic battle gear.

"So," Abaddon, Demon Lord of Destruction cracked his knuckles, "I hear you have a problem with my nephew?"

Chapter Sixty-One

A Fight for the Ages

"What have you done foul demon?!" Arthur Pendragon roared.

"Junior wasn't interested in fighting you, so he called me. And I am more than interested in killing Arthur Pendragon."

"I have no time for this. The spawn of Lucifer must die!"

"And you'll have to get through his uncle to do it."

"I see. Why didn't I recognize you before? You're Abaddon, Demon Lord of Destruction. I remember clashing with you a few times during Armageddon, though there was never a decisive victor," Arthur Pendragon paused, thinking for a moment. "Fine, Lucifer's spawn can wait. I will relish killing you first."

Abaddon's fist came flying out of nowhere. Arthur Pendragon was able to raise his right arm to block just in time, but was still hurled across the throne room by the force of the attack. He rose quickly and retaliated, hurling the red lightning of the sigils of pain at his foe. The energy struck Abaddon in the chest, crackling all through his body, but the mighty demon was not moved from his position. And rather than a scream of pain, he let out a rumbling laugh of distain.

"My big sister hits five times as hard as you do. This barely tickles."

Abaddon rushed forwards, delivering a pair of devastating right hooks. This time Arthur Pendragon raised his left arm. The golden holy symbols flared into light, and a great blinding barrier of divine energy rose to meet the assault. Both Abaddon's fists crashed into the ward, there was a great crackling and sparking of energy as obsidian clashed with holy magic. Abaddon was not repelled. He raised both his left fists this time and delivered a follow-up attack. Arthur Pendragon's ward held up against Abaddon's relentless assault, but the demon could see his foe beginning to be pushed back.

Suddenly the ward vanished, and the former paladin rolled to the side. Abaddon was caught off balance as his next set of punches sailed through thin air. Arthur Pendragon quickly got to his feet and held his left hand outward, mimicking the stance Sophitia and Cassandra used when firing divine bolts of energy. The difference was, when he let loose his attack, it was less of a bolt, and more of a horizontal pillar of light that enveloped all in its path. Abaddon's sixteen foot form was obscured by blinding gold, and when the brightness finally subsided, he appeared, slumped against a wall, breathing heavily.

"So you can hit back with that divine arm of yours?" Abaddon slowly got to his feet, his broken obsidian armor falling off of him in pieces. "Good, I was worried this would be a boring fight. And I haven't gotten to cut loose in a while."

Arthur Pendragon was already charging up another blast. Fire appeared in all of Abaddon's hands. He then struck his palms on the ground and demonic seals were burned into the floor. He then raised his hands up, great chunks of obsidian ripping out of the ground and forming into four massive axes with demonic sigils burned into the blades. The weapons formed just in time for Abaddon to block the next blast. This time the light was cut, splintering like a kaleidoscope and flying in all directions. Great sections of the throne room were crashing down all around them.

Abaddon didn't wait for his foe to attack again. He charged at full speed. As impressive as he had been before, he was that much faster with most of his armor destroyed in the initial blast. He struck down with all four heavy blades. Arthur Pendragon didn't have enough time to switch between offense and defense and so had to leap out of the way. He barely managed to avoid the blades, but as they struck the ground, a massive explosion of hellfire went forth in all directions. Now it was Arthur Pendragon's turn to be hurled into a wall.

The former paladin slowly got to his feet, blood dripping from his mouth. Abaddon took a moment to get his bearings after the smoke died down a bit, then proceed to follow up with another furious charge, this one accompanied by a roar that would put a volcanic eruption to shame. This time Arthur Pendragon was able to put up a ward against the attack. The barrier deflected the worst of the assault, and hellfire was hurled in all direction, even more of the throne room crumbling to the ground. When the dust settled, Abaddon's axeblades were locked against Arthur Pendragon's ward. Arthur Pendragon screamed, channeling as much divine energy as he could muster into his arm, and the great demon before him was forcibly repelled.

Abaddon crashed to the ground, cracks appearing in his axes. Arthur Pendragon readied another blast of divine energy, but this one was clearly smaller. Abaddon got to one knee right as the blast hit. This one he was able to fully deflect, but it shattered one of his axes in the process. His response was to swing another axe around the side, forcing Arthur Pendragon to block with his right arm. The axe managed to dig into the obsidian prosthetic before the force of the blow sent Arthur Pendragon hurtling to the side, tumbling across the floor and crashing against the great throne of bones in the center of the mostly destroyed room.

"You're done for, Pendragon," Abaddon was breathing even more heavily as he got to his feet. "You brought the power of five seraphim and a handful of templars to this fight. That might have been enough to deal with Junior, but did you really think it could beat me?"

"I will not be killed by the likes of you!" Arthur Pendragon hissed from his position on the ground.

"You have no choice," Abaddon slowly descended upon his fallen foe, two of his axes scraping across the cracked floor.

Arthur Pendragon raised a hand. At the same time Abaddon raised his third axe over his head, as though he was performing an execution. As the blade came down, Arthur Pendragon intoned words in the blackest speech. The air darkened around them, the room grew cold. Great chains arose from the ground, lashing themselves to Abaddon's body, halting his attack in mid-air.

"So you can speak the tongue of demons now, human?" Abaddon struggled against the chains. "And how came you by an obsidian arm, especially one with my big sister's magic on it?"

"I don't have to answer you, vile fiend!"

"But I really want to know, I'm curious."

"Well you won't be curious once I have destroyed you. You will be purged from this world by divine light," Arthur Pendragon was struggling to his feet, "and then you will be at whatever peace your wretched kind get."

"That's not a good answer human. You see, my curiosity is the only thing that's currently keeping you alive."

"Me?" Arthur Pendragon laughed, clutching his side. "You are the one who is bound. I can kill you with a single blast straight to the head whenever I please."

"Bound?" Abaddon returned the laugh, only his was a deep rumble, not a wince. "My little brother is the only one with chains strong enough to bind me."

"As if I would believe the lies of a demon. This is just a pathetic attempt to try and intimidate me. You've lost but think you can win by scaring me."

"Foolish human," Abaddon's voice got deeper still. "My weak little brother is the one who resorts to words. I use actions to win my battles."

Abaddon strained his muscles, a deep grunt escaping him as he flexed. Arthur Pendragon had barely gotten to his feet, when the black chains surrounding the demon of destruction shattered and dissipated. Before Arthur Pendragon even had a chance to feel fear, Abaddon's free hand grabbed him by the head.

"Die, mortal scum!"

Abaddon smashed his smaller foe into the ground with all the force he could muster. At least, that was his plan. Just before he impacted into the floor, Arthur Pendragon's body disappeared in a curl of black smoke, leaving Abaddon to stand alone in a destroyed throne room.

"I'll be saved," Abaddon snarled, "Lucifer was right about that bastard."

Chapter Sixty-Two

Resorting to Words

Lucifer stood in the ruins of an old demon city. The crumbling buildings all around him brought back a lot of memories. He distinctly remembered quelling an uprising there about one hundred and fifty years ago. Most of the residents had banded together to assault Pandemonium. He had gotten word of this, came to the city, murdered everyone slowly and painfully, same old same old. No one had come to live in the city after that. Perhaps it had been the bloody death threats on the walls he had written in the citizens' own entrails. Maybe it had been the heads on spikes. For all his rebelling and disagreement with his father, Lucifer had retained a bit of his traditional streak. Heads on spikes were always his go to. Lilith had often made fun of him for that one. Then again Lilith just often made fun of him. Lucifer was snapped back to reality by the figure of Mephistopheles appearing before him in a pillar of smoke.

"I half wasn't expecting you to show up," Lucifer sat on a pile of rubble.

"When my lord calls, I answer," Mephistopheles gave a humble bow. "And you did call indeed. Dressed in full obsidian armor. You even brought Soulcleaver out of its sheath. I don't believe you've used that since Armageddon. I'm almost inclined to think you've come here to fight me."

"I know you don't fight."

"So an execution then?"

"If I tried, you'd just run away. I know you are very good at that. But there is a matter I wish to talk to you about."

"Do tell, my lord," Mephistopheles gave another bow.

"Arthur Pendragon."

"Dead for almost three hundred years at my guess. What do you have to discuss about him?"

"The fact that he is not dead, and both you and I know it."

"Not dead, what do you mean? He was killed during Armageddon, everyone knows this."

"No, after the war was officially over, he led an unsanctioned attack against me."

"I had no idea," it was clear by Mephistopheles tone that he was feigning ignorance. "But if he did something so foolish, then surely you killed him."

"No, I made him fall and left him to rot in the deepest pits."

"Then surely some other demon did him in. A paladin without his powers would not last one day in Hell."

"Unless someone helped him."

"I dare say it sounds as though you are implying something, my lord."

"Yes. My spawn fought Arthur Pendragon not long ago. The former paladin now has a demonic right arm covered in the sigils of pain. He can also speak the tongues of demons. How could he have acquired such abilities?"

"I'm sure I don't have any idea."

"And I'm sure you're lying. You saved Arthur Pendragon's life three hundred years ago."

"Now why in all the pits would I save the life of a paladin?"

"The same reason you do anything: to make a deal. Just think what leverage you could gain from having Arthur Pendragon owe you a favor."

"A fallen paladin has no leverage to offer, I think you need to come up with a better theory."

"Believe me, the moment I suspected you, I thought of that. I asked myself what you had to gain from this. The one thing I could think of was that Arthur Pendragon now had a single-minded hatred of me. So, unless I am much mistaken, you wanted to use him to get something from me."

"Well now, my lord. It sounds as though you are implying that I sent a crazed Arthur Pendragon to kill your spawn. But, if you remember correctly, I represented your son in trial as a result of these attacks. That would be a conflict of interests, wouldn't it?"

"A conflict of Arthur Pendragon's interests, and Abaddon's. But your interests have only ever been your own, so no conflict there. You got a favor from my spawn, and say all you want about Arthur Pendragon's lack of leverage, but you cannot deny the value of that."

"And nor shall I. A favor from Abaddon, spawn of Lucifer, ruler of the Ninth Circle, is something very valuable indeed."

"Too valuable for you."

"Did you come here to get it from me? Well I see no reason to hand that favor over to you."

"Then let me give you one. I know you are responsible for this entire mess with Arthur Pendragon."

"And I'd better give you the favor or else? Is that what you were going to say? Forgive me my lord, but if this is your big play, it is not very well thought out. You are acting as though you have some damning evidence against me, but demons have no need for such a thing. Had you wanted to kill me you would have attempted to do so already. And you said yourself that I would just run away in that event. So I see no motivation to give up that favor."

"You can run from me, but you cannot run from the forces of Heaven, not indefinitely."

"What do you mean?"

"I fully intend to tell Heaven exactly how you were involved in this mess. I will even allow them to move through my circle of Hell to find you should you flee. And at the very least, they will be on high alert. You will be their most wanted criminal. You won't be able to travel to Terra to make deals anymore without risking getting caught by them. A favor from my spawn isn't going to be worth the trouble you will have from them."

"You are probably right about that, my lord. But for Heaven, you *WILL* need proof. I fail to see any, so I don't see how you can muscle me into this agreement."

"I have enough proof for now, enough to know you did it."

"Do tell. I am curious as to what you think you have on me, my lord."

"First, there is Arthur Pendragon's ability to appear and disappear. My spawn mentioned it, and though he may not have realized it at the time, he described him appearing and vanishing using black smoke. This is a type of magic I am aware of only one other individual possessing. That would be you, in case you haven't guessed. Teleportation magic without the use of portals is extremely rare, and your specific signature when you do it, is even more so."

"But that's hardly proof my lord."

"No, that is what first made me suspect your involvement. There is something else that made me positive you were guilty. Arthur Pendragon uses necromancy now. Specifically, he uses it through a small gemstone."

"And what does that have to do with me, my lord?"

"Part of the Armageddon Accords is that I keep the power of necromancy sealed away, never to be used by anyone. However even before that, it was kept under the closest of guard. It was the secret magic of *MY* father, and he was a very jealous demon. There was no way anyone could have stolen it from him. However, when I was little, he used to tell me a bedtime story."

"A bedtime story, my lord?"

"It was a cautionary tale about making deals with you. If I was going to one-day rule over my father's circle of Hell, I would need to not make the same mistakes he had. He told me the story often of how you swindled him, tricked him into giving you the secret of necromancy as part of a deal. As the story went, my father had made a deal with you a long time before that. You gave him a small gemstone that you said would boost his magical powers. But instead it would actually absorb the next magic used by the person holding it. You used that stone to gain the power of necromancy, and my father never knew it. In the deal where you swindled him, you asked for that stone back, and my father agreed. It wasn't until later that he learned what that stone truly was, and realized how you had played a long con on him."

"I see, my lord. So after hearing this story so often, when you heard of the necromantic gemstone you knew I had to be responsible for giving it to Arthur Pendragon. Well, even if that were true, the word of your deceased father is not enough proof for Heaven to declare a witch hunt on me."

"No, you are right about that. But it was enough proof for me to be sure."

"Very well, but I still fail to see how this lets you strong-arm me into making a deal, my lord. For that you would need proper proof."

"And I will have it shortly," Lucifer smiled. "I will get a full confession from Arthur Pendragon any minute now."

Chapter Sixty-Three

Lucifer's Endgame

The rain in New Eden didn't seem to want to let up, but Abaddon barely noticed it. He was still struggling as the two angels pinned him to the ground. He couldn't see very much from his current position, but the blinding pain had stopped, which meant Uncle had probably gotten Arthur Pendragon by now.

One of the angels stood up, grabbing a sword. Abaddon struggled harder, but the combination of the remnants of Arthur Pendragon's attack, and the body still on top of him made it futile. Of all the ways to go, being killed by undead angels was not one he ever would have thought of. Abaddon snarled at his attacker as the sword came down. There was a flash of red.

Abaddon was unsure where the sword had gone. The angels were gone as well, but he had a pretty good idea what had happened to them. The gooey mush that was now covering him and most of the sidewalk was a good indication. Now he just had to figure out what in Heaven's name had happened. To that end he slowly got to his feet. He was greeted by the image of a black-scaled demon in a bright red cocktail dress.

"Aunt Lilith?!"

"How's my favorite nephew doing?"

"I'm you're only nephew- I mean, wait! What in Heaven's name is going on here?"

"This is all part of your father's plan to stop Arthur Pendragon."

"My father's- no, it was my- I mean- Uncle's the one fighting Arthur Pendragon now."

"Yes, but he won't be able to kill him."

"Wait, you think Uncle's gonna lose?"

"I didn't say lose. Your uncle may be a big idiot, but there are few better in a fight."

"So where do you come in? Uncle has this one."

"I thought your father would have taught you better. From what he told me, every time you've tangled with Arthur Pendragon, he's almost killed you, then something interfered with your fight and he teleported away. How's your uncle going to stop him from doing that now?"

"Shit, I hadn't thought of that."

"Well your father did. He was always the smart one. But don't you dare tell him I said that."

"Don't worry," Abaddon winced a laugh, "I've had enough of the sigils of pain for one day."

"That sneaky thief!" Lilith clenched a fist. "I can't believe he stole my secret magic. Having it stolen is bad enough, but by a paladin?! By *THE* paladin? Well, I am going to enjoy getting him back for that. He thinks he knows how to use that magic? Well I'll show him."

"But we'll still need to find him first. Assuming he will slip through Uncle's fingers, we'll have no way of tracking him down."

"I already told you your father thought of that. Follow me."

Lilith turned and held out a hand, a large portal opening up in front of her. She stepped through and vanished. Abaddon quickly followed. When he came out he immediately recognized the Seventh Circle of Hell. The sulfurous air and blasted rock was unmistakable. The red clouds of congealed something off in the distance brought back so many memories from his early centuries.

"You haven't been back here since the last Feast of the Seven Deadly, Right?" Lilith raised a hand, as though introducing him to the place for the first time.

"Yeah, it has been a while. But what are we doing here? I don't even recognize this particular part of your circle."

"Oh, this is the slums. I wouldn't recommend coming here often if you can avoid it. Not much but sulfur pits and feral hellhounds. As to what we are doing here, we're catching Arthur Pendragon; I thought that was clear by now. This way."

Lilith began to walk purposefully off towards her right. Abaddon had to quickly snap out of his confusion to not be left behind. She at least had the courtesy to not unfurl her wings and fly where they were going. Politeness aside, Abaddon always felt self-conscious around demons when they did that, not that he would tell anyone of course. He didn't have wings and had small horns. His dad always said he got that from his uncle, but it didn't help much. Either Abaddon had been lost in thought for a while, or it was a very quick walk, because Lilith suddenly stopped, causing him to bump into her and fall down. She didn't look it, but was surprisingly sturdy.

"We're here," Lilith gestured to an old rundown shack.

"What are we doing in here?"

"Waiting, but hopefully not that long. This place is a shithole. I wouldn't be caught dead here under normal circumstances."

The two went inside the shack. It was made of filthy stone that was moldy and crumbling. Abaddon found an old bench and sat down. Lilith eyed the seat next to him wearily but then seemed to think better of it. and remained standing.

"So, how's life in New Eden? You never send. I was beginning to think you'd forgotten about your favorite aunt, being a bigshot hero and all that."

"I don't think now is the time to be talking about this."

"Nonsense. We have a few minutes at least. Your uncle likes to drag these things out, and he hasn't had a good fight in months, so he was getting kind of restless."

"I know, he threatened to come and visit me at my apartment."

"Oh dear, then I guess this Arthur Pendragon stuff happened just in the nick of time."

"Yeah," they both laughed. "He'd probably start an interplanar incident if he showed up like that."

"Believe me, I love your uncle to death, but he has never been very good at thinking things through… Or holding himself back."

"Well that's just what we need right now."

"You don't have to tell me. I want someone beaten up, he's the first demon I'll call."

"You don't need his help. I saw you take out those angels."

"Yes, but you know me, I don't like to get my spells dirty if I don't have to. I'll let the big muscle-head do all the fighting. I get my enjoyment elsewhere."

"You mean Belial? Or were you talking about someone else in your harem?"

"You're a filthy little bastard," Lilith pushed him away, "And I couldn't be more proud of you. But enough about me, you still haven't told me anything about what you've been up to. I heard from your father that you got into one of the best heroes guilds in the city."

"Well actually-"

Abaddon was cut off as black smoke appeared suddenly in the middle of the shack. A ragged, bleeding figure in a black cloak stumbled out of the smoke, kneeling on the floor.

"When you're father's right, he's right."

Lilith hurled a bolt of red lighting at Arthur Pendragon, and he screamed in agony, before collapsing on the floor. Then Lilith snapped her fingers, and chains of silver and crimson rose from the ground, binding him tightly. Abaddon just stood there, stunned.

"When he wakes up, we are going to have a very pointed conversation," Lilith smiled. "I'm really going to enjoy this."

Chapter Sixty-Three

Striking a Deal

"My lord," Mephistopheles' voice gave the slightest hint of losing some formality, "I have to wonder how you expect to get a confession from Arthur Pendragon. It seems highly unlikely for many reasons."

"My older brother is fighting him right now. Soon Arthur Pendragon will be beaten."

"Ah yes, your older brother is indeed formidable. In fact, he is one of the most dangerous warriors I have seen. But I wouldn't count on him to get you a confession. He is not known for his ability to hold back."

"I specifically instructed him to not kill Arthur Pendragon."

"Well forgive me my lord if I do not trust your older brother to do as you say. I have never known him to be the type to take orders, especially from his younger brother."

"I gave him incentive."

"Oh? And what might that be?"

"The promise that if he leaves him alive, he will get to see Arthur Pendragon horribly tortured."

"Well that would do it. I imagine there are few demons who lived through Armageddon who wouldn't jump at that chance. So that's it then, you have me all nicely cornered. Any minute now, you will get your confession, and I will be at your mercy?"

"You do not sound overly worried."

"Perhaps I am not."

"And why would that be? Do you think my brother will not best Arthur Pendragon?"

"My lord, I only play the odds when they are in my favor. Betting on your brother to lose a fight is not smart. At the height of Armageddon I honestly do not know who I would pick, between your brother and Arthur

Pendragon that is, but now he has fallen, and new powers not withstanding, I do not think he has a chance anymore."

"Then why are you calm? If my brother succeeds in capturing Arthur Pendragon, it's game over for you."

"Well therein lies the issue, my lord. You said that the reason for your suspicion of me, was that Arthur Pendragon seems to mimic my rather unique brand of teleportation magic. Why would he not simply teleport away the moment he had lost?"

"Oh I have no doubt that he would."

"Well then, there would be no way to get the confession. You would need him captured, and alive. But if he just teleports away, there will be no way to find him."

"Well, that's not strictly true, there is one way."

"Oh?"

"You just have to know where the teleporter will appear and be waiting for them there."

"Oh?" this time Mephistopheles gave a very wicked smile. "Unless I am much mistaken, you are suggesting that before setting up a fight between Arthur Pendragon and your brother, you found the exact location of the place he would run to and set a trap for him. I find that rather hard to believe."

Lucifer's next sentence was interrupted by a portal opening up several feet to his right. A black scaled arm extended from the portal, throwing a cloaked figure, feet locked in chains, onto the ground.

"A present for you," Lilith's voice could be heard through the portal. "We really enjoyed having a talk with him. Paladins are so fun to break," and with that the portal vanished.

"Talk about perfect timing," Lucifer smiled.

Mephistopheles retained his usual unreadable expression, "Your sister, Lilith, yes? I see. You did indeed plan on Arthur Pendragon escaping your brother, so you had your sister waiting to catch him. I suppose the queen of pain would be the best choice for an interrogation. You are clever my lord.

Though I have to wonder how you were able to figure out his exact location like that."

"It took a while. I'd actually figured out your involvement in this mess fairly early on. I spent the rest of the time until now trying to track down Arthur Pendragon's base of operations. He had to have one, and I quickly came to the conclusion that it couldn't be on Terra, because Heaven would be conducting a canvased search of the place, looking for him. They would have found him rather quickly. And even with teleportation magic like yours, he would have had no way to get to Heaven. And even if he could have, it would have been way to risky. You would have given him access to Hell, so that was the most likely place."

"But to search all of Hell in such a short amount of time…"

"I didn't need to. The sigils of pain narrowed that search. There's only one place he could have acquired those. I asked Lilith to help me search her layer. After explaining things to her, she was more than happy to oblige, and she found his hiding place. And now here we are."

"I see. Expertly done, my lord. Now all you need is a confession. But he is still a former paladin, and the will of a paladin is not easily broken."

"When it comes to this sort of thing, my sister doesn't do easy."

Lucifer walked over to the figure on the ground. He ripped off the cloak, revealing the gibbering form of a shattered man. Both Arthur Pendragon's arms were missing. It looked as though they had been forcibly ripped from his torso. The rest of his body bore no visible signs of injury, but was still shaking violently from whatever had been done to it.

"WHO ARE YOU?" Lucifer roared at the man on the ground, "SPEAK!"

"A-Arthur, Arthur Pendragon," the man cried.

"WHO BROUGHT YOU HERE?"

"Lilith! It was the demon Lilith!"

"HAVE YOU BEEN WORKING WITH MEPHISTOPHELES TO KILL MY SPAWN?"

Arthur Pendragon tried to speak, but no words came out, his mouth opening and closing soundlessly, "I'm sorry! I'm sorry! Please don't hurt me! I'm trying I'm-"

Lucifer lashed out with a hand, knocking the poor man unconscious. He then turned back to Mephistopheles, who was smiling once again.

"My lord. If it was indeed I who had made a deal with Arthur Pendragon, as you so claim, I would have been smart enough to make him unable to speak of it to anyone. I mean, that's just common sense when engaging in secret activity like this. There would still be no way to get a confession."

"No? I shall simply bring him before a heavenly court and subject him to truth magic."

"You know that will not break a demonic pact my lord."

"It does not have to. If he is forced to tell the truth, then all I would have to do is ask the right question. For example, say I were to ask him the same question I just asked him now. That would prove once and for all if you did it or not. If his answer was no, then you would be in the clear. If his answer was yes, you would be found guilty. However, if he could not answer the question, as just happened right now, then that would also implicate you just as effectively. It would prove you made a deal for his silence."

"I don't know if I would call that proof."

"But Heaven would. That's all that matters. Whether you are guilty or not, as long as they think so, you are in the exact same position."

"As I said, very clever indeed my lord. But I am afraid that all your cleverness has been wasted."

"Really?"

"Yes. I already got my favor from your spawn. You can't take it back now."

"Fine then. I was afraid that might be the case. Let's make a new deal: I do not send Heaven after you for this, and in exchange, we are done. You never make a deal with anyone from the line of Lucifer again. And furthermore, you will never do anything that would knowingly directly or indirectly harm anyone from the line of Lucifer. Do we have a deal?"

Mephistopheles thought for a few moments, clearly weighing his options. He then bowed deeply once more, "Very clever, very clever you are, my lord. Yes, we have a deal," And with that he disappeared in a curl of black smoke.

Chapter Sixty-Four

A Matter of Pride

Abaddon had been sitting in his apartment for the better part of three days now. He had gotten up the energy to walk Boris, but that was about it. On at least two separate occasions he had thought about sending his dad, but couldn't bring himself to do it. He was getting really tired of sitting around and moping, but that seemed to be his go to as of late. Terra was turning him into a real wuss. Before Abaddon could continue on that train of thought, it was derailed by a knock at the door.

"Hi," Sophitia was standing there a bit awkwardly, hand still raised. "I suppose I could have given you a sending, but decided to just fly over instead. Hope that isn't too weird. It only occurred to as I got here."

"Nah, it's fine," Abaddon motioned for her to come in.

"Well something's not fine. You sound like you're in a real sucky mood."

"I guess so."

"What's up? Arthur Pendragon has been dealt with, and turned over to Heaven's custody. And now that he's gone, they agreed to let you off of probation. It must feel good having your magic back."

"Well yeah, that's true. I was just glad they put that binding on my gauntlet so my left arm wasn't constantly being burned. But that is much better. It's just…."

"Yes?"

"The way the whole Arthur Pendragon thing ended is just eating me up."

"Why? We figured out a solid plan for stopping him and it worked. What's wrong with that?"

"My dad figured out the plan. All I did was ask for his help because I couldn't do this on my own."

"Is that all?" Sophitia's voice was a cross between confused and mocking. "You had to ask for help. That is a thing people do. Don't tell me you're moping around because of that."

"Arthur Pendragon attacked me. I was not able to beat him. I had to run to my dad for help. Aunt Lilith, my uncle, it's like I'm still a little kid."

"Arthur Pendragon was the mightiest of paladins. He also had centuries to plot his vengeance against you and your father. He had necromancy and angel powers and demon powers on top of that. Seriously, that's not the kind of opponent you are just expected to beat," to which Abaddon gave her a look that clearly said otherwise. "Wait, you think you are? You think you were expected to beat those odds? What crazy kinds of expectations were put on you?"

"When Arthur Pendragon first showed up, it was the first time I had ever lost a fight."

"Seriously?! That's ridiculous."

"I don't count the sparring matches against Moloch when he was training me, so yeah, that was the first time I had ever lost a fight. But he got away, and I survived. So I knew I could face him again and kill him next time. But I couldn't. He was too strong. He was an opponent I couldn't beat."

"Do you know how insane this sounds?" It looked like Sophitia wanted to slap him across the face. "In two hundred and fifty years, you've never lost a fight, and now that you have you're getting all sad about it? You're acting like a baby."

"I'm the spawn of Lucifer. I am heir to the line of Lucifer. I am not allowed to lose!"

"BULLSHIT!" Both were taken aback by the shouting. "What could possibly make you think that you are not allowed to lose?"

"In Hell, anyone can rule one of the circles. Being an elder demon is not a requirement. All you have to do is beat the previous ruler and take their throne. Because elder demons are, as a rule, stronger than other demons, this means it rarely happens. But it still does. And sometimes, elder demons go into other circles to take over for one reason or another. The line of Lucifer has never been broken. No one has ever taken the throne of the Ninth Circle from us. My grandfather never lost it, my dad never lost it, and I can't be the first of the line of Lucifer to fail like that. The line of Lucifer does, not, lose."

"That's idiotic. I guarantee you that your father and grandfather lost fights before. It happens. And I further guarantee that your father isn't going to disown you or anything because of it. No loving parent would. And besides, you didn't even lose, so what are you complaining about?"

"I- what?" Abaddon just stood there, unsure of how to answer.

"Why do you think you lost to him? You would have killed Arthur Pendragon if Cassandra hadn't interfered with that fight. If you had been allowed to use your restricted magic, you could have beaten him this time too. It's like fighting with a broken leg and then complaining about how weak you are because you weren't able to beat your opponent. Seriously, I never thought demons would get this whiny."

"I-I was really being whiny?"

"Yes. You are one of the most powerful warriors in all the realms of creation. You've mastered one of the most powerful cursed artifacts in creation. Divine entities! You've got a silver spoon in your mouth and you're complaining that it's not gold."

"Well when you put it like that..."

"Yes, it's ridiculous. Now stop all this stupid annoying immature crap and come on," Sophitia grabbed Abaddon's arm.

"Where are we going?"

"Out... Somewhere... I don't know! You're a free demon, your nemesis has been defeated. We need to celebrate."

Abaddon fell flat on his face. It was the third time in twice as many seconds. Of all the A.D. humanity traditions to stick around, roller-skating was the most baffling. Abaddon had read about it before, but never understood why people did it. And now that he was trying it, his confusion was only redoubled. He managed to get to his feet and took one step before falling on his face for a fourth time. Sophitia just laughed at him from her place on the floor.

"Hey, you're falling down just as much as I am."

"Yeah, but it's funnier when you do it. I mean, a 'proud demon warrior' being defeated by shoes with wheels?"

"Yeah, yeah, hysterical. Why'd you even want to do this in the first place? You can fly."

"I wanted to try something new. Besides, you can fly too."

"No, I can't," Abaddon struggled to his frustratingly unstable feet.

"But you're an elder demon aren't you?" Sophitia did likewise.

"Not all demons are born with wings you know! Not having them is actually quite common."

"Geez, not need to get snippy about it."

"I-" Abaddon crashed to the ground again. "Bless these saved skates! When I have the ability to move more than a few inches I just might go over there and punch you."

"Oh come on," Sophitia tried and failed to hold in her laughing. "You have to admit it is funny. I just wouldn't have expected you to have such poor balance."

"I normally don't, but it's like some holy sorcery is at work."

"Holy sorcery?" Sophitia just stared at him.

"I know black magic, and it isn't capable of thi-" Abaddon crashed to the ground yet again.

"Well holy sorcery or not," Sophitia's smile changed from mocking to genuine warmth, "at least you aren't feeling depressed anymore."

Well, Abaddon couldn't argue with that. And maybe it was Sophitia's words from the apartment starting to sink in, or maybe it was just the lack of murderous ex-paladin out for his blood talking, but he felt like things were finally starting to fit into place. He smiled at the thought of all the great things New Eden still had to offer, and tried once more to stumble to his feet, instantly regretting his decision.

Chapter Sixty-Five

Long Overdue

"So how's my favorite spawn doing. It's been two weeks already since we last talked. How's the new job?"

"It's fine Dad. Not much has happened yet. I did get called in to kill a feral griffin the other day, so that was something. But usually the bigger heroes guilds get called in for the really major stuff. I haven't had to fight anymore hellhounds or anything."

"Well, you'll just have to start small. Prove yourself the capable warrior that you are, and people will come knocking down your door to get you to slay monsters for them. You might even get back into one of the bigger guilds."

"Maybe, but I actually like the one I'm at. I'm still in touch with a few heroes from White Pegasus, but I really like the people at this new guild. Well… most of them anyway. Also, at the moment, I'm enjoying some easier work. I think I could use a bit of downtime after the whole Arthur Pendragon stuff."

"That makes sense."

"Whatever happened with that anyway? Last I saw, Aunt Lilith was chucking him through a portal, saying she was giving him to you."

"Well, he was sent back to Heaven. They said they'd take responsibility for the whole mess, but are keeping everything very quiet. I have no idea what they're actually going to do with him. Besides, he might be permanently damaged, I mean, Lilith *DID* get to work him over."

"Yeah, I'll say. I didn't even know you could flay human skin like that."

"Your aunt definitely is something else alright. So I guess he got his just punishment but…."

"Hmm?"

"I just don't like the idea that you almost get killed by Heaven's former champion and they don't even apologize for it. We clean up their mess and they just sweep it under the rug and act like nothing happened."

"Well, it kind of was your mess Dad. I mean, you told me about what you did to him."

"Yes, but that was because he went renegade and refused our peace agreement. I mean I had just killed your grandfather in order to secure this peace. I was in no mood to deal with that shit. I'm not saying this to excuse myself from my share of the blame. But it was a renegade soldier from Heaven that did this. And they're the ones with all the rules and laws. They failed to keep him in check, and I don't think they should get away with that scot free."

"Whatever," Abaddon sighed. "I honestly don't care if anything happens to Heaven because of this. The situation was dealt with."

"By us, not them."

"Yeah, but who cares? Nothing is going to change if they get punished. And besides, they literally couldn't deal with him. Are they at fault because he found a way to steal divine energy? Anyone from Heaven they sent against him would have only made him stronger."

"Well... that's a fair point. I won't fault them for that. But this is just classic Heaven. They have to make sure they rise above it all and never look bad. They have to be the perfect moral beacon. They have to be the ones who are always right. I've heard the line a dozen times before. They are worried what will happen to the mortals if they appeared to be flawed. Seriously, they don't need you constantly holding their hand."

"Okay, I get that. I mean, it's not like I'm taking Heaven's side or anything, it's just that I don't really see how we benefit from them suffering."

"It's the principle of the thing! Even after the Armageddon Accords they still act as though they are good, we are bad, and that's all there is to it. We just witnessed how far one of theirs can fall, and their top priority is making sure that no one finds that out so that they can keep acting better than us."

"Okay, maybe that's taking it a bit far, Dad. I mean, it's not like everyone in Heaven is bad or anything."

"That's my point. They are flawed, just like us. Everyone is. I'm sick and tired of them feeling like they have to act perfect all the time."

"Well, not like there's anything we can do about it now, so no reason to dwell on it. How're things back at Pandemonium?"

"Finally got the saved place fixed. Your uncle really did a number on it when he fought Arthur Pendragon. It would have been quicker to repair if a bunch of demons hadn't seen the wreck and thought it was a sign that I was weak. I had to kill at least seven different demons seeking the throne in the past two days. Seriously, I couldn't get any work done."

"Well, at least you had some excitement. Were any of them particularly strong?"

"Compared to me? None of them stood a chance. This one she-demon put up quite a fight though. I had to pull Soulcleaver on her."

"Impressive. What about Uncle, did he get to join in the fun?"

"Nah. After the fight with Arthur Pendragon he took off to visit the Eighth Circle. I'm not sure how long he'll be gone. I must admit, it does get a bit lonely here from time to time."

"Well, I'll try to send when I can."

"You know I always enjoy talking to you."

"Of course, Dad."

"And just because your aunt and uncle and I stepped in to help you with this whole Arthur Pendragon thing, doesn't mean I think any less of you."

"I... I know Dad, thanks."

"You're my spawn, and you are constantly making me proud of you. One day you will make a fine successor to my throne."

"Yeah, but not for a while. I've still got a lot of exploring to do on Terra first."

"Then I shouldn't keep you from it any longer. Go forth and enjoy, my spawn."

"I will. Thanks again."

"Any time. I love you."

"Love you too, Dad."

Abaddon sighed. This still felt a bit awkward, but he wasn't turning back now. This was something he should have done a long time ago and stalling anymore would only make it worse. He was paced slowly outside the White Pegasus building, for all the good it was doing. He waited for several more minutes before Mary came out and started walking toward him.

"Hey, I got your sending. It's been a while since we talked."

"Yeah. Sorry about that. I was busy with some stuff. But I haven't done a really good job with this from the start. Anyway, I wanted to meet you here to… apologize, for not being a better friend, as well as…"

"As well as?"

Abaddon held out an awkward hand holding a small bouquet of flowers, "I don't know if flowers are an appropriate gift for a golem, but here. The Arcane Theatre is putting on a show about the great magic rift Thursday; would you like to go with me?"

Made in the USA
Middletown, DE
25 July 2019